W9-AHL-934

SOUTH OF AN UNNAMED CREEK

OTHER BOOKS BY ANNE CAMERON

DREAMSPEAKER
EARTH WITCH
DAUGHTERS OF COPPER WOMAN
THE JOURNEY
CHILD OF HER PEOPLE
DZELARHONS
HOW THE LOON LOST HER VOICE
HOW RAVEN STOLE THE MOON
ORCA'S SONG
RAVEN RETURNS THE WATER
THE ANNIE POEMS
SPIDER WOMAN
LAZY BOY
STUBBY AMBERCHUK & THE HOLY GRAIL
WOMEN, KIDS & HUCKLEBERRY WINE
TALES OF THE CAIRDS

SOUTH
of an
UNNAMED CREEK

Anne Cameron

HARBOUR PUBLISHING

Copyright © 1989 by Anne Cameron

All rights reserved. No part of this book may be reproduced or transmitted in any form by any means without permission in writing from the publisher, except by a reviewer, who may quote brief passages in a review.

Harbour Publishing
Box 219, Madeira Park, BC V0N 2H0

Jacket design by Roger Handling

Printed and bound in Canada by Friesen Printers

Canadian Cataloguing in Publication Data

Cameron, Anne, 1938–
    South of an unnamed creek

    ISBN 1-55017-013-9

    I. Title.
PS8555.A44S6 1989   C813'.54   C89-091500-8
PR9199.3.C35S6 1989

for
Alex   Erin   Marianne   Pierre   Tara
and especially
Eleanor

1

The wallahs, goombahs, navvies, and dock-wallopers were working hard to bring in the next century, celebrating Hagmenai with a dedication seldom shown to their church obligations, busily first-footing it from watering hole to watering hole, determined to step into the new year with happiness, joy, and as much song as possible, setting the example for the coming century. It didn't matter to any of them that they were so drunk their first-footing was more a matter of teetering and stumbling, nor did it occur to them that if this was the pattern they were setting, the year following would be twelve months of total hangover. They were, by God, having a good time, and anyone who wasn't could go to hell. Furthermore, any pinch-nosed tight-assed beak who wanted to curtail the fun could expect nothing but a swift kick up the arse, and more verbal abuse in several languages than could be easily endured.

Hagmenai. The Hag's Moon, the last night of the old year, a time for the living to gather together for protection and comfort until after the clock struck twelve midnight. When the last chime sounded, the revel began. Everyone kissed everyone else and wished each other a good New Year, then the festivities erupted and the first-footing began.

The Hag was the death goddess, her hags the priestesses who dismembered the sacrificial victims and chopped them for the feasts, and haggis, the Hag's dish, was made of the internal organs. The Hag and her spinning wheel shone in the sky. Disbelievers called it the Milky Way, but deep in their hearts the reeling drunkards knew the truth, and if this incipient brawl was the last vestige of their traditional honouring of Arianrhod, at least they were busy about it and giving their all to the celebration. The Hag of Scone was attended by swarthy elves, and if she had been turned to stone by a curse or incantation, there was no guarantee she would stay trapped in granite. Certainly the death goddess moved easily in and out of their lives, claiming her own and taking them back with her as she wished. She took newborn and suckling, took child and wife, took the young and strong as well as the aged and feeble, her heavy veils telling all that no one may know her face or the manner and time of death.

But tonight, Hagmenai, was a time a body could get on the good side of her, and if here in this cursed cold terrible strange country they no longer put on disguises and went door to door begging barley and oatmeal cakes, still they could revel and sing, drink and feast, and perhaps charm the old bitch into granting one more year before she came to collect them, take them back to her hel, chop them, and boil the bits and snippets in her big black cauldron, releasing their souls to rise with the steam. A soul freed was a wonderful thing, but the manner of the freeing enough to make a body sit up in bed at night sheened with cold greasy sweat. Besides, once the soul was released the meat and broth were fed to the Hag's pack of black bitches, and what sort of an end was that to a body raised among the tenets of the Church of Christ?

Ceileigh McNab had no reason to believe her fiddle or its song could be heard above the tumult in the bar, but she was being paid by the hour to play the songs these sweating drunks wanted to hear, and there was more money to be made tonight than at any other time of the year. Paid by the hour to play, besides which the men, to follow tradition and culture and to prove something to each other, threw her little bits of metal coin, mostly copper but enough silver to make her smile sincere and her fingers supple. Did they know that before the Christians and their witch fires, money given a bard or troubadour was considered an offering to Ceridwen herself, patron and protector of musicians, poets, and dancers?

Ceileigh didn't care if they knew or not. They were tossing pennies and bits, roaring out requests, and she, by God, wanted to please. Enough pennies, enough bits, enough jobs like this one and she'd have the money she needed for passage. Right now the country was caught in the grip of bestial winter in this unforgiving endless expanse of new land, but soon enough springtime would come, and she, by all the gods of war, would have passage money! Even here, even in a land frozen to ice half the year, there were people who wanted to hear jigs, reels, and ballads, people who wanted to dance and sing, people who wanted to sit with a steaming mug in their hands and weep unashamed tears for the schaelings left behind and never to be seen again. Ceileigh McNab herself gave not so much as a snap of her calloused fiddlers' fingers if she ever set eyes on the Christ-accursed old country again. What had dear Scotia ever given Ceileigh or her kind?

It didn't matter. Nothing mattered tonight but the playing of music and the making of money. Let the old ones know you appreciated life and knew how to live it fully!

She lowered her fiddle, wiped her sweating forehead with the wrist of her bow arm, placed her instrument well away from the pushing and shoving, and quickly scooped up the bits of money tossed her by the loud singing throng. A widely grinning waiter brought her a mug of weak beer. She took it, drained half of it gratefully, and grinned back at him. "Next song is for you and you alone, hinny," she called.

She resined her bow, checked the tuning of her strings, folded a clean square of cloth, placed the cloth on her right collarbone to pad it against the pressure of the wooden body of her violin, finished her beer, and prepared to play for the capering workmen. The poor sods would have one day to recover from this mad enthusiasm, then it would be back to work, the worst sort of work for the worst sort of pay, building the city here in the middle of the frozen prairie, toiling in weather so cold it could crack open the trunks of trees, forcing their bodies to do the most incredible things, the sweat freezing on their faces.

And every one of them glad of the chance of work, glad of a job, glad of a bit of pay, however meagre.

It was warm enough in here tonight! The press of bodies would have guaranteed heat, even without the blazing fire in the open stone hearth. Not that mine host was inclined to be generous with his firewood, but sweating men drink more beer, and it was her job as fiddler to get them dancing, get them sweating, keep them drinking. And she knew how to do that!

It was well after daybreak before the revellers began to wend their way through the frozen streets, back to their cots and pallets in the chilled tenements where they paid dearly for a place to sleep. Ceileigh collected her pay and stuffed it in the sturdy leather pouch she wore against her skin, as safe as it could be from the cut-throats and the light-fingered. Then she wrapped her precious violin in a piece of sheepskin, put it in the leather case her great-grandmother had made, and laid the leather case her great-grandmother had made, and laid the leather case inside the wooden one her brother had made for around the box, hoisted the heavy case, and left the tavern gratefully. She detested the stench of old beer and the sodden sawdust and hay that covered the floor. If there was any other way to make money she'd never set foot in a place like this again.

She was halfway home when two young drunken dandies appeared, suddenly, from the half-hidden side street. They were laughing, but Ceileigh knew better than to trust them. She crossed to the other side of the street, moving as quickly as she could on the frozen ruts and uneven crust of ice. The two men followed her, nudging each other and talking softly. She quickened her pace, cursing the rough frozen ground. In decent weather she would have made it to safety, but tonight, the ice and snow she hated so much betrayed her. She slipped, and in the time it took her to steady herself, the two were upon her, forcing her back into the space between two buildings, tripping her, pushing and laughing. She fell, managing only to protect her violin by cradling it against her own body. Even as she kicked and squirmed, her attention was on the box and the precious instrument inside it. She pushed it across the yellow-stained ice, well clear of the men's elegantly booted feet.

In less time than it would have taken her to fight her way free of them, it was finished. It hurt, but far less than a punch in the mouth. Two thrusts, a lunge, then a gasp and a moment of quivering, like a rabbit, and the dark-haired one was off her and making room for the other one, who was on her before she could struggle free.

Ceileigh rolled to her knees, grabbed her violin box, and struggled to stand up. The blond man was bent half over, fumbling drunkenly with the buttons on his pants. The dark-haired man stood with his back turned to her, pissing against the wall of the building.

Rage exploded inside Ceileigh's head, a rage unlike any she had ever known. The violin box swung and the pisser grunted, the back of his head suddenly bloody. The blond man gasped with surprise and fear, and turned to run, but she swung the box again and the sharp-cornered edge caught him on the cheek-bone. He screamed and fell to his knees, clutching his ruined face, and the wooden box connected a second time, shattering his teeth and chin. The dark-haired pisser struggled to his knees, but before he could rise to defend himself, Ceileigh lifted the box above her head and smashed it down on the back of his head, knocking him face-first into the ugly mess of ice and mud.

Five minutes later she was in her own cold room, panting heavily, her heart racing. She opened the violin box, lifted out the leather case, and brought out her fiddle. All it needed was tuning. She sighed with relief, wrapped it again in the sheepskin, and replaced it in the leather case. Then she turned her attention to the wooden box. She wiped off the blood carefully and examined the scratches made by broken teeth. "May they ache forever," she growled.

She lay in bed shivering with cold, shivering with the aftermath of fear and rage, and knowing she was lucky. If it had to happen, then at least the Crone had arranged for it to happen after a full night of playing music in a large room full of laughter and noise. At least it had happened when she was so tired most of the shock and ugliness hadn't registered. Wide awake and aware, she would have been horrified and close to hysteria. Instead, all she wanted to do was close her gritty eyes and fall into blessed sleep.

When she wakened a few hours later, she was hungry and dull resignation had grown into shocked fury. How bloody dare they! What made them think they had the right to treat another body that way! They didn't have Ceileigh McNab's permission to look at her, let alone touch her!

She lit her little fire, warmed the stew half-frozen in the pot, and heated enough water for a pot of strong tea and a good quick wash. She swabbed the dried blood off her thighs, again cursing the two young bastards. She hadn't won that fight, and they'd got what they were after, but they would know for a long time they had been in a good one. The blond man would always have a three-cornered hole punched in where his cheek used to be and his smile was forever ruined by the solid wood of the violin case. Bad luck to them for all the days of their lives, she prayed.

The hot stew warmed her belly, spreading out to take the bitter cold from her body. Ceileigh took the hot bricks from the small hearth, to wrap them first in sacking, then in sheeting, and tuck them in her bed so she could get a good, long, warm sleep. She would have loved to keep the fire going, but she needed every cent she could save. More than ever she was determined to leave this foul hole.

Ceileigh played in the saloon again on Saturday night, and in the church on Sunday, and the well-to-do listened approvingly. Those who could afford it entertained regularly throughout the grisliness of winter, so there were jobs enough to keep her in food and fuel, to pay her rent on the small, drab room, and to keep untouched her carefully hoarded store of coins from the saloon job. Sometimes she played happy jigs, sometimes they wanted the classical pieces. Thanks to her grandmother, she could read music and play whatever they asked for.

Her father had resented the time she spent learning, but he couldn't argue with his mother-in-law—not while he lived in her house, worked the fields she leased, and ate the eggs from her chickens. "Always make sure you can pay your own way," Ceileigh's grandmother taught sternly. "Give nobody, not man, not woman, any hold over you. No matter how nice it looks, make sure there's a way out of it, make sure you can look after your every need yourself." Every day the lessons, and every day the warning, "It's life, Ceileigh, and not easily lived. Do what you can do as well as you can do it for as long as you can do it and make sure you've saved for the time you won't be young and strong, for nobody will look after you if you can't pay your way."

Ceileigh's mother died, exhausted, after giving birth to two stillborn babies, and when her grandmother knew herself to be dying, she gave Ceileigh a sturdy pouch with a handful of coins in it, told her the heirloom violin was hers, and told her to leave. "Just see me into the ground, Ceileigh darlin', and go." Ceileigh hadn't understood, but she had always done what her grandmother told her. She saw to the burial, then packed her things, tucked the double-boxed violin under her arm, and left in the middle of the night while her father snored off the strong liquor with which he had celebrated the passing of his mother-in-law.

Now, half a world away, her grandmother's music lessons were what kept Ceileigh from freezing, or starving, or having to take to the streets to keep herself alive. The lying bastards had mentioned nothing of any of this! Land of milk and honey, they said. Free land. Opportunity. A new world with a new life for those bold enough to reach out and grasp it. Sheepshit, Ceileigh knew now, but at the time it had sounded like paradise on earth. And really, it was no worse than dear old Scotia where you could work your life away and have nothing to show for it but a few miserable coins and a violin handed down in the family since who knew when. If it was colder here, at least it was cleaner and marginally less violent. And she had followed her grandmother's advice. Ceileigh had her coins, and when the ice broke up she was taking the back door out of this place.

She was on her way back from church, picking carefully among the thawing puddles, when a voice cried, "That's her!" Ceileigh turned to see a blond man with a badly scarred face, pointing at her. Another man, larger, older, and obviously enraged, moved toward her, his cane upraised.

"Po-liss!" she shouted. "Beware! Po-liss!" And then half the crowd was trying to get out of the way while the other half tried to block the way. Ceileigh ran, dodging swiftly. "Militia!"

she screeched. "Po-liss!" and then there were others running: those able-bodied souls who had neglected to report for militia training.

Home again, safe in her cold room, with her heart still pounding fiercely, she leaned against the door and cursed quietly. By the look of him, she'd done a better job than she had suspected or even dared hope. One side of his face looked like something fit only to frighten children into being good. Ceileigh knew the men would be asking questions everywhere. It would take time—the poor are never eager to answer questions put to them by the rich—but sooner or later their money would buy them what they wanted to know.

With any kind of luck except bad, she'd be gone before they tracked her down in this wretched warren of crowded streets and alleys. Anyway, she had worse trouble to worry about. If she paid the abortionist, that would be it for her store of coins, that would be it for her plans. If she didn't pay the abortionist, there she'd be, end of September at the latest, with a howling, wailing brat. What do you do then, Ceileigh McNab? And if you do pay him, that problem will be gone but there's a strong chance you'll lose every other problem, and every joy, too. At home there would be a herb woman to boil up the correct potion. Here, there was a pinch-faced man with glittering metal tools soaking in a basin of water that had never seen disinfectant. Dying wasn't the worse thing could happen. But dying slowly, with lingering infections, or bleeding to death drop by drop, like her mother. . . .

You could always wait, have it, then take it to the closest church and leave it on the altar for the good nuns to raise. Even in this cold land they must have a foundling home. What did Ceileigh care who got the snuffling and shitting little bastard? It was none of her planning and none of her doing, so why should she do any of the worrying?

She had to make up her mind, and make it up fast. Every minute spent leaning against the door, worrying, was another minute the men had to look for her. Every minute she spent doing nothing brought them a minute closer to finding her. And she knew there would be only one kind of justice, meted out by the wealthy against the poor.

2

Aggie had never known her last name. For years she didn't even know people had more than one name. Names didn't mean much to her. People came and people went, some stayed for greater or lesser amounts of time, some were less nasty than others, but none were nice. Aggie didn't even know people could be nice, or clean, or honest, or kind, or even not hungry all the time.

Her father had come from somewhere else, in flight from the old life and in search of a new one, but he had brought his defeat with him. One was too much, a thousand not enough, but he tried. He worked at whatever job he could find to get the money for his passion and poison, and when his drinking interfered with his job, he was fired. When there was no money for booze he endured the snakes, sobered up, pulled himself together, and got another job. He worked like a fiend until he had enough money to quench the thirst in his guts, then the destructive cycle started up again. He was fired again, endured the snakes again, sobered up again, and began to try to pull himself together. Again.

Somewhere in one of these cycles, he met and took up with Aggie's mother, a woman whose thirst challenged his own, and life became the same, only more so. He drank, she drank, they both drank, until harsh circumstance forced them both to sob-

er up, smarten up, tidy up, and act normal until, one way or
another, there was money for booze, and the next bender was
kicked off.

He worked at whatever he could turn his hand to. She worked
as washerwoman, cook, cleaning woman, tavern waitress, or
she worked the streets. Wherever either of them had started,
wherever either of them had once lived, they wound up on The
Flats, a wide and ripely reeking strip of viscous goo on the south
side of the Fraser River, where the flotsam, jetsam, drift-
wood, trash, and low-lifes seethed and suppurated.

The shack they moved into was built on stilts so the river
could lap harmlessly under the rickety structure without actually seeping inside. It was a crazed contraption of poles and sal-
vage, the floor a latticework of boards, broken crate sides,
poles, and branches. The walls were patched with bits of
planking, bits of canvas, bits of whatever they could find in the
mud and mess along the banks of the wide, muddy river. Sometimes one or the other of them sat with a pole and line catching
fish, sometimes one or the other managed to beg, borrow, or
steal a bit of net and lay it more or less in the river to trap
something they could sell for money to buy booze. Failing that,
they could cook and eat what they had caught, and, with any
luck at all, manage to keep it down.

One of their offspring fell from the rickety porch a week
after it had learned to crawl and was found face-down and
stiff in the putrid back goo. One of the others fell into the crazy
contraption that was supposed to be a stove, and was badly
burned. The burns didn't kill it, however, infection did that.
Some townspeople arrived one night without warning, lifted
two of the kids from the festering mess that was their bed, took
them away, and gave them to some other people. And that was
that, there you were, nothing to do but endure and remember
how the ones across the river could just come down as if they
owned the world, steal your kids and not even a thank you or
here have a drink, as if a body had nothing else to do but go
through all that to provide them with the kids they probably
couldn't have themselves, bloodless bastards that they were.

Nobody came to steal Aggie. When she fell down the stairs
she landed on her butt, not her face, and somehow she man-

aged to avoid the stove and the fire that burned inside it. When she got her feet and legs under her and took off toward the river, all she did was stand on the bank and toss stones into the swiftly flowing brown water. She learned to catch fish, and she learned to steal from the other pathetically poor wretches who shared The Flats with the staggering lurching ruins who were her parents. She learned to fight, then she learned to win the fights, and everything she found went into her mouth.

Aggie was seven, filthy dirty, half-naked, fierce-eyed and hungry when her parents came back from a week-long bender accompanied by a down-sliding thirty-year-old. He had managed to hold one job or another for periods of up to two years, but he was obviously destined for a life on The Flats. He smiled at Aggie, spoke to her, then smiled again. "Got a smile for me?" he wheedled. Aggie just stared at him. "Give you a penny for a smile," he coaxed. Aggie looked at the penny, then at him. She knew what you could get for a penny. You could get hot food is what you could get. You could clutch the penny in your grimy paw, make it over to the other side of the river, head into town and get a hot crusty bun from a baker. Or, if you could find a Celestial, you could buy a doughy bun stuffed with meat and spices. She held out her hand. The new-found uncle gave her the penny and Aggie smiled.

A few days later the uncle offered her another penny, and again Aggie smiled for him. He offered her two pennies if she would dance for him, but Aggie didn't know what dancing was.

"Like this." He demonstrated clumsily, his voice quavering in what was supposed to be song. Aggie watched, and as Uncle sang, she danced. And she loved it. If she'd had it, she would have paid him a penny to sing so she could dance. But she didn't have a penny, and he couldn't sing for long before bursting into tears or passing out, so Aggie had to learn to sing by herself.

Music wasn't hard to find. There were people whistling on the docks, there were people singing in the fields, there was the sound of the mouth harp after supper in the work camp where they were laying train track, and there was the sound of Sunday hymns from the half-open windows of the church. Aggie memorized the words and tunes and taught herself to step gracefully and kick easily. Once she found out about them, she spent hours every night outside the town's bawdy houses, peering under the door or through the cracks in the wall at the long-legged dancers.

Eventually she learned what it was Uncle was really paying her for, and her price went up. She would no longer sit on his lap and cuddle for a penny. When her father got knifed in a fight and her mother disappeared with the one who owned the knife, Aggie was alone in the shack with Uncle.

"Aggie," he pleaded, "where's my own sweet girl?"

"No," she said stubbornly.

"Aggie. Please. Just a little cuddle," he wheedled.

"No."

"Two pennies," he begged.

"No," she said, "I want a dress."

"A dress?" He gaped. "Where in hell would I find a dress?"

She never asked where he found it or how much he had to pay for it, or even whether he'd paid anything. She didn't care if he worked for it or stole it. She didn't even care that it wasn't blue. It was a dress, and it almost fit her. Best of all, it had a skirt that swirled when she danced. She put it on, then sat on his lap and smooched him happily.

"Shoes?" he shouted. "What in hell do you want with shoes?"

"I can't tap in my bare feet," she sulked.

The shoes didn't appear for a month. For most of that month Aggie slept in a packing crate she had pushed into the willows along the bank of the river. Uncle searched for her, he called her name, he asked people to let him know if they saw her, and finally he sobered up, shaved, headed across the river, and got a job. After two weeks he collected his pay and bought Aggie's shoes before he bought his bottle.

"Aggie," he called, weaving only slightly, and holding up the shoes for all the world to see. "Aggie, dear."

She moved back into the shack, but the shoes didn't tap very well on the soggy mess of a floor. And Aggie wanted to hear the taps. She went across the river to where they had wooden sidewalks, and she tapped to the tunes humming in her head. At first nobody paid any attention, but Aggie didn't care. She slept in an old barrel behind the chowder house and the Celestial cook gave her leftovers in return for nothing at all except, perhaps, the hope of some future kindnesses from his own gods.

One day as Aggie was tapping in her now totally filthy dress, someone tossed her a penny. She gave it to the Celestial. The next penny she kept for herself. The third penny was for the Celestial, the fourth for herself. Gradually she learned if she danced near a saloon she collected more pennies than if she danced on the corner. She learned how to smile as if life were just one beautiful thing after another, because that parted the fools from their pennies quicker than a serious expression would.

The Salish woman had taken two large baskets of smoked salmon into town to exchange for flour and rice, and was on her way back when she saw the girl moving with an awkward grace, dancing in spite of her obvious hunger. The Salish woman stopped, watching without expression as the child tried to pretend she was smiling, tried to pretend she enjoyed what she was doing. The early darkness of winter was closing around the city, a fine mist of rain starting to drizzle from the low-hanging grey, and the girl's eyes were dark-circled with hunger and fatigue. The Salish woman dug in her hip-bag, hauled out a piece of dried fish, and held it toward the girl. "Come," she grunted, walking away from the sodden corner. "Come," she repeated, patting her hip-bag, indicating she had more fish.

Aggie crammed the fish in her mouth. She had no sooner chewed and swallowed it than the woman handed her another piece. And with no more hesitation, Aggie followed the old woman, stopping only to remove her precious but worn shoes.

She slept that night on a dry floor of rough-split cedar planks in a one-room cabin of cedar posts and large hand-split shakes. A stone fire-pit safely contained a bed of coals and the smoke drifted up to the roof, escaping easily among the planks and shakes. The bed of dried grass and bracken fern was covered with gunny sacking, and Aggie even had a trade blanket and a small cover of soft pelts. Her belly was full, she was warm and comfortable for the first time in months, and she didn't care if she had died and gone to heaven, it was better than anything she had known in her life.

Aggie learned to gut, clean, and fillet fish, how to keep the fire smouldering in the smokehouse, how to build and maintain a fish weir, and how to air-dry fish. She learned to set strangulation snares for muskrat and how to skin and cook the meat. She learned how to swim and she learned how to laugh without sarcasm or fear.

Every morning they rose, put fresh wood on the fire, and went immediately, without speaking to each other, to a special place where the fresh water stream racing for the river widened to form a deep pool of cold, clean water. They stripped off their clothes, walked into the water, faced the wakening sun, and prayed privately. Then they ducked completely under the water, still praying, and surfaced facing south. They prayed again, ducked under the water again, turned again, and stood up, facing the west. Again they prayed, again they ducked under the clean water, and again they surfaced, facing north. There was more prayer and then the ritual was repeated: they ducked under and emerged once again facing the east. They chanted then, together, young voice and old, thanking all levels of creation for the new day. They scrubbed themselves with cedar, dedicating themselves to a good life. When they emerged from the pool they dried themselves with bracken fern, put on clean clothes, carefully cleaned yesterday's garments, and went back to the small cabin, bodies steaming in the cool morning. Their clothes were hung carefully to dry or to air. Only then did they sit by the fire to make and drink kinickinick tea, to speak to each other, to participate fully in the gift and wonder of another day.

Aggie learned to make and use the Salish loom, and she wove for herself a plain, warm blanket. She watched and learned how to shear sheep, how to clean the fleece, how to prepare the wool for the old woman's expert weaving. She learned to choose, gather, and prepare grass and bark for baskets and mats, she learned which wood could be fashioned into plates and bowls. She learned to speak Salish and taught the old woman more English, and she taught English to the children with whom she wrestled, played tag, and raced. Twice a day she ate as much as her belly could hold. And she began to accompany the old woman into town to trade smoked fish, baskets, blankets, or berries for the flour, tea, and salt the aging woman had grown to want. "You're cheating her," she said firmly to one merchant. He glared at her and almost told her to start walking to the ends of the earth, but he had back orders for smoked fish and even if he doubled the barter he paid he would make a healthy profit. So he shrugged wordlessly and added more goods to the pile of staples on the counter.

Aggie willingly dug the garden plot as the old woman directed, then planted the seeds where and how she was told. When weeds sprang up she pulled them. When the ground was dry she carried water from the river. And when the vegetables were ready she ate them, grinning with pride because she had worked to provide her own food. The uncles showed her how to bait a hook so big she was convinced no fish would be stupid enough to try to swallow it, and they showed her how to knot and fasten a line so heavy she shook her head in disbelief. They demonstrated how big and how heavy the weight should be, how to place the weight on the muddy bottom where the line disappeared into the goo. And when the huge sturgeon, old flabbymouth, was caught on the end of her line, the uncles came to help her haul it to shore. She only caught one sturgeon, but the entire family in the village feasted on the rich meat. The children sat with their small hands full of delicious eggs, eating greedily and telling each other it was Aggie caught the feast.

She caught a large, hissing, red-eared turtle in the fish trap, and instead of letting it go, she took it back with her, carrying it carefully by the edges of its shell, avoiding the snapping beak, mildly frightened by the savage hissing. She put it in the creek and watched in awe as it headed immediately downstream, toward the river. She caught it a second time, took it farther up the creek, and again the turtle barely hesitated before swimming off in the right direction, heading for the river and freedom. She wanted to keep it but the turtle was so obviously determined to be free that Aggie just couldn't bring herself to build a weir to hold it captive.

"The world was built on the shell of the Turtle," the old woman told her that night. "The Voice Which Must Be Obeyed saw Grandmother Turtle asleep in the middle of the great lake where all the fresh water in the world gathers. The Creator sprinkled dirt and grass seed, flowers and cedar seeds, and when that was in place, other miracles were put on Grandmother Turtle's back. The sun warmed that small world, the rain washed it, the wind talked to it and night blessed it with rest. The Creator was pleased by the beauty and added more and more. Eventually, Grandmother Turtle wakened and felt the weight on her back. When she turned her head and looked over the rim of her shell to see what this new thing on her back was, the shifting of her body caused the small world to slip off and float by itself. Grandmother Turtle was amazed. She looked at the wonder she had borne so easily and could not believe her own part in this miracle.

"The Creator was amused by the look of wonder on Grandmother Turtle's face and put another small island-world in the water, then another. Some of these worlds floated together and formed a larger world, joined by others and by still others, and Grandmother Turtle's joy grew so much she began to frolic in the water. The Creator was pleased, and to encourage Grandmother Turtle's joy, added more and more of the wonders and marvels of Creation, until finally the world was larger than the great lake and covered it, except in those places where the water burst forth in small lakes, ponds, streams, rivers, and even waterfalls.

"Next time you see Turtle, look at her eyes. Even the many times great-granddaughters of Grandmother Turtle know that the world would never have begun had it not been for them, each of them know that under the soil on which we walk is water. And they know something we do not yet know, something we may never know, and that is why they have that look of wisdom, that look of something secret and precious. All we know about the secret of the turtles is that it has to do with water, with water trapped and hidden under the mountains, under the land, under even the bed of the sea. And turtles are never lost. They always know how to head for the place they need to be. Turtles never stay in a place where there is not enough food for them. They can always find their way to the place they should be living. And," she grinned happily, "a turtle has the most wonderful sex life. She only needs to breed once in her life, and yet she can lay her eggs every year for longer than most of us ever live. She can," the old woman winked, "breed more often if she wants. But she does not *need* to. If she welcomes the male turtle it is because she wants to welcome him, not because her body or her functions require it and force her."

One morning Aggie wakened, reached for her clean clothes, rose from her bed, and turned, expecting to see the old woman waiting by the door for her. Instead, the old woman was still in her blankets, eyes open, face drenched with sweat. She shook her head and flicked her eyes commandingly at the doorway. Aggie obeyed the wordless command. She left the cabin, raced for the pool, stripped off her clothes and rushed through the morning ritual. Her heart pounded, her head felt full of buzzing noise and she shivered, but not from the cold of the pool. She hurried back to the cabin, hung her clothes to dry, then moved to the old woman's bed.

"Grandmother," she breathed, her throat tight and sore. "Oh, Grandmother, what is it?"

The old woman was dead within hours and by nightfall half the village was sick. Aggie did what she could, but the people died as quickly as the old woman had perished. Old men and women, small children, healthy young adults, it made no difference. They took to their beds, pouring sweat, shivering, and puking uncontrollably. Then they died. Nothing helped. Not sage tea, not skunk cabbage, not devil's club. They sickened and died. Aggie wanted to bury them the traditional way, in platforms high in the trees, but the authorities in the town had forbidden the old traditions. She would have cremated them, but how much wood could one person cut, how much would be needed to dispose of so many bodies? Finally, overcome by the enormity of the horror, she went into town, found the office of the Constabulary, and told them.

They sent medical teams to the village but even the doctors and trained nurses could do nothing. So they sent teams of workmen with picks and shovels, to dig a large pit. Then, with only a Christian minister to say words none of the dead would have appreciated, they buried the people who had been Aggie's family. Aggie stood separate from the townspeople, isolated in her own grief and horror, watching but not believing. And when the dead were buried, Aggie gave herself permission to go crazy. She walked away from the only place she had known security or love, taking with her only what she wore, leaving everything else to the fires the townspeople were building, into which they piled everything the family had ever made, or had, or owned. All she took were her clothes, the old woman's blanket, and the blanket she herself had woven.

The townspeople noticed nothing. Without a word to any of them, Aggie walked away, her mind in fragments, her heart turned to a cold lump of stone. She walked away from the garden, away from the stream, away from the river where the great-granddaughter of Grandmother Turtle hugged her secret safe inside her shell. And Aggie headed back to The Flats where the filth and ugliness held no reminders of happiness snatched away by cruel fate.

3

Her name meant Noble Lady. She was neither a lady, nor from a noble family, and the proof of her beginnings moved with her every step of her life.

Long ago, the daughter of the Manchu emperor had been born with grotesquely deformed feet, and rather than have the royal daughter feel ugly, the crazed ruler passed a law that crippled untold millions of girls and women. But the peasants were spared the agony: though their daughters' marriage value was reduced, there is no way a girl child can be worked from dawn until after dark if she cannot stand alone or walk unsupported. So Su Gin's feet were never bound, and that was at once her shame and her salvation.

Even if her feet had been properly bound, she would not have been considered beautiful. The style was for oval-faced, pale-skinned, soft-eyed women. Su Gin had too much of the northern provinces in her features: sharp, flashing eyes, strong, prominent cheekbones, a wild face, more suited to the body of a conquering horseman than a subjugated rice farmer. Perhaps it was the sight of that fierce face decided her parents and saved Su Gin's feet. Perhaps they knew that face would never inspire anyone to offer concubine status, let alone marriage. Perhaps they knew the best their daughter could hope for was life with a humble farmer. With a face like hers, her name was almost a joke. A joke that may have angered the gods, or may have amused them. One never knows with gods.

Su Gin was leading the family ox back to the village from the far fields when the first shots were fired from beyond the small cluster of thatched buildings. She had heard of the lawless ones, she had heard terrible stories of what they could do, would do, and had done. She took the lead rope from the gentle ox, slapped his rump, and told him to save his own life. Then she whirled and ran back the way she had come. On her un-bound feet she ran, away from the village, across the earthen dike that held the water in the rice paddy, to the far field, where she threw herself between the rows of tender green rice shoots, into the thick mud and shallow water.

She rolled herself in the mud, coating her clothing, her hair, and her body, and then lay on her back all day and all night, only her nose and mouth clear of the water, willing herself to ignore the flickering of flames and the smell of the village animals being roasted to feed the bandits. She tried not to hear the screams and the pleading, but she knew the people whose voices were raised in hopeless appeal, and her heart cracked with horror and sorrow. She tried to ignore the shouts of triumph and the wails of despair, but tears leaked from her closed, submerged eyes, and sobs shook her chilled body, for even with mud in her ears she could hear the screams of terror and pain. She prayed to Kwai-Yin, the Lady of Boundless Compassion, the Lady Who Brings Children, the Great Mother of China, whose Gol-den Womb produced the world and all who live on it.

Su Gin stayed hidden as long as she could, even after the shouting and laughing subsided, until she knew if she stayed any longer in the cold mud, manure, and water, she would lose her hold on the spark of life. She moved slowly to the bank, climbed out, and stood dripping and shivering in the angry-coloured sunlight cutting through the thick haze of smoke from the ruined village. The breeze seemed to burn her face and hands, her big bare feet were wrinkled and blue-tinged, and her body ached with every step she took.

Su Gin limped and shuffled her way back to the smouldering wreck of what had been her home, praying with every short, jerky step her stiff legs took. The criminals had gone, taking the prettier young women and some of the strong young men with them. Only the very old and the very lucky were left to bury the dead and try to start again. There was no sign of her sister, her three brothers, or her parents. A young woman lay on her stomach in a pool of blood, her lotus feet unbound, exposed. Su Gin felt her legs weaken, her empty stomach lurch, she sank to the earth gasping, forcing air into her tightened chest. Such indignity, such abomination! Who but a total fiend would dare to do such a thing? She lifted the crippled foot and hastily wrapped strips of cloth around it, hiding it from sight. The three-inch Lotus Hook was stained with blood droplets and something else Su Gin did not have the experience to identify, but still she knew what the raiders had done. Knew they had deliberately unwrapped the delicate atrophied stub and used it to satisfy their perverted lusts. The four smaller toes were folded completely under the bottom of the foot, the big toe over top of them, and the heel bound forward so that the heel and folded toes were brought together, bones broken and curved in what the poets said was a second lotus, a second vulva, one developed solely for the pleasure and joy of the husband, one never used for childbirth, menstruation, or a woman's pleasure. And the bandits had dared vent their lust on a treasure that had been started when the dead young woman was younger than five years of age. Poor soul, to have survived infection, insanity, suppuration, to have avoided gangrene and pain-induced suicide, and then to be used in such a way by men whose own mothers would curse them.

Su Gin covered the violated feet, said yet another prayer to Kwai-Yin, then decided to save her own life. She wanted to fling herself to the ground, to wail and howl, to grieve and mourn, but there was no time. The dead had to be buried, the wounded had to be found and made comfortable and consoled until they, too, died. The living, those few who were not even certain they should be considered lucky, had to do the work.

For a week she moved in a nightmare of terror and grief, eating what could be salvaged from the mess, working to bury the dead, sleeping only when she could no longer stay awake.

And one day, through Su Gin's grief and exhaustion, she heard a voice cry, "Praise the gods you are still alive!" She

turned toward the voice and her father's cousin hurried to take
her in his arms, holding her gently, babbling his thanks to the
few surviving villagers. "Praise and thanks to the gods," he said
repeatedly and loudly. "Praise and thanks to those who helped
this child to survive!"

They went back to the ruined family house, and together they
surveyed what had once been a prosperous farm. Her father's
cousin shook his head and cursed the bandits for ruining the
crops, for killing and eating the chickens, ducks, and pigs.

"I will rebuild this," he vowed. "I will have the family shrine
rebuilt, and pay the priests to bless it. We will placate the
gods. Somehow, sometime, this family must have offended
them, or these bandits would never have been allowed to come
down and destroy everything."

"I know of no offence," Su Gin stuttered.

Her father's cousin smiled. He placed a comforting hand on
her arm and patted gently. "Perhaps it was someone in the village," he soothed, "and the gods were so angry everybody else
had to pay, too. If we knew what offended the gods we would
never offend them. But...we never know what will insult them
and as a result, we suffer." He looked at the land and smiled
again. "Now, my cousin's daughter," he said encouragingly,
"waste no more time in sadness. The land is good and my cousin was a fine farmer! What was built up and cared for over a
twenty-year period is not going to be destroyed for all time by
one raid carried out by a few drunken fools. We will bring
workers from my own village, we will rebuild the house and
outbuildings, we will bring in a crate of chickens and a dozen
good ducks, we will again plant the fields and prosper. This
unpleasantness will become nothing more than a part of the
unchangeable past."

"There is no money for that," Su Gin wept.

"Now, now," he scolded gently. "This talk of money does not
belong in the mouth of a woman. Money is something for men to
worry about. Leave things to me."

"But..."

"We are family," he said simply. "It is our duty that our
family survives, and that they survive for as long as is possible.
There was a time your father, my cousin, helped me, and

now..." He shrugged and Su Gin felt herself fill up with relief, gratitude, and pride that there was a man like this in her own family, a man not only successful in business, but also of high morals. Her mother had told her the two did not often go together but here was proof that they could.

"You!" he called to his workmen. "We need food. We need tea for my cousin's daughter before she is overcome by all this upset. Quickly, now, quickly!" And the way the men moved to do as they were bid told her just how successful and important her new-found kinsman really was.

There was already a cleared place in the ruins where they could sit together and drink tea, and her father's cousin again reassured her that combining the family resources would benefit and protect them all. "And you," he smiled, "as my cousin's only surviving child you will be cared for as if you were my own. You will not be impoverished or bereft. Now you will prosper and when your heart has healed and you are ready, we will make a good marriage for you, and then you will have a family of your own again."

A workman brought them food and they ate together, Su Gin marvelling at the delicious meal. Her father's cousin insisted she refill her bowl, and then with his own hands he handed her a cup of hot liquid. "This will help you relax," he promised. "You will sleep soundly tonight. You look as if you've hardly slept for the past week."

"There was so much to do," Su Gin said, hearing her own voice tremble. She swallowed quickly. The hot drink burned like fire and brought tears to her eyes. She coughed and almost choked. Her father's cousin laughed and refilled the cup, telling her she had to get used to the taste of the drink because all the successful people drank it all the time.

When Su Gin became sleepy, her father's cousin again told her she was like his own daughter, and he wept to think of all she had lost, all she had endured. "The thought of you being tormented with nightmares hurts my heart," he insisted. She could not remember telling him she had been tormented with nightmares but she did not want his heart hurting any more than it already must to see his cousin's family so reduced. So she drank from the cup he held to her lips and lay down to sleep on the quilt which had appeared from nowhere, as if by magic.

When she wakened, she was lying on a cold metal floor, her stomach heaving, her head thick and sore. All around her men and women puked and wailed, gagged and cursed the gods. It took hours of terror, panic, horror, and confusion before her questions were answered. Only then did she learn that the floor heaved because they were in the belly of a ship. The air was foul and the bodies soaking wet because everyone was seasick and there were no facilities of any kind. You pissed and shat where you were and if you stepped, sat, or slept in your own or someone else's mess, your condition was no different from anyone else's.

Nobody had to tell Su Gin she was here because her father's cousin had drugged her and smuggled her away from everything and everyone she had ever known. Nobody had to tell her she was here because her kinsman had no intention of sharing anything with her. The taste in her mouth and the fuzziness in her head told her she had been drugged. Her surroundings told her everything else. She knew it was the end of the Old Times. She did not yet know it was the beginning of what she would one day think of as the No-Time, the Dead Time.

Once a day, if the weather permitted, they were taken on deck and allowed to clean themselves with sea water. The foreign sailors aimed hoses into the ship's belly and flushed out the hold until filthy water poured from vents in the sides of the paint-flaked monster, taking most but never all of the slime and horror from it. And as the hold was sluiced, the captives were fed a disgusting mess of boiled oatmeal and chunks of salt fish. When Su Gin looked at it the first time, her stomach heaved. She considered her choices. She could fling herself over the side into the frigid grey water. She could refuse to eat and die slowly. She might be able to swallow her own tongue, or find a way to slice open her veins. And who would know, or care? Who would go back and slit the traitor cousin's throat?

She ate the vile mess and forced her stomach to accept it. Then she moved back to the vats of cold salt water and once again cleaned her hair, skin, and encrusted clothes as best she could. She was determined to live. Whatever she had to do, she would live. Whatever she had to endure, she would live.

While others sat and mourned, or stood at the deck looking back toward the place they would never again see, Su Gin forced her stiff body to move in the patterns of T'ai Chi, trying to convince herself she was back in her own village, safe and warm, moving through her work with her mother and grandmother, following the centuries-old traditions with her family.

The foreign sailors then went down into the hold long enough to burn lengths of rope to try to kill the stench, and before the smoke had cleared, the captives were herded back down into the darkness. Su Gin's eyes stung, her throat was dry and raw, the mess of mush and salt fish threatened to come back up again, but she found a quiet corner and sat with her back against the cold metal plating. She made herself discipline her emotions, made herself achieve calmness of purpose and clarity of thought. It was the duty of every member of the family to survive as long as possible. Otherwise the family would perish and the spirits of the dead would never rest.

Day after day, night after miserable night, she endured. When there was no room to practise T'ai Chi she flexed her muscles to their utmost and held them rock hard for ever-increasing lengths of time. She pressed against the sweating metal sides of the ship and imagined herself pushing it apart, straining her body, silently concentrating in every cell, in every drop of blood, pushing in futile attempts that did no harm at all to the ship but, over the long weeks of her captivity, hardened her muscles.

When the two captive men came at night to rape her, she fought silently. Her peasant hands, still calloused from a lifetime of work, closed around the windpipe of one man. Closed, squeezed, then tugged, as if Su Gin were ripping the head from a chicken. The man gave a single, agonized gasp, then flopped onto the floor, strangling in his own blood. The second man scurried away in panic. When the foreign sailors roused the prisoners and herded them out onto the deck to feed them and clean the hold, they found the rapist lying on the floor, his eyes bulging and his throat swollen and blackened by the blood beneath the skin. There were no questions. The sailors simply picked him up, carried him on deck, tied a weight to his ankles, and threw him over the side. More than anything, that disposal told Su Gin how the foreigners felt about the people who had to live or die in their own mess below deck. But nobody bothered her after that.

Gradually she lost all concept of time. She almost lost her memories of green fields, blue skies, and the scent of clean garden earth. Day after day she ate the foul food, slept in the disgusting mess the captives shared, and passed her time doing her exercises. Sometimes, when there was no light anywhere, when she could no longer tell up from down or left from right, sometimes, when she felt sure her next move would send her tumbling and falling, floating and out of control, she would almost think she could hear her mother's voice talking to her, telling her again the stories of the peaches of immortality, the stories of the monkey king, the stories of the fierce white-haired warrior woman who lived in the mountains and had dedicated herself to vengeance against those who had persecuted the weak and the innocent.

When they landed, Su Gin had no idea where they were. The foreign devils shouted orders nobody understood. As they pushed, shoved, hit, kicked, and flailed with lengths of knotted rope, the captives went over the side down rope nets, to smaller boats that transported them to a night-dark beach. There, with the Lo Fan, was an interpreter. Su Gin considered him a traitor but guarded her face carefully, knowing she would survive by appearing passive. She did as she was told, went where she was told, all with what looked like obedience and numb fatalism.

Into a wagon, crouch against the side, then bounce through the long night, obeying the order to be quiet. Su Gin studied the stars, trying to figure out where under the dome of the sky she might be. But the stars and their patterns were different. All she recognized was a sliver of what she prayed was the same moon she had seen at home.

As the sky lightened, the wagons left the road and bounced across rough grass-covered ground. They drove into a grove of trees, then crossed a shallow stream and stopped near a large, barn-like building.

"Out," the interpreter hissed, pointing at the open door. "Inside. Quiet."

Su Gin went inside the barn, found a place to hunker against the wall, and waited quietly. When they were finally given food and water, she ate and drank, then returned to her place. The captives were there all day, and Su Gin slept most of it. She was warmer here than she had been for weeks, and the smell of straw and hay was like a promise of life after the stench of shit and vomit. The hard-packed earth floor seemed as soft as her own long-lost bed, and her clothes no longer felt as if they would never again be dry.

She wakened when the Lo Fan brought in more of their strange and disgusting food, and even if she had no idea what it was she was taking into her body, she ate it. When they ordered her back into the wagon, she moved quickly, quietly, and willingly, to sit with her back braced against the rough-sawn boards, bouncing silent and passive through the dark night, under the grim guarding eye of a bearded man with a loaded shotgun. Before dawn she could smell the tar and shit of the docks, the sickish odour of intoxicating liquors. Then she could hear the rumble of drunken voices, a burst of discordant music, and a muted laugh. The dirt track became a road that ran through the stench of the outskirts of the city, past tents and shacks, down dark streets where privies festered behind crowded buildings.

There was too much to look at for Su Gin to see anything clearly. Buildings that looked nothing at all like the buildings of her own village, even before the raid. Streets totally unlike the ones she had known, wagons unlike the ones at home. And, everywhere she looked, evidence of the bearded Lo Fan.

When the wagons stopped behind a large building, a door opened. Lamplight flooded from inside, spilling on the dirt and garbage of the back alley. "Out," the interpreter yawned. "Inside. Silence."

Several men and a woman with bound feet, long painted nails, and rich clothing were standing in a large room brightly lit by a number of hanging oil-burning lamps. The men were dressed in foreign clothing, the woman in traditional clothes, wearing more jewels than Su Gin had ever imagined existed, jewels Su Gin knew were real jewels, not imitations. One of the women, beautiful and well-dressed, supported on either side by attend-

ants, moved past the uncertain and frightened people. She
seemed neither impressed nor unimpressed by any of them.

In this room Su Gin almost made the mistake of relaxing,
almost let herself believe she had been saved. But the memory of
her father's cousin was still too fresh and too painful for the
sight of Chinese faces to reassure her. What her father's cousin was capable of doing, anyone was capable of doing. So she
stood, her head slightly bowed, watching the well-dressed
ones, keeping her face devoid of expression, guarding the light
in her eyes. Until she knew more about them, they would know
nothing about her. She saw that there were doors out of this
room, but she had no idea where they went, and she was not
going to waste time, energy, and perhaps even her own life in a
vain attempt to get from where she was to some place she did
not know.

The women captives were taken away from the men, led up a
flight of stairs to a large room, and told by the beautiful woman's attendants to strip off their filthy clothes. Su Gin did not
appreciate standing naked and vulnerable in a room with half a
dozen other naked women, but there she stood, quietly, head
bowed, eyes hooded, while buckets of hot water were emptied
into large galvanized wash tubs. And when she was told to
climb into one of the huge tubs, Su Gin climbed in obediently.
To her surprise, there were attendants to help her. They undid
the long braid of her hair and washed weeks of filth and salt
from it. They helped her scrub herself repeatedly, then, when
even she was satisfied she was truly clean, they rinsed her hair
over and over, helped her from the tub, and handed her an
enormous, white, soft towel. She dried her body and would
have wrapped her hair in the towel, but there were women to do
even this for her. It seemed as if dozens of helpful women
were busy in that room, though not one of them spoke to her.
She was given clean, fresh clothes, of good quality cloth. Her
hair was dried, brushed free of tangles, and skillfully braided.

And just when all of this help and comfort began to over-
whelm her, the door opened, and huge bowls of deliciously
scented steaming hot food were brought in. Rice, for the first
time since the false cousin had drugged her, and bits of pork in
a hot pepper sauce.

"Eat," an old woman urged repeatedly. "Eat, so you smell like yourselves, and not like those big-nosed curd-scented barbarians." Su Gin asked no questions. She ladled pork and pepper sauce on top of her rice, sniffed it as if it were closer to salvation than she dared hope, and began to eat. She ate until she thought she would burst, and then she ate some more. Throughout the meal, the beautiful woman in the beautiful clothes sat on her beautiful chair and watched them with glittering eyes.

Su Gin almost fell asleep sitting there in that big room. Women were clearing away the baths, pailing out the water and tossing it out an open window, going back for bucketful after bucketful. Su Gin could tell by the number of stairs they had climbed and by the time it took for the water to splash on the ground, that they were too high for her to take a flying leap to freedom. Besides, she was so sleepy. She was warm, she was clean, she was full, and her eyes just didn't want to stay open or even to focus. She would gladly have lain down on the damp-spotted floor and slept for hours.

And that is when the gorgeous painted woman snapped her fingers. Two attendants rushed to help her stand, and within a few short minutes Su Gin had learned the price she would pay for her bath, her clothes, and the delicious food. She would have a bed to herself in a room with three others. Her clothes, her food, and her bedding would be provided. She would be warm, she would be clean, she would be protected, she would even have a few pieces of money for herself each month. In return for her body. For seven years.

Su Gin wasn't surprised. Somewhere inside herself, she had known this was not sanctuary, that these were not noble and spiritual people appeasing their gods through charitable works. She was no longer sleepy. But she was warm, her belly was comfortably full, the taste of the food lingered pleasantly in her mouth, and the memory of that stinking ship was still painfully fresh in her mind. She considered her options coldly. She could leap out that window and try to ensure she landed on her head and killed herself. Or she could try to escape. To where? She didn't know where she was, let alone where to run. She didn't understand the language of the foreigners and she knew nothing about their laws, if they had any. And until she knew that, there was no place to go and no place to hide. So she swallowed her growing anger and decided to wait.

One of the attendants showed Su Gin and three other women the room they were to share. Four beds, one in each corner of the room, and four very small, very plain wooden chests in which to keep their things. None of them had any things to keep in the chest, but it was nice to think that maybe one day.... The bed had fresh sheets and a warm blanket, with a second blanket neatly folded across the foot. Su Gin climbed into bed and slid under the covers, the taste of pepper sauce still in her mouth.

The world could have come to an end in the middle of the night, and Su Gin would not have known. She slept as if someone had cracked her on the back of the head with a length of sturdy stick. She wakened clear-headed and calm, knowing all her decisions had been made even before she had dropped into sleep. Breakfast was like nothing Su Gin had tasted before in her life. Even the food she had shared with the traitor cousin, delicious as it had seemed, could not compare with the meal waiting for them in the big kitchen downstairs. White rice, as much as a person wanted, meat in spicy sauces, vegetables steamed and sauced, it was inconceivable that ordinary people would ever get the chance to eat like this. But Su Gin was the daughter of farmers. She asked no questions. She took what was there, gave thanks to the gods, and wasted no time in indecision or doubt. She ate steadily, her mind racing, her eyes carefully examining the faces of the other women. Almost two dozen of them, and not all of them Celestials. Women with skin darker than any she had ever seen, women with skin as pale as the skin of the foreigners, tall women and short, all of them obviously well fed, well cared for, and seemingly content. Only the newcomers were dressed in plain trousers and tunics. The others wore clothing such as Su Gin had never imagined. They seemed incredibly cheerful considering they were to be slaves for at least seven years.

When she had eaten all she could, Su Gin was taken to the bathing room. The washtubs were still lined against the wall, but the window was closed and the curtain drawn. The beautiful woman with the tiny feet sat again in her gorgeous chair, flanked by two attendants. Su Gin was ordered to strip. Then, to her horror, she was carefully examined from the top of her head to the soles of her feet, examined as carefully as she herself had once examined animals in the market.

The beautiful painted woman was more than pleased to discover that there had never been a man in Su Gin's life or in her body. "Perhaps," she laughed, "we will get back our investment much quicker than I had dared hope." She frowned slightly at the muscles corded in Su Gin's back and shoulders, cluck-clucked and shook her head at the callouses on Su Gin's hands and feet, and stared for long minutes at Su Gin's face. "She looks," the painted woman said with a brittle laugh, "as if she was fathered by a wild animal." Su Gin flushed with shame, but the painted woman seemed not to notice, and continued to speak to her attendants as if Su Gin did not exist. "She is too tall," the painted woman decided, "and too raw-boned for any chance of making her appear beautiful, so we must make her look as wild and as fierce as possible. There are always some," she decided, "who consider savage appearance to be exciting and who get a great deal of pleasure from pretending they have managed to tame the fierce."

Nobody asked Su Gin any questions, nobody seemed to care whether she could hear what was being said. They might have been examining a piece of wood.

The painted woman waved her hand and Su Gin was led from the room, still naked, her clothes carried by the old woman who accompanied her down the hall to the bedroom she shared with three women she did not know. Someone had been in the bedroom. The lid of the wooden chest beside her bed was hinged open, and inside the box were towels, a face cloth, a small piece of soap, a little brush she knew immediately was for her teeth, and a small pile of plain dark blue clothing. She looked at the old woman questioningly, and the crone began to laugh. "Whether it was lack of opportunity, morality, or a protective family, your virginity has ensured your comfort, and you are lucky you did not lose it before you arrived here. Most do." She laughed again. Su Gin almost told her about the two men on the ship, but keeping quiet was a habit she had learned too well. Why tell anyone, especially those who might be the very ones she had to escape, that she knew how to defend herself? Why give potential enemies a weapon against her?

"The Lo Fan pay a high price for virgins," the old woman cackled.

"Lo Fan!" Su Gin gasped, horrified.

"Who else could afford it?" the old woman shrugged.

Su Gin had learned that No-Time is never so bad it cannot get worse. With no conscious decision on her part, she began to protect herself and her sanity by shutting off her mind and emotions. Sun and rain were the same to her. She didn't care if the flowers bloomed outside or not. She became so deliberately passive she was almost an observer of her own existence. All of it was happening to someone else, and all of it was timeless, it might have been one day or one decade. She didn't care. She wasn't there anyway, she was searching for her own peaches of immortality, travelling with the woman with the white hair, looking for Kwai-Yin the Compassionate.

4

Lily Nelson was born in a room above the dirt-floored hovel that was the closest thing to a saloon or tavern in a three-day ride. Her midwife was an Ojibway woman who cooked, did laundry, and tried to clean up after the drifters, boozers, trappers, prospectors, Hudson's Bay Company agents, and general arsel-tarts who came to this spot on the face of nowhere to drink, fight, and spend paid time upstairs with women who might have chosen another life if there had been any other life available to them. Since nobody, least of all her mother, had any idea who her father might be, she was given a name of her own, and her mother's maiden name.

Lily Nelson squalled and howled through her first week of life, her body tight, her knees drawn up to her distended belly. Minutes after nursing she spewed a thin stream of curdled milk all over herself. Day and night Lily howled, until finally the Ojibway woman lifted the taut-bodied infant, wrapped her in a blanket, and walked off with her. She came back two days later with a quietly sleeping, fuzz-headed blonde baby, and a young woman with a child of her own strapped to her back. The young woman lived downstairs, sleeping on a pallet on the pantry floor with her own child.

Lily Nelson's mother stopped her mild fretting about the absence of her first-born. She got out of bed, walked up and down the corridor holding tightly to the arm of her best friend Sally, and happily accepted the fact someone else was going to nurse the child, someone who wasn't nervous, who wasn't dying for a drink, who wasn't prone to weeping, who ate more than one meal a day, who slept soundly at night, and who never needed a good stiff shot of laudanum to bring the comfort of sleep. Two months after the child was born, Letitia was back at work, playing her mandolin, singing in her high, thin voice, dressed in her simple, child-like gowns, reminding the men of a life they had left behind or never known in the first place.

By the time Lily could walk, Letitia was drinking before supper, and by the time Lily could talk, her mother's thirst was flaring before the noon-time meal. Lily didn't care. She loved to clamber up the stairs and run up and down the long splintered hallway, laughing happily until a door opened and one of the doxies held out her arms for the child to run into and be swooped up, cuddled, almost suffocated in soft flesh and the scent of perfume, and taken into the room. Lily didn't care whose room it was. All the girls smelled the same, all the beds were soft and rumpled, and a cuddle is a cuddle is a cuddle. She played with powder puffs, she played with yards of soft, thin cloth, she bounced on well-used feather-stuffed beds which the whores laughingly called work benches, and she was smooched, tickled, cuddled, fussed over, and teased. She ate in the kitchen, and she ate well. She was washed in the laundry tub. She hardly had time to know she wanted something before it was given to her, and she learned early not to get upset by Letitia's flurries of scalding tears.

Letitia's collection of bar hooch empties was augmented by increasing quantities of small vessels which had once held laudanum. Her hysterics became less frequent. She spent more and more time lying on her bed, staring at the ceiling. Within a few years, Letitia stopped working except for her mandolin and guitar playing, which still enthralled the bearded and often grimy men, because few of them were enthralled by what happened once she stopped singing and took them to her work bench.

One day when Lily was six, she sat on the front steps of the saloon, playing with a corn husk doll someone had given her, moving the doll's stiff legs in the pattern of the dance Frenchie did at night, if enough men threw enough money into the pot. The horses tied to the hitching rail stood hip-shot and lazy, swishing flies and snorting dust from their nostrils, and from inside she could hear the soft murmur of voices as Madame and 'Gatha went over the books. The books were a constant source of dispute, and from hearing the heated discussions, even Lily knew they stayed off kilter and would not balance. Lily knew about balance. It was what Cookie could do with glasses, piling them in more shapes than you would believe possible, and when Cookie did it, the glasses stayed piled. When Lily tried, everything fell, things broke, and Madame roared with anger. She didn't roar when 'Gatha couldn't balance the books, though. She just puffed on her stinky cigar and squinted her eyes, muttered about finding the culprit and scalping him. If it was a him, it was a bartender, or a bouncer, or maybe a card player, the one Madame called a thieving scat.

Lily watched incuriously as a coach made its way down the bare ruts that pretended to be a road. The coach was big, it was black, it was gorgeous, and it was drawn by four of the fanciest horses Lily had seen in her brief life. It stopped right in front of the Mad Dog, the driver refusing to so much as look at the place. Then the coach door opened and a middle-aged woman got out. She sailed past Lily without even looking at her, and went inside the roadhouse. There was a short silence. Then the woman spoke briefly, her voice low and strong, and then Madame answered, her voice sullen and harsh, as if she had been caught doing something she shouldn't. But that was stupid, Madame could do anything she wanted, and usually did.

The square-bodied woman came back out of the Mad Dog and went to the open door of the coach. She spoke briefly to the person inside, and a small, grey-gloved hand appeared. The big woman protested, the small hand gestured demandingly, and the middle-aged woman grumbled but supported the tiny hand and stepped aside for the person inside. It was a tiny woman who looked like a bird, a fierce-eyed, small-bodied hawk or a furious bantam hen. She was dressed in pearl grey: dress, hat, veil, and gloves, but her beautifully shined little boots were black. She moved toward the Mad Dog as if she had bought it and

intended to burn it flat to the ground, and almost walked right
past Lily the way the middle-aged woman had.

The old woman stopped and looked down at the girl who sat
gawking, the corn husk doll almost forgotten, her bare legs and
feet coated with dust.

"What is your name?" the hawk-woman asked, her voice
strong and clear.

"Lily," the child answered. "What's yours?"

"Mind your manners!" the middle-aged woman snapped.

"Did anybody ask you?" Lily did not look at the big woman, she
was locking glances with the old lady.

"Bite your tongue, Miss Smart-Mouth!"

"Why'n't you shove your head up your arse and roll back off
down the street?" Lily suggested amicably. "I don't need no shit,
so you don't need to open your mouth. Do I want shit, I'll just
squeeze your head." The old woman coughed suddenly, her
hand over her mouth, her face reddening. The large woman in
the swishing black dress sniffed, tossed her head, and moved
forward, as if tugged by the frail old lady.

The women swept into the roadhouse. Lily listened to their
voices, wishing she could hear the words. But she wasn't allowed in the front door. Any time Madame found Lily in the
saloon, Lily's arse burned, so she didn't dare go any closer to
the half-door than she was. After a few minutes, she got up
and moved around the side of the building to the back door. She
went into the kitchen, intending to make for the stairs where
she could sit and eavesdrop, but she was distracted by the smell
of stew and dumplings, fresh bread, and cake.

"Any extra?" she grinned, openly flirting with the new cook.

Lucy smiled, reached for a bowl, and ladled stew into it. Lily
sat on a stool spooning stew into her mouth, mopping up her
gravy with a sandwich made of fresh bread and sliced raw onion. There was nothing in the world better than a raw onion
sandwich and if it made your eyes water sometimes, or your
nose run, so what? It was more than worth it.

She heard Letitia's voice, then the sound of hysterical weeping, punctuated by loud shrieks of protest and the usual threats
of suicide. Lily almost got off her chair and went to tell her
mother to put a plug in it, but all the noise was coming from the

saloon, and Madame was there. The last thing Lily needed was a warm arse, a thing like that could ruin the entire day. Besides, Letitia was always on the verge of either depression or hysterics. Lily heard Letitia run upstairs, and then there was more yelling, more howling, more weeping, and more screeching. Lucy shrugged expressively, making Lily giggle and almost choke on a big piece of cooked Swede turnip. "Having herself a real fit this time," Lucy chortled.

"Is there more?" Lily hinted broadly, peering in the direction of the bubbling stew pot. "It sure is good."

"You must have worms," Lucy decided. "No child could pack away this much food if she didn't have to feed a belly full of worms."

"Everybody has worms," Lily lectured. "Mabel told me worms were here before people were."

"Mabel ought to know, she *is* a worm."

"She's got the clap," Lily confided.

"How do you know? Was I asleep and missed the part where Miss Smarty went to school in the East and came back a doctor?"

"I know because I heard Madame yelling at her," Lily responded easily. "What's clap? I mean, I know how people clap, but..."

"May you never have to find out," Lucy prayed.

"How d'you get it?"

"You don't need to know."

"I might," Lily contradicted, "I might catch it. 'Specially if I don't know how *not* to catch it."

"Stay away from men," Lucy pronounced, laughing bitterly.

"Oh." Lily nodded, understanding everything.

And now Letitia was back in the saloon, carrying on again, hollering insults, shouting curses and weeping between accusations. Then Madame was shouting, 'Gatha was yelling, and Letitia was racing back up the stairs, screaming about the absolute unfairness of everything. They all came into the kitchen then, and everyone stood looking at Lily as if none of them had ever seen her before in their lives. Letitia charged back down the steps, pushed through the small crowd, raced forward dramatically, flung herself on her knees, and pulled Lily half off her stool.

"My baby," Letitia wailed. "My poor little baby girl."

"Lemme go, you're squeezing me," Lily protested, pushing her head against Letitia's forehead, bending her mother's head so far back Letitia had to let go or wind up with a damaged spine. The old woman smiled broadly at this, but the middle-aged woman sniffed disapproval.

"How can you?" Letitia howled, turning to the old woman. "You're supposed to be my grandmother! How can you do this to me?"

"Quite easily, my dear," the old woman said kindly. "I am not only your grandmother, I am this ragamuffin's great-grandmother, and, as has been said several times already, this is no place and no way to raise a child."

"You never did love me!" Letitia raged. "Everything I . . ."

"She's gotta go," Madame said flatly.

"Why?" Letitia snapped. "She isn't in anybody's way."

"She's in everybody's way," Madame contradicted coldly. "You barely justify your own keep lately, and anyway, even if you were working and bringing in good money, I'm not havin' no kid underfoot! She's getting too big for the customers to over-look, and should any of them get ideas . . . who needs that kind of aggravation. She goes."

"I might not go nowhere at all," Lily said, sliding from the stool and edging toward the back door. "I might not do no such thing."

"Your loss," the old woman said clearly. She looked at Lily, then, and smiled, a wide and already triumphant smile. "After all, you'd have a room of your own, you'd have clothes, and shoes, and your own books and music lessons. You'd have," and she drove in the telling nail, "your own pony."

"Pony?" Lily paused, tempted.

"Child." The old woman stepped forward and stood close, but not so close as to invade Lily. "Nobody wants to make your life miserable, but . . . your mother is not well. She cannot look after you properly."

"We're doing just fine!" Letitia screeched, but nobody paid her any attention.

"She drinks," Lily admitted.

"Yes," the old woman sighed. "Her father did, too. And the

other women can't . . ." she let it trail off, and Lucy sighed, turning away, leaving Lily feeling very alone and very helpless. "You're going to come and live with me," the old woman said firmly. "One way or another, sooner or later, the hard way or the easy way, you're coming to live with me."

They left within the hour, and Lily tried not to cry. When the traitor tears slid down her face, the old woman wordlessly handed her a small lace-trimmed hanky, and patted her arm comfortingly.

For months, Lily dreamed of her last sight of Letitia, kneeling in the dirt, wailing like a madwoman, screaming that it wasn't fair, she had done all the hard and dirty work and someone else could just walk in, steal her baby, and not pay so much as a penny for all her time and trouble.

The heavy-bodied, middle-aged woman had her own ideas of how Lily ought to behave, and before nightfall of the first day, war had been declared between them. Lily did not move like a lady, did not sit like a lady, did not talk like a lady, and most certainly did not eat like a lady. Lily didn't even sleep like a lady. She squirmed, twisted, kicked, and even went so far as to sit up, pull off her nightgown, and lie back down again in nothing but her own bare skin.

Great-grandmother napped during a great deal of the trip, and was thus unaware of how bitter a war was being waged. When awake, she spoke quietly and comfortingly to the confused and increasingly resentful child, and mediated effectively between her and her enemy. But Great-grandmother's intercession only meant that as soon as the way was clear, the enemy redoubled her efforts to civilize Lily.

Lily could not believe she was going to live in the house when they finally arrived. It was bigger than any building she had ever seen, bigger than all the buildings at the roadhouse, almost as big as all of them pushed together. And out behind the house, on the far side of a broad expanse of neatly trimmed grass, there stood a barn and a stable, and two smaller houses where the help lived.

Unfortunately, The Witch lived in the big house, in the room next to Lily's, and their rooms were joined by a common

door. She ate two meals a day with Lily, and opened the door and
entered any time she wished, without knocking. Lily liked the
new clothes: new shoes, a coat, mittens, and a hat. But she did
not enjoy learning to wear gloves, nor did she enjoy the lessons
in how to walk, how to sit, how to get off a chair, how to stand.
And The Witch wasn't the only person who was less than kind
to Lily. There were aunts and their husbands, uncles and their
wives, and more cousins than Lily knew what to do with, all of
them resentful, all of them disapproving, and even scornful.

"Just like her mother," they said. "No gratitude."

"Her mother never learned how to behave, either."

"I'll never understand why the old lady favoured her, or
why..."

"Why? Everybody knows why! Of all the eligible young men,
Letty had to fling herself at an absolute villain!"

"He was no such thing! Immature, perhaps, and undisci-
plined, but not a villain. If she hadn't been such a fool...the
pressure was just too much for him."

Lily was quick to realize they said none of those things when
Great-grandmother was in the room. When the old lady appeared, everyone was soft-spoken, the frowns vanished, the
smiles appeared. Cousins were pinched or pushed lightly,
urged forward to show their talents, to display their school-
work, to bring a smile to a faded face.

"Sucky baby," Lily growled in the playroom.

"You shut up!" they said. "You're just a charity case!"

"Oh yeah? She came lookin' for me. She got stuck with you!"
But all that did was turn The Witch loose, and Lily's palms
smarted bright red from the strapping. "You can't make me
cry," she vowed. But at night, in the bed they had said was
hers, she pulled the pillow over her head and wept for the roadhouse and the life she had known.

In spite of her misery, Lily learned to read, and then there
was no stopping her. Great-grandmother didn't care what
books Lily read, as long as she read. And the library could have
kept anyone busy for years. Lily learned that as long as you had
your nose in a book, nobody accused you of daydreaming, or of
being ungrateful and pining for a way of life infinitely inferior
to what was now being offered. And Great-grandmother was

no fool. She may not have known the extent of the persecution, but she knew it existed and she did everything she could to make up for it. It was she who walked with Lily to the stables, it was she who spoke with the senior groom, it was she who approved the choice of the small mare, and it was she who agreed with Lily there was no need for a special riding habit. A pair of pants would do.

"Simply disgraceful," one of the aunts sniffed.

"As indulgent with this one as she was with her mother!"

"I suppose the little vixen will inherit her mother's money as well as her position as pampered Sugar-Pie."

"Trousers. Did you ever?"

By this time Lily knew there was a price to be paid for everything. The price of riding lessons was to take deportment lessons, the price of reading the books in the library was to read the Uplifting Literature The Witch provided, the price of music lessons was the envy of the cousins and other relatives, and in wintertime, when she learned to skate, the price for that was learning embroidery. If some of the prices seemed dreadfully high, others were cheap. Anything given had a price. Only Great-grandmother gave open-handedly.

When Lily was eleven, her life changed again. She was sent off to school, for her own good, she was told. She expected to detest it. The cousins had gleefully warned her she would hate it, and certainly they all did. But Lily loved it. No more sudden appearances by The Witch, no more waking up at night to find the glowering woman standing by her bed checking to see if she was sleeping with her hands outside of the covers. Lily had a room to herself, she had a letter from Great-grandmother giving her permission to read anything in the library, and arrangements had been made for her to have her own horse in the school stables. She had piano lessons, she had mandolin and guitar lessons, she had violin lessons, and she knew it pleased Great-grandmother to receive embroidered samplers and other examples of Lily's increasing skill with the needle, so even that seemed less than onerous. An hour a night of determined focused attention was more than sufficient to get a good report from the teacher. It also provided Lily with a steady supply of gifts for Great-grandmother, a small price to pay for being free of The Witch. Lily was becoming an expert at paying whatever price was required.

Every summer she went to the cottage by the lake to spend her holiday with Great-grandmother. The cottage was as big as the houses most people lived in, and Lily knew it. She knew she was lucky. She didn't even miss her old life any more. Christmas and Easter she spent at the big house trying to ignore the relatives, and trying not to notice that Great-grandmother was smaller and frailer every time she visited.

"Lily," Great-grandmother said quietly during one of these visits, "you won't be going back to school this year."

"Yes, Great-grandmother," Lily agreed. "Might I ask why?"

"I'm going to die," Great-grandmother said firmly, "and with me gone your life would be hell."

"No," Lily gasped. "No, please..."

"Nothing any of us can do," the old lady laughed softly. "When it's time, it's time, and I've had more time than most. But I'll miss you."

"But...we'll get doctors, we'll..."

"Lily, darling, don't waste your time or mine with futile protest. We have very little time left together, and I don't want to lose one minute of it. Here, hold my hand. That's my good girl. I want you to know why I went to get you, why...I had to go so far to find you."

"Yes, Great-grandmother." Lily moved quickly, took Great-grandmother's hand in both of hers, and waited, blinking rapidly against the hot scalding tears.

"Your grandmother was the most wonderful child in the world. The most obedient, loving, joy-filled child I ever saw," the old woman sighed. "And when she married, she married a young man we all approved of totally. She was six months pregnant with your mother when the young man simply vanished. With everything of value he could lay his hands on, I'm afraid. Your grandmother pined terribly, and, shortly after your mother was born, your grandmother..." The old voice faltered, quavered, then strengthened determinedly. "Killed herself."

"My God," Lily gasped.

"I'm afraid I took it very badly. Your mother became the

focus of my life. And I spoiled her. No matter what she did I excused it by blaming the tragedy that had left her motherless. It was inevitable. There was a scandal, and I excused it, there was another, and I excused it, too. She was asked to leave every school she attended. And then...she threw herself at the wrong man. Absolutely the most unsuitable man anyone could have imagined. And I knew she did it more to punish me than because she loved him. I never understood," she sighed deeply, "why she felt she had to punish me. And then," again the deep sigh, "she did exactly what her father had done. She left." Great-grandmother patted Lily's hand and stared out across the lake, but Lily knew the old woman wasn't looking at the trees. Her eyes were unfocused, she was looking at scenes inside her head, in her heart. "I found her very early on, actually," she laughed softly, "but I'm not the fool now I was a few years ago. I knew it would be no use bringing her home, she would only leave again."

"Do you know who my father is?" Lily dared ask.

"Darling," the old woman laughed, "not even your mother knows that! But it makes no difference. I know you're Lily, my great-granddaughter, and I know it because you look so much like my daughter...your grandmother....She was more laughing than you are, but then she didn't have a horde of jealous relatives sniping at her." She looked at Lily then, and smiled gently. "Oh, I knew, my dear. But I didn't dare make all the same mistakes again, I didn't dare protect you, pamper you, cosset you, and ruin your character."

"It's not important," Lily smiled, feeling as if a weight had been lifted from her shoulders. "They have to live with themselves and each other all the time," and she was happy to hear her great-grandmother chortle agreement.

"You're educated," the old woman said firmly, "and you'll have a small annual allowance, there's nothing they can do to stop that. You're qualified to get work as a governess or a teacher. Or," she winked, "you could open your own dressmaking business."

"I'd rather put on a bright red costume and sing and dance on stage," Lily vowed, "with men staring at my legs and thinking evil thoughts."

"Why not?" The soft laughter flowed again. "Evil is in the eye of the beholder, not necessarily in the heart of the one dancing. And," she winked, surprising Lily totally, "one of these days, if there's time, I might tell you what a time-honoured if unfortunately secret family tradition it really is. I had," she confessed, "the finest legs in Dublin!"

There wasn't time for Lily to learn the unspoken history of the family. They left the cottage early the next day to go back to the big house, and the doctor was called. Lily spent hours by her great-grandmother's bedside, and in all those hours, the old lady only spoke once, with her lawyer as witness.

The afternoon of the funeral, after they had returned from the cemetery and the relatives were publicly mourning, privately wondering about the terms of the will, Lily left her great-grandmother's house for the last time. She took her clothes, she took her personal things, she took her jewels, she took the money the lawyer had given her, and she took two buggy horses, the small buggy, and three riding horses chosen by the senior groom.

"They're too good for those who think a horse is nothing but a dumb and soulless creature," he said. "You'll be good to them. I'm quitting as soon as you leave. They can bring in their own people, most of us won't work for them."

Only the servants saw Lily leave, her trunk and two valises packed in behind the buggy seat, the riding horses following easily on long leads. The family would have had a fit if they had seen her, dressed absolutely inappropriately in riding boots, tan-coloured travelling skirt, and a plain white cotton shirt, open at the throat, the cuffs rolled back. Her violin, guitar, mandolin, and lute rested under the seat, each in a strong case, each wrapped in a thick blanket.

"Eeeee-up, horse," Lily said softly. "Away from here! Ee-eee-up!"

5

The small cabin was cold and damp, and Mary Morgan's toes curled away from the chill of the bare plank floor, but she hurried to the small stove to get the fire going and breakfast started. Carefully she pokered the small bed of coals, the ashes falling through the grate to the metal box below, then she laid kindling sticks of dry cedar on the cluster of glowing embers, blew gently until the flames began to flicker, and added several larger pieces of dry cedar. There was just time, then, to hurry outside to the privy.

Mary put several sticks of dry wood into the stove. She hugged herself, shivering as the first faint heat touched her. Within minutes the kettle would be hot, and the big pot of oatmeal put on the side of the stove the night before would be cooked. When the kettle boiled, she made tea, put the skillet on the stove, and laid in thick strips of cured pork jowl to fry.

The old man got up then, pulled on his clothes, moved to the table and sat, sodden with sleep, his eyes swollen, his face sullen. She put the big mug of tea where he could close his thick fist around it, and waited. No use putting a bowl of oatmeal in front of him until he'd had his tea, you might wind up wearing it, and wearing a blue eye as well.

He stirred honey in slowly, spoon clattering against the side of the mug, then he slurped noisily, and sighed in weariness.

One hand stroked his balding head as he sighed again, and Mary wished for the thousandth time she could just reach out, hand him a great heap of money and tell him to go back to bed, he'd never have to work again. He'd been working since he was twelve years old and every hour of it showed. He looked at her then, his eyes clear, the lifetime of sullen anger tamped and controlled for another day. He nodded, even managed a small smile. She filled his bowl with oatmeal and put it in front of him. He stared at it, then laughed softly, without humour. "One of these days," he promised, "I'll come in that door, grab the sack of oats, and heave it out into the rain. And we'll never eat this slop again!"

"There's some milk," she offered. "Put some milk on it, Da, it's impossible without it."

"If there's milk," he growled, "someone in this house hasn't drunk her share."

"You know I don't like milk," she lied, "I drank what I could."

She turned the strips of jowl, crisping them carefully, then cut thick slices of bread and dropped them into the sizzling fat to brown. She heard him pour the milk, stir it into the thick porridge, then eat steadily, swallowing noisily. She lifted the cooked bread from the pan and laid the crisp jowl on it. He held out his tea mug and she refilled it almost automatically. Then she poured the rest of the tea into his round, flat-sided canteen. Two spoonfuls of honey dripped through the spout, and she screwed on the cap, shaking the canteen to mix the sweetener.

"Well, I'm off," he grunted, pushing back his chair. She quickly wrapped his sandwiches, such as they were, in a soft clean cloth, packed them in his kit, then stood by the door with the kit and the canteen. He got his soft cap from the peg, put it on his head, grabbed his ugly safety hat, and reached for his lunch.

"God be with you," she said formally.

"And with the house," he answered.

She opened the door for him. He stepped out, looked around at the faint grey of pre-dawn, and moved from his door, walking toward the mine, joining other thick-bodied men as exhausted as himself. Mary watched from the top step, the door closed to save heat. She shivered, but not only from the cold. The men flowed slowly into a double column, their feet moving as if there were a band, or at least a drummer, playing music she could not hear, marching them off for another long session in the bowels of the earth, another twelve hours of toiling and struggling, another shift wrenching out the coal the company would sell to the steel mills of Pittsburgh, the comfortable householders of San Francisco. The ones who did the work would be paid a pittance; the ones who sat safe, warm, and soft would get the profit. The rich get richer, the poor get children. And the women of the poor die having the children, the way her own mother had died.

She went back into the small company-owned cabin, poured the last of the milk into the oatmeal pot, and ate hungrily. She tidied the house, washed the few dishes, then pulled on the thick sweater which no longer fit the old man because it had shrunk from so many washings. With sacks and a small, short-handled shovel, Mary hurried from the cabin to the creek. The path along the banks of the creek was rough, but at least there were no shin-busters or foot-tanglers to make life miserable. Where the creek flowed into the river, the path widened, and she could run instead of walking. Here the fish had long since moved downstream or upstream, or died. The river was coated with coal dust from decades' worth of coal being hauled from pits, carried to the harbour in massive train cars, and dumped into colliery barges. The beach here was clean, but closer to town it, too, was encrusted with a glittering layer of black dust. The leaves of the trees glittered between rains. Even the grass grew through a blanket of the black grit.

Mary looked for the little holes in the sand, the sign there were clams buried in the damp. Her shovel blade slid into the dark grey, there was a sucking sound, then the white shells showed in the scoop she turned. She pulled out the large ones, left the small, and dug again. It wasn't hard work but it was wearing, the waves bitterly cold on her bare, chilled feet, the wind whistling around her legs, the damp numbing her flesh, reaching for her very bones.

At first she thought it was a log washed onto the sand at high tide. She might have walked past it without really looking at it except her back hurt from stooping and digging, from bending and sorting clams. She dragged the half-full sack behind her and moved toward the damp shape, meaning to sit on it and tuck her poor sore cold feet under the hem of her skirt. But it wasn't a log, it was a canoe, one of the dugouts of the local Salish, used for everything from fishing to war. Chiselled to no more than two inches thick, steamed and given shape by the insertion of crossbars of yew, it had no seats of any kind. Natives knelt to paddle, or, if it was a large thirty-puller G'lwa, they stood to paddle. There was no sign on it of any kind, no design, no mark. Two leaf-bladed paddles, short ones, with hand grips, rested on the bottom, and near them lay a coil of line. Not twisted nettle fibre line like the Salish used, but the strong, green-coloured cord from the Hudson's Bay Company store in town. The hook was metal and still wickedly sharp, but the flashers were made of polished abalone shell.

No footprints in the sand, no sign of anyone up the beach, just the dugout. And Mary Morgan was never one to look a gift horse in the mouth! She heaved the sack of clams into the small craft, pushed the canoe to the water's edge, and was in it, kneeling, paddle in hand, without hesitation.

Mary had little trouble balancing herself, little trouble learning how to use the paddle, and no trouble at all accepting her good luck. She split open clam shells, threaded the clams as best she could on the hook, dropped the gooey mess over the side, and in less time than she thought possible, she had a large rock cod.

The dugout took her quickly back the way she had so slowly come, and the river current hardly bothered the light craft. She stroked upstream, to the creek, and the dugout managed that shallow water, too.

When she got home, she had half a sack of clams and three cod. She cleaned the fish quickly, saving the guts and heads for the next day's bait, and traded the clams for potatoes and onions. When her father stumbled in from his back-breaking toil, there was as much supper as he could eat, and a fish left for breakfast.

"How'd you get fish?" he managed, unable to believe what he was seeing.

"With a line and a hook," she answered, smiling. It was only half the truth, but it was no lie, and he questioned her no further. He ate hungrily, hugely, then went to his bed and was asleep before the dishes were cleaned and the stove banked for the night.

In the morning, she had his tea ready for him, and a crisp, cooked cod for his breakfast. He looked better already, and patted her shoulder affectionately when he left the house to join the others. Mary watched them walk to the pit head where the great cage would lower them down to the timbered shafts, where they traded their youth and good humour for coal. Coal that profited the owners, most of whom had never seen the inside of a mine, or even this poor island, so recently beautiful, so quickly sullied.

She left the housework for later, and hurried to the creek where she had her dugout hidden behind a moss-covered fallen log. She hauled the craft to the water, got in, and pushed off eagerly, the dugout bobbing easily and swiftly down the creek, past the thick wall of forest, to the heaving green ocean. There she caught several cod, two green-eyed, lethal-looking small sharks, and a salmon, then beached the dugout and lit a small fire. For her lunch there were oysters, picked from the barnacle-coated rocks and placed around the periphery of the fire to open in minutes, steamed in their own juices. She had no need of salt, pepper, or anything else. She ate them as they were and ate until her belly was as full as it had ever been.

The cod got her a guarantee of a quart of milk a day for the next week, the small sharks made the Celestials grin happily, the salmon she took home and baked in the oven, stuffed with bread, sage, and onions. The old man ate until she thought his skin would split, and then he ate some more. He even had enough energy to roll himself a cigarette and sit smoking quietly before taking himself to his bed.

It became her life, getting up and sending him off to work, then going to where the dugout was hidden. Stroking swiftly, with increasing sure skill, she sped down the creek to the river, down the river to the ocean. She learned where the cod gathered in pools whose depth she could only imagine, she learned how to troll for salmon, she learned that almost anything she hauled out of the sea would be welcome in the cluster of houses where the Celestials lived segregated from the white miners and their families. Some of the creatures she hauled out of the rolling grey waters were so strange she had no idea what they were called, and she might never have eaten them, but the Celestials never once refused anything she had to offer. She had steady milk, now, and vegetables from the gardens the Celestials tended so expertly. She even had some money hidden in a small bag stuffed in her mattress, in the corner where the stitching had pulled loose. She no longer looked like a fledgling bird, and the old man looked younger than he had looked for most of her memory.

On Thursdays she stayed longer, knowing she could sell anything she caught because the Dogans were supposed to eat fish on Friday. Or not supposed to eat meat. Or something. Whatever it was, rule, regulation, or superstition, it meant she could sell clams, oysters, cod, salmon, snapper, or whatever else grabbed at her hook. Sell it to the Dogans on Thursday night, then, on Friday, she could take the money into town and buy a piece of meat for herself and the old man, and she could buy more fishing twine, more hooks, some tobacco for the old man and some candy for herself. They stared at her, but that cost her nothing. People were always staring at her. Let them stare and be damned. One day she'd have some decent clothes and the staring would stop. Until then, it gave the fools something to do, as if there wasn't enough in the world to do already.

Mary experimented until she could run a main line down with several long auxiliary lines coming from it, each line hooked and baited, each weighted with a small piece of rock or lead shot, each flashing a piece of brightly shined mother-of-pearl oyster shell. The entire rigging trailed behind the dugout, secured to the back end through a little treasure she'd liberated from the coal company, a screw with a ring on top. It had been part of the gear on a piece of machinery, the use of which she couldn't even guess. She ran her line through the ring and tied the end of the line around her ankle. When the drag on the line told her there were fish caught on the hooks, she stopped stroking and carefully hauled, stuffing her catch into wet gunny sacks. When her sacks were full she headed for shore to gut and clean the fish. Only the storms of springtime kept her from heading out onto the surface of the sea to pull from the water a security never provided by the mines.

Some of them were scandalized. Someone is always sure to be scandalized. But they kept their muttering to themselves, and just as well, too, because Hugh Morgan wasn't one to accept any criticism of his daughter. He was eating better than any of them and the improved diet gave him the energy and strength of a younger man. He was cutting coal with the best of them and his pay packet had never been thicker.

"It's daft," he said thoughtfully, sitting on the back steps and puffing happily at his pipe. "When we had sore need of money, we had none. Now that we spend practically nothing and still eat better than the lords and ladies, I'm making more than I've made since I was eighteen. Them as has," he decided, "gets. Them as hasn't does without."

"Celestials eat funny," Mary told him. "They said I should use the heads and the guts from the fish and make a kind of trap thing. Put the guts and all in it and when the scuttlers come to eat the mess, I should catch them and they'd buy them from me."

"Crabs," Hugh told her. "The kings eat crabs."

"And the wiggly things?"

"Octopus," he explained. "I never heard of anyone eating them."

"The Celestials do."

"Ah, well, poor buggers," Hugh sighed. "They've a hard life of it. They do the work of men but get the pay of boys. And their women denied entry."

"There's women down there," Mary scoffed. "I've heard them. Laughing."

"Not wives," Hugh flushed.

"Oh." Mary looked away, watching the streaks of pink and light blue tinge the clouds above the western mountains as the darkness of night swelled up from the forest.

Spring gave way to summer and the water turned from grey to blue. One of the scandihoovian women set up a small shed and started smoking and salting the fish Mary sold her. She told Mary to be sure to wear a hat, told her to spread lard on her face and arms to protect her skin from salt and sun, told her to smudge charcoal on her cheekbones to stop the glare from the water, told her she'd be out on the sea, too, if she were twenty years younger, if she didn't have so many children.

They had eggs now, too, and meat as often as fish. The Celestials showed Mary how to cook the hard-shelled crabs but Hugh didn't like them much, said it was too much work to get at the flesh inside. Mary had new clothes, decent clothes, fit to wear to chapel. In the dugout she wore a pair of the old man's threadbare trousers and a thin shirt; one wave taken the wrong way and she'd be in the water, not on it, swimming for her life, and if that happened, she didn't need however-many pounds of water-soaked skirt dragging her down to where the cod and crab would feast on her flesh as gladly as she feasted on theirs. Of all the things Mary Morgan was, stupid was not one of them.

She was nearly home with a fine catch, supper planned, and a sure market for her fish, when the ground rumbled and shook, the surface of the sea flattened and dimpled, then heaved. The sound was like a big fist in the side of her head, and she knew, she knew. By the time she had the dugout secured, the sirens were howling, the bain sidhe giving warning to those who already knew the same thing Mary Morgan knew. "At least," she told herself repeatedly, "at least he died well-fed and warmly clothed."

One hundred twenty-one men, fifteen mules, and nobody knew how many Chinese. She wanted to ask when the Chinese had stopped being men, stopped being human, but that was foolish, they had never been counted human, had always been numbers, not names, paid half what a white man was paid without even being eligible for a company house. Now there was equality for them, under tons of fallen rock, with the fire burning them all to cinders, white and non-white, human and mule, all of them, down there forever now, and Mary with twenty-four hours to leave the company cabin, leave the company town, go with the other widows and orphans, away from the property of the almighty company.

The town was split by a tidal ravine, with the decent and hard-working living on the northern side, in the townsite, and the lower classes keeping their place on the southern side. At full tide, the ravine could be crossed only by means of a small boat manned by a nameless crew of silent Salish; at low tide anybody who wanted could walk across the mud. Of course, the better quality people seldom had reason to cross to the south end, and if they did cross, they did not wade through ankle-deep scunge; the Salish provided piggy-back rides for the same pittance they charged for the boat ride. The lower classes had no such qualms and were as likely as not to turn up in the townsite with spatters of mud and daubs of tidal goo stuck to their feet and clothes. Mary crossed the ravine whenever she wanted, sometimes in her dugout, sometimes in the mud. She sold her fish to the cooks and housekeepers who came from the back doors of the large, solidly built homes.

And she sold fish to the women on Fraser Street, which was on the south side of the ravine, so the women in the houses had probably never been respectable. Doing business on Fraser Street did nothing at all for Mary's tattered reputation. And though she insisted to herself she didn't care a fingersnap for the opinion of the nice people, she did care very much.

She rented a small shed, built as a net loft. Gradually she accumulated such luxuries as a small stove, a mattress for the floor, a table, two chairs, and a few kitchen goods. It was bare, it was uninsulated, it was anything but homey, but to Mary, it was as close to home as she could get, and anyway, she was only there to eat and sleep. She was up early and out on the water, high tide or low, and she fished steadily until it was time to sell her catch. "Fish, get your fish," she called. "Fresh caught today, get your fish." Up and down the streets, her wet gunny sacks on a small, rickety wooden wagon she had put together with bits of board scrounged from the dump and a set of wheels she had bought at the store for more than they were worth. "Fish, get your fish." Back and forth she went, up streets and down alleys, calling loudly, watching for the back door to open and the cook or house-keeper to move toward the gate. "Fresh caught today, get your fish."

Friday, without fail, she went up the river, then up the creek to Company Town, and she moved past the very house in which she had once lived, moved up one side and down the other of both streets, offering her catch to the miners' wives who had once been her neighbours. When she had sold all her fish, she turned her back on what had once been her home, went down to the creek, got in her dugout, paddled down the creek to the river and down the river to the sea, and followed the beachline to the small net shed where she lived as frugally as she could, eating what she couldn't sell, eating fish too small for the families who lived well in warm houses. The old man's last pay packet and her own small savings were carefully hidden in the false bottom of the stinking, heavy-lidded box where she kept the entrails she used as bait.

"Why don't you get married?" the young man asked, his smile wide, his eyes cold.

"Me," she laughed. "Why would I want to do that?"

"Stop taking the work away from the rest of us!" he snapped.

"Don't be a fool," she glared, "I've as much right as anyone to do my work and earn my bread."

"Do women's work then," he hissed. "Sew dresses, or whatever it is women do. Fishing is men's work."

"Oh, listen to the foolishness of you," she mocked. "And was it not Boann herself gave the secrets of mathematics and navigation to women? Was it not Boann who disguised herself as a tree, gave the secrets to the salmon, who gave it, in turn, to the women who caught the salmon and ate of its flesh?"

"Pagan slut!" he cursed, white-faced with anger and insult.

"Christian fool," she laughed, and pointed her fingers at him, her little finger and index finger pointing out like horns, her middle fingers folded to her palm, held by her thumb. "G'wan," she laughed again, mocking him. Idiot that he was, thinking she could really hex him. Superstitious ninny, as if two fingers of a woman's hand could bring bad 'cess to anyone.

The next morning she found her beloved dugout ruined, axed repeatedly, the bottom of it smashed. She stared down at it and burned with fury. So that was how it was to be, then.

Mary knew she could get another canoe. All she had to do was go to the Salish and for almost no money she would have another, probably bigger, better balanced. But she would have to take it inside the loft with her at night, and who knew what else the jealous ones would think of to make it impossible for her to work? She knew they were watching. She couldn't see them and wouldn't give them the satisfaction of openly looking for them. But she knew they were watching. She gathered dry beach wood, started a fire, then put her beloved dugout on the flames and sat watching the cedar burn. Let them think whatever they wanted to think.

When nothing remained but ashes, Mary Morgan went back to her loft. She took her reeking bait box with her. Minutes later she reappeared at the top of the steps and tossed the bait box down to the rocks and sand. Then she went back inside, closing the door.

They told each other she had eaten the guts, told themselves she had probably tried to do magic with them, told themselves they had showed her what happened to pagan sluts.

Three hours before the passenger steamer left the island, Mary moved cat-like through the velvet darkness of night, her bare feet making no sound. It was easy work to slip from the wooden dock, her hand-auger held tight. Easy work to brace herself against the piling and drill below the water line, easy work to haul herself back up to the dock and slip the lines securing the young idiot's fishboat, easy work to give a good solid push that sent it drifting with the changing tide. She ran back to her little shack, unconcerned about the wet footprints on the dock, footprints already obscured by the thin film of falling rain.

When the passenger steamer left the island, Mary Morgan was on it, wearing her good clothes, her decent stockings, and her sturdy, respectable shoes. She had a small bag containing her few worldly possessions and the money she had retrieved from the bait box. She stood on deck in the dark of pre-dawn, her shawl drawn tight against the rising wind and pouring rain. She would have loved to see the fishboat low in the water, slowly going down to the bottom, but she had done her work of vengeance well, and there was no sign of it to be seen.

6

Cora Tandy was born in a dark soddie dug into a prairie sidehill while a thunderstorm rumbled and the rain pelted sideways, soaking the sod roof of the primitive shelter. Her mother lay on a bed of poles and rawhide lacings, grunting and straining, her wide face flushed with the effort and drenched with sweat. Cora's father sat on the stool he had made and trembled with fear and hope; fear, because he hadn't the slightest idea what to do to help, hope because he was certain he was about to become father to a son who would grow tall and strong and help with the endless work which came with a homestead.

Jack Tandy's help wasn't needed. Cora was determined to come into the world, and all her mother had to do was endure the labour. Esther had no intention of not enduring, and if she had no more idea than Jack of what to do to help speed the birthing process, her body did know what to do. The child emerged, lay still for a heart-stopping moment, then squirmed, choked, gasped, and drew breath, her tiny chest heaving.

She walked at thirteen months, she was chasing the hens by fifteen months, and by four years she was helping Esther care for Jacob, the son whose arrival Jack celebrated with such glee Esther made herself bite her tongue. Jack celebrated the third and fourth children but did not celebrate the fifth, and by this time Cora was old enough to know why Alice's arrival was almost ignored and why her own arrival had not kicked off a fresh pork dinner or a small bottle of dandelion wine.

When Cora was eleven, Jack sold the farm, loaded his wife and children into one wagon and their few possessions in another, and headed deeper west, Esther driving the wagonload of goods and Cora driving the wagonload of children. Jacob rode the dun gelding, Jack rode the bay mare, and they talked easily together, sharing something Cora knew she could never share. They left the old place at the beginning of April and slogged through melting snow, mud, and cold until mid-May, when the broad prairie was dotted with small blue flowers and humming bees, and they arrived at the new place. Even before they started building a shelter, they put in the garden, using the big ground-breaker plow to cut into the earth, lifting the sod carefully, piling it in the shade of the willows near the year-round stream, their arms aching, their backs screaming protest. When they had enough sod for a house, the garden was big enough to get them through the winter they knew would be both fierce and long.

And then they started the soddie, butting it up against a small hill. There were no big trees but there were plenty of small ones, and Jack cut them as close to the ground as he could. He marked off the space, put up the corner posts, and started yelling orders. When the basic frame was lashed and knotted in place, the crosspoles were laid. Then the ugly job of transporting sod, lifting it, laying it in place, and going for more sod. The dirt sifted down and got in their eyes, in their noses, in their mouths, but complaining about it didn't get the work done, so they blinked, wept, sneezed, coughed, and ached in bitter silence.

The warmth of the small stove kept the sidehill thawed enough that most of the winter was spent digging into the hill to provide more space. It was dark in the soddie, it was damp, it was always chilly, and they were crammed in together so tightly they got on each other's nerves and in each other's way. If spring had been even two weeks later they might have gone totally crazy and chewed out each other's throats. But the wind stopped howling, the snow stopped falling and drifting, the soddie roof began to leak even more than before, and they could spend more and more time outside, looking for edible greens.

Jacob went hunting with his father and came home with several rabbits, their fur just starting to darken from the winter white. He bragged so much about the tough, stringy, skinny creatures that Cora would gladly have shot him and put him in the stew pot, too. Instead she smiled and congratulated him on his prowess. But when the buffalo arrived, Jacob was sick with a cold that made his breathing rough and his fever high. Jack couldn't take the chance that his son would have a coughing fit and scare off the meat they so desperately needed. So he took Cora and left Jack in bed, weeping with disappointment and aching bones. Cora sat on the dun gelding, wearing an old pair of Jack's trousers held up with a piece of rope, and a warm shirt rolled up at the sleeves. Her feet were bare, the callouses split with chilblains.

She knew she did well. She knew she moved quietly, waited patiently, aimed carefully, and shot skillfully. She knew it even though Jack didn't once praise her or pat her back the way he had patted Jacob when he held up his skinny, winter-bitter rabbits. She cared, she knew she cared deeply, but nobody else would know how bitter Jack's treatment was. She used her disappointment, her jealousy, and her anger as fuel, and with that fuel she sharpened her reflexes, moved even more quietly and carefully, aimed even more steadily, shot even more accurately.

The small herd moved on, but the meat left behind was the difference between health and hunger for the desperately poor family of sodbusters. They all feasted on fresh liver, then they worked like possessed people to smoke, dry, and salt the mountain of meat. What they couldn't find the time or energy to preserve or the room in their bellies to eat, they cut into hunks and lay in the trenches they dug, then planted their potatoes and turnips in the already fly-blown meat, turned slickery and unpleasant in the increasing heat.

They enlarged the garden, again cutting strips of sod, again using it as building material. They repaired the roof and added a small room to the soddie, so Jack and Esther could sleep separate and private, and they even put together a small stock shed. Jack and Jacob rode off with the buffalo hides and the little money Jack admitted he had, and when they came back three weeks later they had half a dozen laying hens, a milk goat, and wonderful things like salt, tea, flour, baking powder, and dried fruit. There were lengths of stiff, thick cloth and even some sugar and two peppermint candies each. Cora knew Jacob had been given candy for himself, candy he gobbled greedily, candy he didn't even think of sharing with the others. She sucked her candy and remembered the skinny rabbits, the proud pat on the back, the grin of pride.

The buffalo passed on their way south, and again there was a mountain of meat to salt, to dry, to smoke, and it was Jacob went with Jack to take a wagonload of salted meat to sell in town. Cora burned with anger but there was no place to direct it. The rules had never been spoken, but they were rules, and they were obvious. When Jack and Jacob returned, the wagon was half-filled with necessaries for winter, and Jacob had new pants, new shirt, new boots, and a thick, warm jacket. He even had a new hat, which he wore as proudly as if it were a full-sized man's hat instead of a half-sized boy's hat. Cora hated Jacob, his hat, his new boots, and her father for his obvious favouritism.

Their second winter was much more comfortable than their first and Cora took what pleasure she could in her mother's words of praise for the skill with which Cora stitched clothes for the smaller children, the patience she showed when dealing with the babies, her willingness to gather grass tips for the chickens. One morning she found one of the hens frozen to her perch, dead. Without even asking, she plucked and cleaned the dark reddish-brown bird, saving the liver, the lights, and the bright yellow cluster of undeveloped yolks. Jack cursed the bad luck that had killed the hen, but gnawed happily on a drumstick, spooned more delicious gravy on Jacob's mound of potatoes, urged his oldest son to take more of the savoury sage-and-onion dressing.

Their third spring, summer, and autumn were so like the first two Cora began to wonder if she was losing her grip on reality. She wasn't sure any more how long they had lived here in the middle of what seemed to be nowhere at all, she didn't know whether she was eleven or fourteen or if this was their first soddie or their third. Everything seemed like everything else, every day the same as the one before and after. At least there was no new baby to drain Esther's strength and bring even more work. There wasn't time enough to get all the work done and Jacob was as tired as anyone else. He was big enough to cut wood, to help in the field, to work on the stock shed, to chop, saw, dig, and hoe. He was big enough to lift pails of water from the stream, fill the dark-soaked wood kegs in the wagon bed, and drive the wagon to the garden to water the crop, lifting buckets of water from the barrels, pouring water carefully around each flourishing plant.

Cora took the younger children with her in the other wagon and went out on the prairie, gathering buffalo manure, stacking it in the wagon, lifting it with her hands, hunk after hunk, plop after plop, until the wagon was full and it was time to go home, unload the winter fuel, scrub her hands, and help her mother with the mountain of chores that never quite got finished.

And when she got home, there was Laughton Davis, a thirty-two-year-old widower, visiting with her father. Helping Jacob with his chores were Laughton's three small children. They looked so little like him Cora knew they had to be the spitting image of their dead mother. "You children unload that wagon for Cora," Laughton ordered, and the three quiet children obediently hurried to do a job everyone except Laughton knew was too much for them.

"Jacob," Jack said quietly, "you and your brothers help, Cora's needed in the house." That meant, Cora knew, that Laughton and his brood would be staying for supper.

Laughton's children sat on the floor, eating hungrily, saying nothing, watching their father nervously. Cora knew Laughton was intolerant of noise, and as intolerant of mischief as her own father was. Children should be seen and not heard. Train up a child in the way in which he is to go and when he is old he will not depart from it. Fathers, discipline now your sons and let not your heart refrain from their weeping. Suffer little children.

Laughton and his children slept in the fresh hay in the stock shed, and Cora listened to the faint conversation from her parents' small adjoining room. Esther's voice was low, and thick with unvoiced sobs, Jack's voice was sharp, commanding, and firm. When the conversation stopped, the other noises started, and Cora hated them even more than the sound of Jack's unemotionally demanding words.

After breakfast in the morning, Jack and Laughton went outside for a long conversation, and after Laughton and his children had left, Jack told Cora what had been decided.

"No," Cora said flatly.

"You'll do as you're told," Jack warned.

"No," Cora repeated.

"You'll have your own home," Jack bargained, "your own kitchen, your own things. He's built up his place, he's got a real house instead of a soddie, he's got ducks for his pond and . . ."

"And what do *you* get?" Cora demanded hotly. Jack drew back his hand to slap her, then thought better of it and lowered his hand.

"You'll change your mind," he said, and it sounded more like a threat than a promise.

There was no candy for Cora when Jack, Jacob, and young Tom came back from the autumn trip to town, no cloth for new clothes, and no winter shoes, and the white-hot silence flared every time Jack glared at her. Once every two weeks, right up until the time the snow flew and the temperature dropped, Laughton and his quiet children arrived, often bringing large mutton haunches with them, some ducks hanging dead by their necks from the pommel of Laughton's good saddle, a small bottle of distilled liquor the men shared after supper.

The winter was hell for all of them, trapped in a dark soddie with a man who glared constantly and refused to speak to his oldest child. Cora worked harder than she had ever worked in her life, trying to show him she was needed at home for her work, her strength, her willingness, but Jack could not forget she had defied him.

Laughton was back at the first thaw, smiling at Cora as if he knew something she would soon learn. After he and his children left to sleep in the barn there was another argument, with Jack roaring at Cora and Esther weeping quietly. "Selfish bitch!" Jack raged. "Fill your face with food the others could use, take up more than half the bed so your little sisters sleep crowded. And no way you'll do what's reasonable and best for all! Selfish, selfish little bitch."

"What did Laughton promise him?" Cora wept, wishing her mother would think to hug her just once.

"Four cows," Esther said wearily, "each of them pregnant. And an unbroken yearling stallion."

"I don't *want* to!" Cora wailed.

"Well," Esther said stoically, "Want hasn't got much to do with anything. It's a good strong house, with a real roof and windows. You could do worse. I did."

Laughton grabbed her as she walked back from the outhouse, her feet damp with morning dew. There was no warning. One minute she was watching the lightening sky, the next his hand was over her mouth, his other arm was around her waist, and her feet were kicking uselessly in mid-air.

"Why are you being so stubborn?" he demanded, his beard rough against her face. "You're just being silly."

He took her to the willows beside the stream. There he pinned her easily and, one hand over her mouth, he raped her. Twice. When she was finally allowed to run away from him, her thighs stained with her own blood, her stomach heaving with revulsion, his wagon was already loaded, his children sitting in it quietly and obediently, and in the wagon bed was a small bundle she knew contained her clothes.

"You aren't coming back into the house," Jack said firmly. "You go with him or you go to hell."

Laughton laughed, grasped her by the waist, lifted her with insulting ease, and dropped her, sobbing, into the wagon bed. Then he climbed up, took the reins in his hand, and clucked commandingly. The horses moved off quickly and Cora knew Esther was lying on her bed, sobbing hopelessly.

Laughton's farm was pockets of money and years of skilled work ahead of Jack's. There was a permanence Cora had never seen before, the house square and solid, the barn big and well-built. There were ducks in the pond, and geese, too, there were horses and pigs, there were sheep and two dogs to guard them, there was even a barn cat with a litter of kittens. And cows. Not milk cows, as Cora had imagined, but long-horned wild-eyed beef cattle spread out across the rolling grassland.

"Take care of the horse and wagon," Laughton grunted, jumping from the wagon and handing the reins to his oldest son. The boy nodded, eyes downcast, and took the leathers. Laughton grabbed Cora, lifted her from the wagon and carried her into the house. She wriggled and squirmed, she struggled and strained, and finally, she started hitting him as hard as she could. He put her down briefly, hauled back his huge work-hardened hand, and slammed her across the side of the head. Her ear burned, her face throbbed, her head pounded, and all she could see were a zillion little dancing black dots in a sea of grey. She felt herself being lifted again, and carried, then dropped onto a bed. She tried to focus her eyes, tried to lift herself, intending to run, but her arms and legs didn't remember how to move, her body could do nothing but lie there gasping for breath.

Then Laughton was on top of her again, positioning her, thrusting. She was already sore, and torn, and swollen, she was still bleeding from his first assault, and it wasn't over quickly this time. She moaned with pain, she tried to twist away from the demanding, painful intrusion, but he only grabbed her by the shoulders and shoved her down to meet his up-thrusting body, his enraged lunge.

"Get up," he told her when he was finally finished. "There's water in the bucket, there's a basin in the wash house, there's soap, and there's a new dress waiting for you. Fix yourself up, then get busy in the kitchen."

"I hate you," she sobbed.

"See if I care," he laughed. "Just see if I care." And he stretched lazily, settling himself for a rest.

She was so shocked and stunned that she did exactly what he told her to do. She took water to the wash house off the kitchen, and she scrubbed herself from head to toe, even washing and rinsing her hair. Then she pulled on the dark brown dress which fell loosely from her shoulders to her ankles. When she was dressed, she went to the kitchen and looked carefully in each canister, amazed at the amount of food. She got the fire going in the big stove, she peeled potatoes, she asked one of the children to bring in more wood and asked another to go for fresh water, and she started making biscuits.

The children ate hungrily, smiling shyly at her, wanting her to like them, and Laughton amazed her by complimenting her on the meal she had cooked. He told the children to do the dishes. Then, his arm around her waist, he led Cora around the farm, pointing out his wealth, his obvious success. She wanted to ignore it all, but she was impressed, and she knew he knew it.

In the barn the stalls were wide and there was still plenty of hay in the loft, proving he had put away more than enough for the long, cold winter. "The mares with young ones are in here in the winter," he bragged, "so they don't have to fight the weather. Makes 'em profit," he explained, "and makes 'em tame, too, easier to halter break than if they're out there like the wild ones, fighting to stay alive." He laughed. "Everything tames down when there's lots of food, lots of shelter."

"Not me," she vowed, but he only squeezed his arm tighter around her waist.

The dishes were done, the kitchen tidy, and the children washed and ready for bed when they got back to the house. Laughton gravely kissed each child on the head, wished them a good night's sleep, then patted each one gently on the bum to start them on their way to bed.

"Come on," he said, when the children were out of sight.

"No," Cora pleaded, "not again. Please."

But her pleas might as well never have been uttered. He just led her to the bed, pulled off her dress, and stared at her, grinning widely. "Take off my shirt," he said quietly.

"No," she said. And he hit her. Hard. Not hard enough to stun her, not hard enough to knock her back on the bed, but hard enough that her hands reached out in defiance of her own wishes and began to unbutton his shirt, then remove it.

"Now my pants," he said.

"No," she wept. He hit her repeatedly, never hard enough to knock her down, never hard enough to send her unconscious, never hard enough to make her bleed, but hard enough that she unbuttoned and removed his pants, then his one-piece warm underwear. And when he told her to stroke him, she stroked him. When he told her to kiss him, she kissed him. And when he told her to position herself the way he wanted her positioned, she did. Her sobs of pain and horror were muffled in feathers plucked from the bleeding breasts of the white geese she had seen swimming contentedly in the pool.

7

There was a small pot-bellied stove set up in the middle of the bare car, and every once in a while a uniformed railroad employee came in with a small scuttle of coal which he grudgingly dumped into the stove. Those sitting close to the squat black burner had to remove their coats and jackets and wipe the sweat from their faces, those sitting farther away hugged themselves to keep warm. Ceileigh moved twice before she found a seat where she was warm enough to take her plaidie off her shoulders and wrap it around her legs and feet. After more uncomfortable hours than she would have thought possible, she finally drifted off to sleep.

The movement of the train made her uneasily nauseated, the acrid reek of burning coal made her head ache, and the odour from the sweating bodies near the stove didn't help. She wakened with her legs cold from the knees down, her plaidie slipped half to the floor. Ceileigh thought briefly of trying to move closer to the stove, but abandoned the thought, knowing any increase in the sweat stink would have her heaving up violently.

Twice that night the train stopped and more people got on. The car became even more crowded, and Ceileigh heard more languages than she had known existed. Some of the immigrants had baskets of food with them, so the smell of hard-boiled eggs and pickled fish was overwhelming. Several times Ceileigh put her violin on her seat to save her place, then went to the little cubicle marked 'Ladies' at the back of the car to wash her hands and face in the cold water trickling rustily from the tap, but the smell in the washroom nauseated her even more. As soon as she had drained her bladder, she hurried back to her seat, more miserable than before.

Eventually she slept again. When she wakened, the car was jammed with people, the air stifling and sour. Children wailed and howled. One of them had puked and the stink lingered in the air. People were eating in spite of the constant stench, and those who had stuffed the eggs down their throats were farting. Ceileigh gasped, lurched to her feet, rushed to the Ladies', pushed open the door to the stinking cubicle, and retched drily into the foul chute that served as a toilet. She huddled miserably on the hard bench, her feet resting on her wooden violin case, her plaidie wrapped around her legs. There was water in a big tank at the end of the car, but to get to it she would have to pass the stove and the sweating people sitting near it. The aisle was thick with discarded egg shells and slippery with melted snow, mud, and probably crap which had slid down the legs of the miserable children. She decided she really didn't need a drink that badly. Besides, she would probably just sick it up again.

The train stopped in the middle of the afternoon to take on water and fuel. Passengers poured from the car to stand gasping in the cold, clear air. Ceileigh felt better immediately. She watched as the railway crew disconnected the empty coal cars, then pushed them along a siding and left them to be refilled. Huge, patient horses pulled loaded cars from a second siding, hauled them close to the engine, and were led away as men pushed the coal cars the last few feet to the coupling. The shaggy horses plodded off, tossing their heads, and Ceileigh almost wished she could follow them.

When the whistle sounded she made her way up the steps to the immigrant car. Nobody had done anything about cleaning up the mess, so as soon as the train started moving, Ceileigh felt sick again. So sick, in fact, she didn't even regret not having any food with her. The next time they stopped, she was the first one out of the car, moving along the track, cursing angrily. She scooped up snow, washed her hands and face with it, even put some of it in her mouth to quench her thirst, and eyed the front cars bitterly. Inside those cars the better-off sat on comfortable plush-covered seats. They ate in a dining car, eating good food from clean plates, staring with unseeing eyes at the poor, who stared back in envious frustration. Ceileigh turned suddenly and raced back to the immigrant car, grabbed her violin and her plaidie, then hurried back outside again. The crew was busy filling the boiler of the engine, struggling to get their work done quickly so they could hurry the immigrants back into the stinking cars and chase off in pursuit of their precious schedule. Ceileigh dodged up the steps and across the metal platform, pushed open the door, and was inside the passenger car. She slipped into the Ladies', went inside a cubicle, closed the door, and sat down gratefully on the clean toilet. God, to be one of those fortunate enough not to have to crap in a festering midden!

Ceileigh dozed until the train moved off again, and sat in the cubicle hugging herself with glee and fear. Nobody knocked on the door and demanded to see her ticket, nobody ordered her out. When she dared leave the toilet and move to the basin, the water that ran from the tap was warm and only slightly tinged with rust. She scrubbed her hands and face with a sliver of soap she found, then dampened her hair and pulled it back, tied it, and folded the unbrushed tangle under her fleece-lined jacket. Now she looked almost respectable. There wasn't much she could do about the wrinkles in her skirt, but if she spent most of her time in the toilet cubicle, nobody would notice. She drank warm water from the tap, scooping it with her hand and sucking thirstily. When her stomach cramped, she waited fearfully, but the cramp passed and she drank more water, then more.

Ceileigh went back into the toilet cubicle, lowered the lid, and sat down. It was at least as comfortable as the bench in the immigrant car. There was a draft along the floor, but she didn't care, she just wrapped her plaidie around her legs, put her feet up on her violin box, and went to sleep. The next time she wakened, she changed cubicles, believing she would be able to hide longer that way. Then she slept again, fitfully and uncomfortably, but she slept.

When the train stopped the third time, Ceileigh moved out of the Ladies' and walked down the aisle as if she owned the entire train. The porter looked at her and grinned slightly, then looked at her violin case.

"Excuse me, miss," he said quietly. Ceileigh knew she was caught. Knew she ought to have stayed in the Ladies'.

"Yes?" She tried to appear haughty and unconcerned.

"I believe you're looking for the club car." He stared at her and she gave herself over to whatever was starting to happen.

"Thank you."

The porter led the way down the aisle, through the door, and across the small platform to the next door, which opened into yet another passenger car.

"You got a ticket?" he asked without moving his lips.

"Yes," she said desperately.

"But not for here?"

"I can't stand the stink in the other car," she blurted.

"I can understand that well enough," he agreed.

He reached into his pocket, pulled out a stub, and handed it to her, grinning widely. "Ask no questions," he warned, "and be sure to give it to me when I ask for it."

"Why?" she asked stupidly.

"You're going to split your take with me fifty-fifty," he said sternly, "and if you go to a sleeping compartment with any of the gentlemen, you split that with me, too."

"I'm no harlot!" she hissed.

"I don't care one way or the other," the porter laughed. "Make more money if you are. And don't think I won't know if you do. I know everything that happens on this train. Even," he laughed, "in the Ladies'."

She was the only woman in the club car. Men sat with glasses by their hands, playing cards at tables lit by overhead lights. On the wall beside every table, a large sign warning the world that consumption of alcohol and gambling were not to be tolerated by the railway company. Two men in white coats moved among the tables with large pots of tea, pouring the glasses half full whenever one of the card players gestured. As soon as the waiters turned away, the bottle appeared from the inside pocket, the glass was filled to the top, and the liquor flask was returned, out of sight, out of mind, what the eye does not see the heart does not grieve over.

Ceileigh opened her violin case and took out her sheepskin-wrapped instrument. She tuned the strings quickly, then re-sined her bow, flexing her cold-stiffened fingers, and began to play. First she played slow and quiet pieces, then, as her fingers relaxed in the warmth of the comfortable club car, she played faster, more intricate tunes.

After she'd played for two hours, the porter motioned for her to follow him. "You can make five dollars," he offered.

"No," she said quickly.

"You want more?"

"I don't do harlot's work. I play my fiddle," and she grinned suddenly, "but I don't fiddle around."

"Suit yourself," he shrugged. "You got money for food?"

"No."

"You're a fool," he laughed. But he took her to his little room and gave her a cup of tea and a thick beef sandwich. In spite of the steady rocking of the train, Ceileigh ate and kept down the food. Then she went back to play for two more hours.

When the club car finally emptied the porter gave her another thick sandwich and another mug of tea, then counted her tips and handed her exactly half. "How much for the food?" she asked warily.

"I'm a fool too," he shrugged, "and a bigger one for telling you that you'll be safe sleeping on the floor here. Not so big a fool, though," he laughed, "as to give you my couch!"

She slept soundly, her belly full, and in the morning there was coffee in a mug and a plate of leftovers from the dining car. She rummaged openly in the porter's things and managed to pull his comb through her hair and tidy herself, but her clothes were beginning to look as if she'd been on a train for three sooty days and nights. She rolled her cuffs back to hide the grime, and watched through the window as the flatland rolled past. By mid-afternoon the first of the hills were breaking the horizon and Ceileigh could feel the first stirrings of excitement.

After darkness fell she was back in the club car, playing her fiddle for the men with their half glasses of tea and the cards they played for matchsticks. The men gave her money. Good money, real money, and the more of the half glasses of tea they drank, the more generously they tipped.

"You want to make twenty dollars, darling?" one of the men asked.

"Sir," she replied clearly, "I'd love to make twenty dollars but I'm not in the line of work you seem to think I'm in. I play music, sir, and that is all I do."

"Not even for twenty dollars?" he asked.

"No, sir," she answered. "I know you think me a fool, but...could I play you a song, instead?"

"If that's all I'm going to get, then that's all I'm going to get," he laughed.

The train stopped before midnight and took on another engine to pull it up the increasingly steep grade, and twice during the night there were brief halts while the crew got out to clear fallen snow from the track. None of the card-playing men seemed the least inclined to stop their game and go to bed. They concentrated on their cards, but darted nervous glances toward the windows. Ceileigh was as frightened as they were. The wind buffeted the train until it swayed dizzyingly. More than once she realized they were twisting and turning almost back on the route they had just covered. The windows threw back the reflection of the inside of the car, as if there were nothing at all on the other side, as if they were moving slowly and painfully through absolute black, coming from nowhere, going nowhere.

When dawn paled the sky, they could see the world beyond the windows was thick with snow. Ceileigh concentrated on ignoring it. She knew it was no accident they had gone through the mountains at night! Had any of them seen how precariously the tracks were perched on the rail bed, how steep the slopes were, how deep the crevasses or ravines, there would surely have been panic among the passengers. It seemed that on every side of them there were rough patches where snow had slid away, filling the valleys with dirty heaps of rock, gravel, and broken trees. And still the train toiled slowly upward and forward.

They stopped mid-day to cool the engines, refill the water

tanks, and exchange empty coal cars for full ones. Ceileigh got out of the train then, and stood beside the track, staring down at the valleys unfolding to the west. Rich, green lowlands, and dark-treed slopes, and saw-toothed ice on mountaintops hard-edged against the blue sky. The tracks ahead ran level, but she could see where they started to twist and turn their way down the slope, vanishing into the dark green and frozen white, reappearing on the valley floor, then heading up the side of a hill. There the trees thinned again and the tracks reappeared briefly before they wound behind another slope and, she knew, went down the side of it, closer every foot of track to the coast. Almost directly below them she could see a small frozen lake, and in the lake snow-covered islands sprouting the bare winter bones of trees. Even as she watched a patch of snow slid from the boughs, dropped silently to the ice-encrusted ground.

"We'll be there this time tomorrow," a voice said. Ceileigh turned. The middle-aged card player with the greying hair and neatly trimmed moustache smiled at her and nodded as if he himself were directly responsible for the scenery. "Beautiful," he breathed.

"I've never seen anything like it," Ceileigh admitted.

"That's a rare thick accent you've got," he teased. "Have you been over here long?"

"Och, aye," she laughed. "Almost a year."

"That's not long."

"It can seem like forever," she contradicted gently. "Every day seems longer than the one before when you're cold and hungry and far from your people."

"And are you?" he asked. "Alone, I mean?"

"I am now," she answered curtly.

"Do you mind me asking your name?"

"No," she shrugged. "Ask if you wish."

"And if I ask will you tell me?" he laughed.

"Why should I?" and she laughed, too, that he not think her angry.

The whistle sounded and they went back to the train. Within minutes the engines were moving again, and Ceileigh was in the club car, playing. When the card game ended early, she went to the porter's little room, wrapped herself in her plaidie, and slept on the floor. She woke to the smell of real coffee. "You've been very kind," she said quietly.

"No, I haven't." He shook his head. "I've made good money on you. I bet them they'd have no luck at all trying to get you into bed, and you won me a fair pocketful."

"Then since I had to give you half my tips, you give me half what you won!"

"Don't be stupid," he mocked. "You've got the satisfaction of knowing you're still pure; that's worth more than money, isn't it?"

"Och, you're a dreadful man," she laughed. "There's no shame in you at all!"

By afternoon there was almost no sign of snow, just miles and miles and yet more miles of deep green forest, and meadows already rich with new grass. The river tumbled eagerly westward, muddy brown and full of bits of broken tree branch, stumps, and large twisted tangles of root balls. There were houses now, and barns, with fat brown and white cows grazing in pastures. Horses raced, frightened by the train, and children waved from their perches on split rail fences.

"Is it what you expected?" a familiar voice said softly.

"Better," she said happily. "Better than I'd dared dream."

"And what will you do when you get to New Westminster?" he asked.

"Och," she teased, "pick gold from the streets if the stories are to be even half believed. Although if they're paving the streets with it, it can't be worth much."

"My name is David Brownley." He handed her a small card. "Come see me tomorrow and I may have a job for you."

"Sir," she said firmly, "it must be understood right at the start that I'm not the least bit interested in some kinds of jobs."

"Do I look like a whoremaster?" He was laughing at her, she knew.

"I'm not sure I've ever seen a whoremaster," she said clearly, "but if I ever did I would expect him to look very much like you."

"Well, I'm not," he nodded, smiling slightly. "What I do might be barely respectable in the eyes of some, but it is respectable. And it pays, madam. It pays much better than you would think."

"Ceileigh," she said, surprising herself. "Ceileigh McNab."

"Come see me," he urged.

8

Su Gin lived and worked in the House of All Races for three and a half years. She slept most of the day, rising in time to bathe and have a delicious meal before the first of the Lo Fan arrived. She smiled at them, she learned the language and spoke to them, she went upstairs with them and did what they wanted her to do, and she did it energetically and skillfully. When the last Lo Fan left in the pre-dawn grey, Su Gin went to the large bathing room and soaked all memory of their touch from her body, then spent an hour or more doing T'ai Chi, cleansing her mind and emotions as scrupulously as she cleansed her body.

She was trusted now, and allowed to walk on the beach with several other women, none of whom knew she spoke and understood English as well as she did. After the daily walk there was a hot, delicious meal, and then Su Gin went to bed, to sleep until it was time to get up and prepare for another night with the Lo Fan. Some gave her presents, which she was allowed to keep. Some gave her money, which she hid with her things. She kept her eyes downcast, she answered politely and promptly, she argued with nobody, and she waited.

One morning when the world was swathed in fog, Su Gin made her move. She ate breakfast as she had done for almost four years. She went up to her room as she always did. She got into bed. She even closed her eyes and napped for almost an hour. Then she slid out of bed and minutes later she was dressed and moving quietly down the stairs. The kitchen was empty and from the basement, through the open door at the top of the steps, she heard the voices of the women doing the daily laundry. Su Gin quickly stuffed a napkin around the clapper of the bell above the door; seconds later she was outside and down the few steps, her bare feet making no sound.

She kept the woodshed between herself and the House of All Races and went over the fence easily. Then she slipped down the alley, moving confidently, moving as she had imagined herself moving a hundred times. Between the buildings, noiselessly, never showing herself to those who walked along the street. She hugged the outer walls and blessed the gods who had sent the thick white and grey mist.

When the morning train headed north out of the city, Su Gin was hiding in a box car. She kept out of sight behind a pile of crates and heavy boxes until the train stopped in a town whose name she never knew. There she slid the box car door open, jumped into the darkness, took the time to slide the door shut again, and melted into the shadows, whispering prayers of thanks.

Su Gin passed the night in an alley, her eyes fixed on the small store across the street. When the owner arrived in the morning and lit a lamp against the lingering darkness, she moved from the alley, crossed the street, and went into the store. The storekeeper wasn't surprised to have a well-dressed, heavily-veiled woman for his first customer. The girls from the Palace were always careful about hiding their faces, and it wasn't the first time one of them had arrived to buy clothes for a customer who had been in a fight, or swallowed too much booze and puked over himself. He wrapped Su Gin's purchases wordlessly, took her money, made change, and watched with absolutely no interest as she left the store and walked across the street toward the saloon.

Su Gin went back into the alley. Less than five minutes later she emerged from the far end and moved behind the buildings, back toward the train station.

The ticket agent had never seen a woman of her people before. He was expecting a man, so he saw a man.

"Where to?" he growled.

"Seattle," she whispered.

"You ride in the stock car," he warned. "No Celestials allowed in the passenger cars." Again she nodded, and again he saw only a frightened, humble Chinese youth with one long pigtail down his back, his hat pulled low over his ears, his clothes loose-fitting but clean.

The stock car smelled of straw and hay, of grain and manure, and Su Gin was pleasantly reminded of the time she had spent with the gentle ox she had known for most of her life and all of his. She turned her gaze from the strips of light coming through the cracked wall and blinked, adjusting to the dimness. The stalls were narrow. The partitions pressed gently against the sides of the horses, which were tethered by short, strong ropes to the thick beam along the wall. Each stall was fitted with strong webbing across the opening instead of a door. Every effort had been made to ensure the horses would not lurch or stagger or, in case of an accident, tumble loosely, fall, and break legs.

Su Gin reached out tentatively to stroke the closest, a large dark brown mare with black mane and tail. "Oh, Friend," she whispered, "oh, look at you. So beautiful, so gentle, so wonderful." The horse turned her head, stared at Su Gin for long moments, and whuffed expressively. The large head turned again, lowered, and nosed demandingly at the bucket fastened to the back wall. Again the mare whuffed, again she nosed the bucket, and then she stamped once. Su Gin raised herself on her tiptoes, looked at the empty bucket, and grinned widely. "You don't need to learn to talk," she laughed softly, "you do fine with what you already know."

There was a barrel in one corner of the stock car, and next to it a small bucket lying on its side in the scattered straw. Su Gin ran to the bucket and scooped water from the barrel. She held the bucket over the partition wall, where the mare could sink her nose into it and drink noisily. "This way," Su Gin confided, "you have to acknowledge me as the one who gave you a drink when you were thirsty."

The other horses smelled the water and stirred restlessly, stamping and whuffing, tugging at their tether ropes and de-

manding their own share. Su Gin waited until Friend was
satisfied, then she moved to the next animal, a mottled grey
mare. There was no way Su Gin could get to the mare's head or
the bucket without going into the stall, and no way she could get
into the stall without unfastening the safety webbing and exposing herself to the back end and the sharp hooves of the horse.
"You kick me," she promised, "and you will go thirsty. In
fact, if you kick me, I am apt to kick you right back." She
unfastened the webbing and moved gingerly forward, squeezing between the side of the mare and the solid plank wall. "If
you heave yourself against me and crush me," she whispered,
"I promise you I will spill every drop onto the floor before I
die, and you will still get nothing to drink." The mare laid back
her ears and raised them again, and Su Gin very carefully held
the bucket where the mare could drink. "See," she reached out,
stroking the mare's shoulder, "I am no threat to you. And if
you crush me on my way out, this is the last drink you will get
from me. But you aren't going to crush me, are you? You know
who your friends are."

One by one she watered the horses, marvelling at the beauty
of them. She knew that these were brood mares, that someone
had paid good money for them and then paid more money to have
them shipped. Lesser animals would have been herded, but you
don't send first class stock that way.

By now the light was fading. The cracks which had allowed
her to see the countryside were now grey strips through which
the chill night air came freely. Su Gin pulled her jacket tight and
put her hands in her pockets, but still the draft eddied unpleasantly around her ankles, found its way through the layers of
clothing, and chilled her skin. She gathered armloads of the
straw and piled it in the space between the end wall and Friend's
stall. She pushed straw up the wall and stuffed it into the
cracks, then made herself a cozy nest of fragrant dried prairie
grass. She was warm in minutes, and with the warmth came a
doziness she didn't even try to resist. She snuggled deeper into
her little burrow and slept, comforted by the scent of horse.

Su Gin was jolted from sleep when the car suddenly rocked
crazily. All hell was busting loose. The metal wheels screamed
on the rails, the floor beneath her shook and shuddered. She

heard gunshots, then an explosion. A series of crashes and bangs followed. By now the horses were hysterical, but the sound of their stamping was drowned out by the loud roar of another explosion that shook the very sides of the stock car.

Su Gin lay stiff with terror in her nest. There was light now, flickering outside, but not moonlight, not sunlight, not comforting light.She reached out to pull part of the straw plug from the crack in the wall and saw the bright glare of fire. There was an acrid reek of explosives, and she could hear screams, yells, rifle shots, and revolver shots. Her flesh cringed, expecting any minute a bullet would rip through the planking and tear her belly open or blow her head apart. She waited for the stock car door to open and bandits to pour in, bandits who would find her and make her pray for death.

The stock car doors stayed shut, but still Su Gin lay frozen with fear, seeing only the flickering flames and the shadow-figures that moved rapidly in the narrow slice of her vision. From somewhere up front there was a loud yell of triumph, a muffled explosion, the sound of men cheering and laughing. Su Gin crouched in her little burrow, uttering prayers she had not spoken for over a year. She heard voices raised in protest and fear, voices pleading, the sounds she had heard in her village when the raiders struck. And then the voices were cut short and more gunshots echoed long and loud.

"That's it," a voice yelled, and the gravel railbed clattered and grated as the metal-shod hooves of horses slipped, slithered, then pounded away, the sound fading rapidly.

Now Su Gin heard the hiss of flames, the crackling and snapping of burning wood. The horses screamed in terror, and it was their terror helped her overcome her own. She scrambled from her nest in the hay and threw her weight against the door. For one horrific moment she thought the door had been locked, but then it moved. She got her fingers in the open crack and heaved again. The door slid open and Su Gin dropped to the floor to peer out at a scene of total destruction.

Ahead of her, the express car was burning. Several of the passenger cars were off the rails and lay tumbled on the slope. Su Gin dropped to the ground and raced along the length of the train, unable to believe her eyes. The mail-safe doors gaped open to reveal the mail car empty, except for the blood-drenched bodies of two men. The baggage man lay sprawled in the flickering light of the fire. Farther along, the conductor lay crumpled, his blood pooling around him. In the passenger cars there was more blood, and horror, the bodies of men, women, and children fallen to the floor, draped over the blood-soaked plush seats, half in and half out of the smashed windows. The fire from the express car was spreading, and a new fire in the tangled wreck of the engine flicked at the wooden roofs of the freight and baggage wagons.

Su Gin raced back, horrified, to the baggage car. She cursed herself for not having a knife, she cursed herself for being clumsy in her haste and fear, she cursed the bandits, she cursed the world. And she unfastened the safety webbing of each stall, untied the tether ropes, and backed the terrified animals out of the death trap. Friend pulled back, afraid of the light, the smell of fire, the stench of blood. *"Go!"* Su Gin shouted, slapping Friend's rump as hard as she could. The mare jumped with surprise, out the stock car, and over the railbed, landing on the gentle slope from the tracks to the grassy field below, where she skittered and kicked, then stood waiting, her rope hanging. Su Gin reached for the grey mare's rope and repeated the shouting and slapping. When Grey jumped from the stock car, the other mares followed. Su Gin was the last to leave. She landed on her feet, lost her balance, fell, and rolled down the slope, skinning her elbows and the palms of her hands. For several seconds she lay, winded, then made herself sit up and watched the fire eating at the passenger cars.

She wanted away from here. She wanted far away from here. She stumbled to her feet, turned, and almost walked right into a bulky shadow. A horse, saddled, standing obediently where its reins dangled, shivering with fear, but too well-trained to flee. Not four feet away a body lay sprawled, face down, and still. Su Gin didn't have to think about it. She grabbed up the reins, put her foot in the stirrup and was up on the saddle, urging the horse forward. As soon as the horse started to move, Friend moved with it, and when Friend moved, the others followed. Su Gin had seen the outlaws race along the tracks in the direction the train had come, and she had no wish to meet up with them, no wish to go pelting at full speed into the middle of a circle of resting madmen. So she kicked her horse gently and it responded at once, racing along the grass in the direction the train had been taking before it had slammed into the ambush.

But something was screaming, scrambling toward her, something small and pale. Su Gin felt the blood rush from her head, she thought she would fall from the horse's back. Were the spirits of the dead coming for her, jealous because she had escaped what had overtaken them? Then she saw the terrified face turned up to her, tears glistening on chubby cheeks, small hands held up pleadingly. Without thinking Su Gin leaned to one side, reached down to grab the child's clothing, and heaved herself upright, pulling the traumatized child from the ground. The child, still screaming, clutched hysterically at Su Gin's jacket, squirming closer, hiding her face, sobbing uncontrollably.

Somewhere in that inferno a mother had managed to think before dying. Somewhere in that mess, before death stopped all thought and movement, some mother had smashed out a window, lifted her darling, and heaved her out into the unknown, risking everything, risking it all for the slim chance that her child would live. She had even slipped a small brocade purse onto a ribbon, and over the child's head and one shoulder. The little purse now dug into Su Gin's belly. She shifted the child's weight, moved the purse, settled the toddler sideways between herself and the saddle horn. With one arm around the child and the other holding the reins, she rode away from the destruction scattered along the tracks, away from the blazing fire and the stink of burned bodies. She wanted away from here, she wanted far away before anybody else arrived. Whether the next to arrive were bandits or lawmen, her fate would be the same.

Heading north, the noise and stink rapidly vanishing, they moved away from insanity toward the promise of peace and safety. The child fell asleep, her little body warm against Su Gin's fear-chilled body. Finally Su Gin stopped and dismounted, stooping to lay the child on the ground. Straight brown hair, singed on one side. Oval face, serious in sleep, scraped and crusted with dried blood. One shoulder had been scratched and there was a nasty cut on her arm. Her dress, once expensive and beautiful, was ripped and singed. Her pantaloons and stockings were filthy, ripped, and stained where she had lost control of her bladder as fear swallowed her world. She was not a beautiful child, but her body was strong and well-formed. Su Gin gently took the small foot in her hand and as she gazed at it she knew what the child had suffered. More than anything else, the cut, burned, bruised little foot told the story. Broken glass, bits of hot and jagged metal, burning coals and cinders, sharp rocks and sticks had all left their mark. No wonder the child had been screaming as she raced toward the horses and the unknown figure who represented her only chance for safety. It was one of the wonders of the gods that the child had been able to move at all.

Su Gin checked the horses, soothing them, caring for them as she would care for any frightened animal on her parents' farm. She cupped her hands on either side of each horse's muzzle, lifted, and whuffed gently in her nostrils, identifying herself. Each horse whuffed back. Su Gin accepted their introduction, then whuffed again, knowing that for the rest of their lives the animals would recognize her by her scent.

The child stirred, sat up, and looked around, her eyes round with terror. When she saw Su Gin she relaxed. She did not smile, she did not speak, but her light grey eyes lost the wild look of horror, and something inside Su Gin's chest cracked forever. She knelt and held the child close.

"Hush," she soothed, "hush, now."

"Cold," the little girl said clearly.

Su Gin removed her jacket and wrapped it around the child. The little girl nodded, lay down on the ground, closed her eyes, and sighed deeply. Su Gin hunkered beside her, patting her gently, until she knew the child was again asleep. And then she took stock of her situation. She had horses, more than she had ever expected to have. One saddle. One bridle. Two water canteens, both full. Saddlebags laid across the back of one horse. Behind the saddle, a rifle in a scabbard and a canvas travel bag tied to the horn. Tied with leather thongs through metal-rimmed holes in the saddle skirting, a warm, thick woollen blanket wrapped in a black slicker. Su Gin unfastened the bedroll and lay the slicker on the cool ground and the blanket over it. She lay the sleeping child on the blanket, then wrapped her up, enclosing the little girl in a cocoon of warmth. Next Su Gin opened the saddlebags to examine the contents. Dried beans in a cloth bag, rice in another cloth bag, strips of dried meat, dried fruit. A coffee pot, soot-blackened and battered, and inside it a small bag of dark brown ground coffee. In the other saddlebag, more rice, more beans, and several metal pots which fit one inside the other and were neatly wrapped in a spare shirt. Stuffed in the bottom, a roll of clean clothes and woollen socks.

When she found matches, she quickly gathered enough dry grass, small sticks, and branches to make a decent fire. She didn't want to take the time to soak and cook beans or rice, but she needed nourishment and she was certain the child needed something hot in her belly. She poured water from the canteen into one of the blackened pots, added some dried meat, and put it near the fire to simmer into soup. She pulled a pair of warm socks onto her bare feet, then went to check the canvas travel bag. Inside the bag were two other canvas sacks, and when she opened one of the sacks, all she could do was stare. Su Gin had never seen more than a few pieces of money at one time, and in the canvas sack were sheafs of bills, each held together by a small strip of white paper. She knew she was looking at money that had been in the mail car not too many hours ago. She knew she was looking at money stolen at the cost of far too many lives. She pulled shut the canvas pouches, stuffed them back into the travel bag, and decided to concentrate on something she could handle.

Su Gin had never saddled a horse in her life. She had never even unsaddled a horse. She spent several minutes studying the bridle, how it fit, where it fastened. Then she removed the rope from the bridle and tied the rope around Friend's neck. Friend was used to the bit, used to the bridle, and accepted it easily. Transferring the saddle wasn't as easy. Friend seemed placid enough, but each time Su Gin thought she had the saddle snug, she discovered it was loose.

"Ha," she hissed. "You think because I'm not experienced, I am a fool?" and she started tightening the cinch for the sixth time. Then, with no warning at all, she fired up her knee, catching Friend in the side. Friend gasped, Su Gin tightened the cinch, and this time the saddle stayed in place. "Don't forget that," she suggested. Friend just eyed her, then looked away, switching her tail.

The meat was softened and the water a thick soupy broth when Su Gin wakened the child and offered her food. The child smiled and drank the rich hot mixture greedily. They scooped the meat from the warm pot with their fingers, chewing and grinning at each other.

"Pee?" the little girl asked.

"What?" Su Gin stared, uncomprehending.

"Pee!" the child insisted, struggling her way out of the blanket. She got to her feet, winced, stumbled and limped a few yards, fumbled with her soiled, torn underwear, then gave up and began to wail. Su Gin cursed her own stupidity. She helped the child pull off her stained rags, then grasped the child by the legs, lifted her, and grinned. Sitting comfortably in mid-air, the little girl flooded happily, sighing with relief. "Grunt," she then decided, looking up questioningly. Su Gin nodded, and waited until the child was finished and squirmed to be set free.

Friend shifted anxiously, sniffing the wind. Su Gin stroked her head, looking across the landscape. Ahead of them the green grass sloped down to a valley where darker green marked bush and glinting silver indicated water.

"Yes," she assured the horse, "yes," and she turned to the child, smiled at her, and patted the saddle. "We go," she said.

"Go," the child agreed, limping bravely.

Su Gin tied up the bedroll, packed away their few things, scooped the child up, set her on the saddle, and swung up beside her.

"My name," she said conversationally, "is Su Gin."

"Elizabeth," the little girl answered, fighting a yawn.

9

Laughton showed her how he liked his porridge cooked, how he liked his eggs poached, how he liked his biscuits still soft and lightly browned. He explained how he liked his clothes washed and then dried outside, in the fresh breeze, and how he liked something sweet for dessert after both the noon meal and the supper he told her how he liked cooked. And every night he told her what she was to do to pleasure him, and she did it. She did it with the same frightened desperation she did everything else, trembling, not in eagerness to please him, but in fear of the heavy numbing slaps, the shaking that bruised her shoulders where his fingers pinched. As long as she did things the way he liked them done, he was polite, even kind. Like his children, she learned how to anticipate his wants, how to leap quickly to do his bidding. Like his children, she made sure all he saw were smiles and respectful expressions, and like his children she worked from the time she got up until it was time to go to bed. Then, unlike the children, she continued to work.

Her father and brother arrived unannounced and unexpected. Laughton made them welcome, even though their arrival put a decided crimp in his plans for the day. Cora was more desperately grateful than ever when Laughton did not blame her for the unwelcome visit. She turned herself inside out cooking the noon meal they shared, and Laughton's children helped her without being asked. She made sure she cooked enough extra biscuits that neither Jack nor Jacob could eat them all before they got home, and she carefully wrapped several fertile goose eggs in thick pieces of cloth. She didn't tell Jacob to be careful with the eggs, she didn't want him to deliberately shake them and kill the fertilized spot inside. She just put the bundle in a small box and put the box under the wagon seat, knowing her mother would find them and be smart enough to put them under a broody hen to hatch.

"If I'm providing goslings," Laughton said mockingly that night, "then I want some kind of payment for my charitable generosity. I want," and he lay on the bed, naked, grinning up at her, "some enthusiasm from you. Pretend you aren't paralyzed. Pretend you want me to be happy."

When the buffalo reappeared, Laughton surprised her totally. He handed her new boots, flannel pants, and a flannel shirt. "You might like to come," he said softly.

"Oh! Thank you, Laughton," she blurted. He smiled, her happiness pleasing him, and she didn't care that there was a price to pay. An enthusiastic price to pay. If it was pretended enthusiasm, he didn't care, the pretence was almost as good as the real thing.

Cora rode a light-bodied, strong-muscled buckskin mare, and sat easily in the gleaming leather saddle Laughton told her would be hers from now on. In the saddle scabbard a near-new rifle rested, lighter than Laughton's, but definitely not a toy. Cora knew without Laughton having to say it or even hint at it that she had more, already, than the sum total of everything her mother had ever had. She also knew that the price tag Laughton demanded was less than half the price her mother had paid and was still paying.

They placed themselves where Laughton directed, then sat, each of them alone and quiet. Cora half-dozed, enjoying the sun on her skin, the breeze on her face, the entire day light on her heart, the boring sameness of endless work and chores left behind at the farm. When the ground beneath her began to tremble, she knew the herd was close. She roused herself, checked her rifle, crouched behind the large rock and watched anxiously for the cloud of dust.

It was a small herd, but to Cora it seemed endless. Each beast weighed more than half a ton. It was a storehouse of meat, fat, tallow, and hide. She sucked in her breath and waited, heart pounding, mouth suddenly dry. Oh, please, God, not that, not what her father called buck fever, please, if she froze and let the animals go by without firing a shot, Laughton would never allow her to accompany him again, and she would die within spitting distance of that kitchen she knew would never be truly hers. She heard the sound of Laughton's voice and the fear was gone. She focused on a young cow, the rifle barrel resting on an outcropping of rock. Lying on her belly, propped up on her elbows, steadying her gun on the rock spur, she fired. The young cow bellowed, stumbled, and fell to her knees, shaking her head. Cora aimed again, fired again, and the young cow fell to her side, legs thrashing. Cora could hear other shots, see other animals falling, but she paid no attention. She picked another young cow, aimed again, fired again, and then the animals were charging madly across the grassland, heads down, tails up, and she knew it would be a waste of expensive ammunition to try to fire again.

Laughton didn't slap her on the back the way Jack had slapped Jacob, but he did put his arms around her thin shoulders and squeeze approvingly. And he gave each child a brusque, proud hug, told them they had done well. "It's a wonderful thing," he assured them, "to sit at a table and eat a meal you know you provided yourself. Food earned by good honest work tastes better than food given in charity." The children nodded, and Cora knew they had heard this same assurance all their short lives.

The meat was loaded on wagons and taken back to the farm, and then the long hours of hard, bloody work began. When it was finished and the meat was safely stored, Laughton allowed them two days' rest: reward, he told them, for a hard job well done.

"What will we do?" the middle child asked, his small face puzzled.

"What will we do?" Cora repeated, almost unable to believe the little boy had no idea of how to play. Then she hugged him tightly, kissed his ear, and took his hand in hers. "What will we do? We'll get fishing rods and go to the stream, we'll lie on the grass and watch the hawks, we'll cook our supper over an open fire, and we'll tease each other. And tickle!" She grabbed him, her fingers digging at his ribs. There was a brief moment of shocked, uncomprehending silence, and then the little boy giggled.

They made a ball by stuffing sand and grass into a sock and knotting the top securely. The children chased after it, their laughter loud and shrill. They caught fish, cooked them over the fire, and Laughton pretended to enjoy the meal. He even agreed to allow them to sleep out under the stars, although he grumbled they were turning into wild savages. "You'll be living in skin huts next," he warned, "become little more than pagan sinners." But he threw the grass-stuffed sock for them. Then he went to the barn, got a long piece of good rope, knotted the ends to a strong branch, cut notches in a board, set it on the rope, and grinned with pride as the children thrilled to their first swing.

There was a price to be paid for the days of fun, but Cora knew now how to behave, how to tighten her muscles and bring him gasping to climax, how to turn off her head, ignore her own revulsion, and snuggle close to him as if content, until his breathing slowed and he was asleep. Then she could roll to her own side of the bed, away from his hairy body, his bristly beard, the sharp salt-tang male smell of him.

Summer passed in a blur of hard work, and then it was harvest time, and she was busy canning from first light until she was too tired to move.

She was so tired she slept through the first ruckus, slept through the sound of a madly galloping horse, slept through the thunder of feet thumping across the porch, a fist pounding on the door. She didn't waken until Laughton came back to the bedroom and shook her awake.

"You're needed," he said softly, "there's been an accident."

It wasn't an accident. Jack, Jacob, and Tom had gone to town, and Jack had been razored across the throat in the hallway of the whorehouse. He had bled to death before anyone thought to go for the doctor. By the time the box had been hammered together and the carpenter paid, the grave dug and the gravediggers paid, the doctor paid for declaring Jack dead, and the minister paid for saying a few brief words about the wages of sin being death, there was no money left for the boys to take home.

"Lucky those townies didn't take the horses and wagon, too," Jacob cursed bitterly.

"Not to worry," Laughton said. "We can combine the two places. We'll just move you all here and use your place as a line-shack for the beef we'll run on your land. A place for you to stay," he explained, "when you're over there checking the herd."

"I don't know anything about beef herds," Jacob said uneasily.

"You'll learn," Laughton promised.

Cora had company now, and her mother made no secret of her joy and relief. Not that she was joyful about Jack's death, but if he had to go to the whorehouse and get his throat slit, at least she and her children weren't left alone and helpless on the bald prairie with the weather turning colder every day. She had a room nicer than any she had known in her life, she had a kitchen the likes of which she hadn't even imagined possible, she had bins of vegetables, a cellar full of preserved vegetables and fruit and pickles and relish, and there were plenty of children to help with the many time-consuming small chores.

By Christmas time, Esther looked better than she had looked in anyone's memory. She had put on weight and she had begun to relax. The lines on her face were only faint traces, not deeply cut furrows.

"I didn't know your mother was such a good-looking woman," Laughton remarked casually.

"I didn't, either," Cora replied.

"If you showed half as much enthusiasm as she did," he grumbled, "life around here would be ideal."

Cora almost said that her mother's enthusiasm probably came from sleeping alone and unbothered, but she didn't want another slapping around, didn't want him to grab her shoulders and shake her until she felt as if her teeth were going to pop out of her gums.

When Laughton and the older boys rode out at the end of winter to check the herds, Cora, Esther, the girls, and the younger boys amused themselves happily. They made ginger snaps by the dozen, and gingerbread men for the children to play with while nibbling hungrily.

"Is he a good husband?" Esther asked.

"How would I know?" Cora replied tartly. "I've no other to judge him against."

"Is he kind?"

"I suppose."

"You're very lucky," Esther beamed.

"Lucky," Cora snorted. "I was traded away for a few cows and an unbroken colt. And now he's even got them back again! He always gets everything his own way."

Esther ignored Cora's anger. "I never thought I'd have a place like this to live in," she sighed, staring contentedly at the shining kitchen, the large stove, the shelves and bottles, the canisters and jugs, the plates and mugs. Cora looked around her jail-kitchen bitterly. Esther would have gloried in less than half of what Cora so thoroughly detested. Nothing Cora ever said could explain to her mother how trapped and sullied she felt. And no use telling Esther about the slapping, the pushing, the hitting, the shaking; Esther would only sigh and tell Cora to please Laughton more, to stop being stubborn, to try harder not to make him angry. Esther would tell Cora to have some appreciation.

Laughton and the boys returned with good news. The herd had survived the bitter cold winter. The wolves had been busy hunting elk, moose, and sheep and had ignored the beef, or hadn't come down low enough nor close enough to the house to be tempted. Supper that night was a near feast, prepared because the favoured few were back, and planned and supervised by Esther, not by Cora. Laughton and the boys ate as if they had to fill hollow legs before they would be able to stand up and walk away from the table, and Cora watched everything with her sense of isolation renewed and magnified. Everyone else was having such a good time, eating, laughing, even the children were talking happily. When had Laughton begun to relent and allow his children to be people, instead of possessions? They hardly resembled the frightened little things Cora had so pitied. They were as free-moving and relaxed as her own brothers and sisters, all of whom had profited from the move to the big house, the soft beds, the abundant food. Even Jacob and Tom had changed. They no longer spoke to Esther as though she were a dog or a horse. Laughton insisted they follow the injunctions honour thy father and mother, respect your elders, and a good woman is without price, and whether it was his example, or the realization that a back-handed slap along the side of the ear would hurt a lot more if Laughton let fly than it ever had when Jack had hit them, the boys were actually becoming pleasant.

Esther was laughing softly, smiling often, encouraging the children to eat, offering Laughton another cup of tea, another slice of apple betty, and when Laughton protested he would get fat if he ate any more, Esther replied easily that he worked far too hard to get fat. "There aren't many men can put in the day's work you do," she said. Cora took a good look at her mother, a good look with fresh eyes. Laughton was thirty-four now, about her mother's age. The two of them never ran out of things to talk about. Instead of being full of strained silences and nervous behaviour, the after-supper interlude before bed was relaxed and pleasant. Laughton even put the kettle on for another pot of tea and took a honeyed cup of it to Esther as she mended one of his shirts. "There," she smiled, "I turned the collar and sewed a strip of strong material on the inside, where it won't show, but the buttons are sewn to it. You'll get a full six months' wear out of it. After that," she warned, "it's into the rag bag and you won't see it again until it's part of a thick winter quilt."

Esther went to bed with the children, and Laughton sat staring into his tea cup. He rolled and smoked one cigarette after another and didn't even notice when Cora went to bed. She snuggled gratefully into the empty bed, wishing she could sleep alone all the time, but when she wakened in the morning, Laughton was there, sprawled on his back.

It was Esther spoke to her about it first, and all Cora could do was stare in surprise, then laugh with relief, nodding her head happily, almost babbling with joy. By the time Laughton brought himself to speak of it, Cora's mind was made up and she had her own plans. Better late than never, there's no time like the present, a stitch in time saves nine, early to bed and early to rise gives a woman time to do what needs done. She went to bed soon after supper, pleading cramps and a headache. Then, when she heard Laughton go to Esther's room, Cora got up and dressed in the pants and shirt he had given her for the buffalo hunt. Carrying the sturdy boots under her arm and her warm jacket in her hand, she sneaked from the bedroom to the kitchen and went out the kitchen door. She sat on the top step, pulled on the boots, shrugged on her jacket, and headed for the barn.

The saddling took only a minute. Everything was exactly where she had hidden it, her clothes in the canvas bag that fit easily in front of the saddle horn, food in the saddlebags, cooking pots wrapped in sacking so they wouldn't jangle and clank and maybe warn Laughton he wasn't getting everything his own way after all. She had ammunition, she had the rifle he had said was hers, and she had money stuffed between her stockings and her boots, more money than she had known one person could have, but hardly any money compared to what she had left behind in the box Laughton thought she didn't know about.

She took the mare and the two-year-old roan stud, part of the bride-price Jack had received for her, and only when she was sure she was far enough from the house not to be heard did she mount up and urge the mare forward. There was no road, but Cora didn't need a road. There was no path, but Cora needed no path. She knew the North star, and she knew where the sun came up in the morning and where it went to sleep at night. She headed west, leaving Laughton with his idea of having two wives and Esther with her new life. Laughton might be angry about the horses, the rifle, and the money, but Cora didn't care, and she didn't care that Laughton might waken at night sometimes remembering with regret the young body he had used so freely. Esther would mourn briefly, because she really did love Cora, but Esther was nothing if not sensible. Better to be the sole wife of a man getting wealthier each year than be one of two wives. Especially in a country where more than one wife is not only a sin but a crime.

"Anyway," Cora said to the buckskin mare, "it's not as if we were ever really married. Not really. No minister, no prayers, no nothing except being grabbed by the outhouse. That's not a real marriage. And if it wasn't a real marriage, then I'm not doing anything wrong. And if I am," she said, urging the mare forward, "I don't care."

10

The representative of the Coast Steamship Company frowned thoughtfully and studied the application form he held in his soft hand. "Your father is a miner?"

"Was, sir," Mary answered, looking down at her white-gloved hands. "It was a cave-in, sir, the ceiling fell and the beams and trusses broke..."

"And when was that?"

"Almost a year ago." She lifted her eyes briefly and looked down again. "I was going to start a little business of my own," she explained, "over there, but not in Company Town. I thought..." She swallowed nervously, then looked into his eyes. "I had no family, and a woman without a family is a woman without protection. There are some places where a woman should not go at all, especially unescorted."

"Was your father a union man?"

"I don't know." Again she looked up, her eyes wide. "He was a Welshman and a digger. He was paid top rate. I never heard him talk union, and as near as I know, he never went to a meeting."

"And what experience do you have, Miss Morgan, that would qualify you to be a stewardess on our northern run?"

"Well, sir, I've looked after people all my life. First my mother, God rest her soul in heaven, then, when she was gone, my Da. And any time any of the wives was sick, sir, they sent for me, to look after them and keep house and all. I've experience with boats." She smiled slightly. "Not much, but some. Enough I know I wouldn't get sick. And I'm a good worker."

"I'm sure you are," he agreed. He studied the application form again. "Your references seem to be in order. The only hesitation I have is that your previous work experience was..." He cleared his throat. "Frankly, you worked for yourself, and we prefer..."

"Let me work for a month for nothing," she dared him. "One month, and all it will cost you is meals and a place to sleep. Ask everyone I work with, and if they don't tell you I do a good job, I'm on my way with no hard feelings, and it hasn't cost you anything in wages."

She left two days later on the coastal steamer that ran between New Westminster and Skagway. She worked harder than she had ever worked in her life, knowing she had to prove herself, knowing she needed friends and allies among the other workers, knowing that if the company did a proper check of her letters of recommendation she would need more than friends and allies, she would need divine intervention. She had bought the letters from a Water Street sidewalk scribe who, for ten cents a page, would write anything you wanted written and sign it with any name you ordered.

Six women to a crowded room, two tiers of bunks, three high, and Mary got the top bunk, where she lay with her face so close to the metal-plated ceiling that she began to feel she was going to be smothered. They got into and out of bed one at a time, moving carefully, struggling into and out of their clothes, and no matter how carefully they moved, they banged their elbows on the bunk frames, knocked their shins against corners, and had to step out into the narrow corridor to smooth and arrange their long skirts. A month of the most foul and nasty jobs, and Mary did them, knowing the others had been put through the same trial by nausea. If a passenger became seasick and puked up supper, it was Mary got to change the bed, wash the cabin walls, swab the puke from the floor. If a child turned itself inside out with the wave-tip skitters, it was Mary got to clean up the shitty mess, rinse out the stained bedding, and stand over a bucket washing the child's filthy clothes. Female passengers watched her carefully for any sign of disrespect, any hint she might welcome or even provoke advances from husbands who, when the wives weren't looking, smiled and winked and watched for the same hints their wives feared. Single male passengers invited her to walk the deck or to meet them in the cabin for wine or tea, and even asked openly how much she would charge for what they called a bit of fun. Mary ignored it all and concentrated on her work.

When the month was done, she was back in the company representative's office, her stomach a tight knot of fear. If they had contacted any of the people whose names were on those letters of recommendation, she was sunk. Not only out of a job but possibly in trouble with the law for misrepresentation, even forgery. But ten minutes later she walked out of the office, her feet barely touching the muddy street. The job was hers!

Mary made two more trips to Skagway, then decided the last thing she intended to do was spend her life cleaning up other peoples' messes. Her fourth trip north, she kept her eyes open for every possible opportunity.

When it happened, Mary didn't see the opportunity, it saw her. She was walking down the mess that passed for the main street in Skagway when a native woman approached her, smiling, holding out a magnificent otter skin.

"It's lovely," Mary breathed, touching the gleaming pelt, stroking it gently.

"Trade?" the woman grinned, pointing at Mary's hat.

"Trade?" Mary gaped.

"Trade," the woman said.

Mary walked back to the ship bareheaded, a prize pelt draped over her arm. She managed to get to her cabin without being seen by any of the other stewardesses, and there she quickly stuffed the pelt in her dunnage box. She sat on the box, thinking furiously, then threw all good sense and reason to the winds, stood up, opened the box again, and began to haul out her dresses, her other hat, her new coat. She folded them carefully, put them in a small cloth satchel, and once again left the steamer, hurrying back down the street to where she had met the Chilkat woman. "Trade?" Mary asked, smiling. The Chilkat woman eyed her suspiciously, clutched her hat protectively. Mary opened the cloth satchel, and pulled out a lace-edged petticoat. The Chilkat woman grinned happily, nodded, then reached out to touch the lace.

"Trade," she said firmly.

Back in New Westminster, Mary took the otter and seal pelts to a furrier. Half an hour later she was shopping like a crazed fool for hats, petticoats, even bolts of cloth, the brighter the colour, the better for her purpose. She met the Chilkat woman and her husband behind the wharfinger shed in Skagway and in spite of the language and cultural barriers, there was no misunderstanding or disagreement. The Chilkats were overjoyed and the New Westminster furrier beamed gleefully.

"How many can you get me?" he asked greedily.

"I don't know," Mary answered. "But I suspect if we can better the prices the company is offering, we can at least get the prime ones, if not all."

The furrier would have loved to find a way to underpay Mary or even cut her out of the business altogether but Mary had learned more selling fish than how to make change. She went to several furriers and got offers from each of them, then went back to the first and told him what she wanted. He protested only until she let him know he had competition. There was no way he could squeeze her out of things, she was his contact and she was the only one the Chilkats trusted. Mary had to smuggle the trade goods off the ship, then smuggle the furs back on again, and she knew there would be no second chances. If she was caught she was fired, in court, in jail. She made one trip after the other, each trip teaching her more about what the Chilkats needed, what they wanted, what they would be most eager to trade for.

She had more than eight thousand dollars in the bank when the news came from the north that gold had been found in the Klondike.

Mary pulled her money out of the bank and invested it in silk cloth, cotton cloth, five hundred hot water bottles, and as much flour, rice, coffee, tea, sugar, and beans as she could get. She paid her freight bill in advance, ten cents per pound, delivery guaranteed. Not delivery to Skagway. Delivery to Dawson!

The freight was heaped in nets and lowered over the side of the freighter into small boats, which ran up as far as possible at high tide, then off-loaded the boxes, bales, crates, and barrels onto the ground. Powerfully-built Chilkat men pulled the freight from the nets, loaded it on horses, mules, oxen, and the backs and shoulders of other powerfully-built men, and it was packed the mile and a half in to Skagway, where it was dumped on the ground so that the owners could rummage through and find their own gear.

Mary checked in to the first hotel she found, and spread her down-stuffed quilt over one of the many bunks in the long narrow room. The bunk was only a canvas rectangle stretched over a rough wooden frame, but it was off the floor, and there was no way it could be less comfortable than the rock-hard bunk in her steamer stateroom. The wind whistled around the frame and board buildings, the drafts blasted cold air through the cracks in the walls, and the floor creaked with every step. Between the cracks in the floor she could see water glistening a few inches below the building, and she knew she was in for a cold, damp, uncomfortable night. The dining room had a big stove in one corner and the tables were covered with oilcloth. She picked a plate from the stack on the end of a table and went to the stove. The cook, wearing thigh-high boots, an untrimmed beard, and a harried look, piled boiled potatoes, stewed meat, gravy, and baking powder biscuits onto her plate. She found a space at the table, pushed her way in between two men, sat herself on the bench and ate eagerly as men streamed constantly into the noisy and crowded room.

Mary went to bed early, fully dressed, with her skinning knife under her pillow and every intention of using it. Either the other hotel guests were decent men or they were exhausted men, because nobody even seemed to notice she was a woman. She slept like a baby and wakened early in the morning, well rested and almost shaking with excitement. She ate a huge breakfast and hurried to the freight site to check on her goods.

Two hours later she was leaving Skagway, heading toward the Chilkoot Pass. A fine mist drizzled steadily, the mules and horses steamed with their efforts, and Mary prayed she had managed to rub enough oil into her boots to keep her feet dry and warm. The trail followed a river bed, over stones tumbled round and smooth, made slippery in the rain, crossing and re-crossing from one bank to the other, back and forth, back and forth. The group picked carefully for the easiest passage, sometimes moving on ice and snow, sometimes wading in slush, sometimes stepping from boulder to boulder, and always the mist and chill. Except for her size and her hairless face, Mary looked like any of the packers handling the freight from Skagway to Dawson. Warm long underwear, woollen trousers tucked into heavy wool socks, and the boots, almost knee-high, laced from toe to top and well greased against the wet. A thick flannel shirt and over it a warm hand-knit sweater. Tied to the pack she carried on her back was a fleece-lined jacket, and on her head a fleece-lined cap with earmuffs and neck guard which could be folded up and out of the way if the weather warmed up.

At first, all Mary did was walk and carry her small pack. She had worried she wouldn't be able to keep up, but months of constant work, walking back and forth, back and forth all day long, up and down narrow steep steps, in and out of cabins, bending, lifting, carrying, stooping, had honed her strength and endurance. By mid-afternoon she was helping with the pack mules. Mary knew not to step on a round rock, knew to stay away from anything even remotely resembling lichen or moss on a wet rock, knew how to walk and how to climb. Best of all, she knew how to keep her mouth shut and save her energy for walking.

They went through Canyon City in late afternoon and camped on the far side, putting up their tents and carefully stowing all the freight and gear under canvas, safe from the rain, the fog, and the snow. Supper was quickly finished and Mary was glad to get into her tent, change her sweat-damp clothing for dry, and crawl into her comforter. At daylight they were up and packing their gear, loading up the horses and mules, moving toward the base of the pass. When the misting rain turned to huge wet flakes of snow, all Mary could do was hold on to the tail of the mule and push doggedly forward, her warm cap pulled over her ears, her collar turned up, her nose colder than it had ever been in her life. Hour after hour, up one hill and down another, up grades at least as steep as any roof, past dozens of tents pitched in the snow, a moving column of determined fanatics. Up long, steep slopes with only the barest downgrade on the other side before starting up the next slope, moving through the broken country, moving with men, dogs, and mules, moving with horses and oxen, moving with wagons and hand-drawn sledges, moving stubbornly. Here the trail was six feet wide, and minutes later it was sixteen feet wide. Here three fifty-pound sacks waited for someone to return for them, and somewhere else several tons of gear sat unmolested and unguarded. Men walked, men rode horses, men led mules, men followed dog teams, and through it all, Mary trudged quietly, a forty-five pound pack on her back, following the mules which carried her gear.

At the Scales, at the foot of the pass, the North West Mounted Police weighed the gear each packer was taking over the summit, checking to make sure that everyone heading to the Klondike had at least 1500 pounds of provisions. Mary had ten times that amount, and every pound of it freight pre-paid from New Westminster to Skagway, from Skagway to Dawson. Now all she had to do was make it up and over the pass, then walk the soul-scorching miles of fractured country between where she was and where she wanted to be. The town was a small one of rough buildings, canvas tents, and saloons where the weary could get something to make them forget the agony of the trip. Dominating it all was the transportation miracle. Mounds, heaps, even mountains of material piled wherever there was room, and, blessedly, two cable lines hauling supplies to the summit of the pass. Mary watched, smiling widely, as one cable line moved forward, the hanging cords like her fishing lines, all pulling sleighs that were piled with tons of freight. The other cable line moved upward carrying packages or bundles attached to strong lines, the load dangling in mid-air, moving slowly from the loading spot, going up to the top of the pass, disappearing into the clouds.

Mary sat on a box to catch her breath while the freight master did the talking with the police. Mary would gladly have fallen asleep, but there was too much to watch, too much to hear, too much to try to understand. Two Chilkat packers with crates strapped to their backs talked easily and quietly to each other, moving up a slope so steep it would make a goat think twice. A woman riding a horse and leading two others with heavily-laden pack frames went past. Mary tried to catch the woman's eye and smile but a dog fight broke out and demanded her attention, and when she looked back again, the woman was out of sight, moving with the steady push and shove of the inward bound.

The freight master emerged from the NWMP shed and waved his arm, and in minutes their gear was being heaved and hauled, pushed, shoved, tossed, and bundled onto one of the huge sleds. When the sled was full, the tramline worker grabbed a passing cable, snapped it to the front of the sled, and their first load of gear was on its way to the top of the pass. Another sled was loaded, another passing cable attached, another load on its way to the top. And then they, too, were on their way to the top of the pass, climbing up on the notches cut into the ice and frozen mud a rough-hewn flight of hacked gouges, like stairs, up more than 1600 feet, and neither the room nor the time to stop and take a rest. Mary moved grimly, doggedly, her breath coming hard, her lungs aching in the cold, her back sore, the muscles in her thighs and calves screaming, and when she was sure she couldn't go another step, she went that other step, and another and another until there was no sense to any of it, no rhyme or reason, no going forward or going backward, no up and no down, just the fire in her muscles and the frantic sense that she would spend the rest of her life in this idiotic hell, following someone she didn't know, followed by someone she didn't know.

Then, mercifully, there was the Canadian Customs shed, and she was almost falling inside it. Someone handed her an enamel mug full of hot tea. She drank, nearly scalding her lips and tongue, almost weeping with joy at the taste of sugar. Afterwards she could never remember whether anyone had asked her any questions. But what did it matter, she was a Canadian, coming by way of Alaska, back into her own country. She did remember the warmth, the hot sweet tea, the sudden manic exultation. She had made it, she was at the top of the Chilkoot Pass, she was where nobody she knew had ever been, she was there and her next steps would take her into the Klondike.

11

Ceileigh had no trouble finding the address David Brownley had given her. All she had to do was show the card to passers-by on the street, and one after the other, they pointed out the way. Once she knew where the building was and what it looked like, she dared to look for a place to spend the night. That was easy, too. Every street either ran uphill from the river, or crossed another which sloped down to where the wide and muddy Fraser moved determinedly westward to the sea. She hurried downhill, past the houses and stores, past the shops and businesses, past the warehouses and railway tracks, to where the willows grew thick and the grass was too green to be believed.

She had no food and nothing to cook it in, she had no blankets, no pillow, and no extra clothes. But she did have some money hidden in the pouch against her skin, she had her warm plaidie, and she had her violin. All she had to do was watch the sun set, pass the night, then make her way back to Brownley's office. And if she was hungry in the morning, she would buy something to eat, something which would taste all the better for the wait.

She sat for more than an hour with her arms wrapped around her knees, watching the sky slowly change colour, watching the birds skim the surface of the mud-coloured river, only partially aware of the sounds that meant other people, too, were settling themselves in for a night under the stars.

"You play that thing?" a voice asked quietly. Ceileigh's head snapped in the direction of the voice and her hand reached for a rock or a stick with which to defend herself.

"You scared me," she confessed.

"Didn't mean to. You play that thing?"

"I do."

"I've a big piece of smoked fish here." The dirty-faced youngster pulled a canvas-wrapped piece of something from the pocket of her oversized work pants, the bottoms casually and inexpertly cut off and fraying. "I'd share it with you if you'd play something."

"What would you like?"

"I don't know any names of songs. Anything."

"Anything?" Ceileigh opened both cases, pulled out her violin, tuned the strings, then brought out her bow, tightened the horsehair, and rubbed it with resin. "Slow or fast?"

"I don't mind." The girl sat down, eyes bright with excitement. "I don't care."

"What's your name?"

"Aggie."

"Aggie who?"

"Aggie None-Of-Your-Affair," the girl snapped. "Are you going to play?"

Ceileigh grinned, nodded, tucked the violin under her chin and began to play softly. "This is an old, old piece," she said. "It's about a girl named Mary." She watched the pleased hint of a smile replace the sullen frown on the girl's face. "Mary of Argyle," she elaborated. "Argyle is a place in Scotland. It's a love song. I don't know who wrote it. I ought to know, but..." She let her voice trail off, played to the end of the song, then started again at the beginning. "It's a song sung by a young man who is in love with a girl from Argyle. He says, I have heard the mavis singing, it's love song to the morn...a mavis is a bird, you see, I don't know if you have them here or not....I have seen the dew drop clinging to a rose but newly born," she sang softly, and the dirty girl's face softened as she leaned back against a willow, swaying gently to the sound of the music. "But a sweeter song has thrilled me," Ceileigh crooned softly, "at even's gentle close, and I've seen an eye still brighter than the dew drop on the rose. 'Twas thy voice, my gentle Mary, and its goodness was the wile, that made thee mine forever, Bonny Mary of Argyle."

"What's a wile?" Aggie asked, blinking the tears from her lashes.

"A sort of a wee bit of a bribe...like the fish..." Ceileigh laughed gently. "It's something that gives you a nudge to do something you wanted to do anyway, but you might not have done if it hadn't been for the wee bit of a wile that made the wanting and the wishing impossible to ignore."

"So he wanted to tell her he loved her, but he was scared, and then he heard her talking and...?"

"Maybe," Ceileigh suggested, "maybe he heard her singing...he says he's heard the mavis sing...and says he's heard an even sweeter song...it might be she was, oh, it might have been she was working and singing and thought she was alone...and he heard the song and knew there was no way he could just pass on without declaring his love."

"It must be like a miracle to be able to make music like that."

"Miracle, is it? Well the world itself is full of miracles and magic. Can you dance, now?"

"Me?"

"Who else? I doubt the smoked fish can dance," she winked, and her fingers began moving quickly. Aggie laughed, jumped to her feet, and began to caper to the happy jig.

"I can dance," she said, "but I don't get half enough chances! And never any chance at all to dance to real music!"

Ceileigh played two more jigs, then put her violin back in the case, loosened the horsehair of her bow and put it away. "You said something about smoked fish, I believe," she reminded the girl. Aggie sat back down on the damp grass, hauled out the canvas-wrapped package again, and opened it. They shared the fish, and Ceileigh could hardly believe the flavour of it.

"I don't know if it's just that I'm half famished," she admitted, "or if this is the best meal I've ever tasted."

"It's the best thing you'll ever eat if you live to be a thousand," Aggie vowed. "And thank all the saints in heaven, it's free."

"How can anything this good be free?"

"They haven't found a way yet to make the poor pay for it."
Aggie glared up at the town. "They will, but not for a while.
The river is too big, there's too many fish come up it, and all you
have to do is stand on the bank with a dip net and haul them out.
Then, even an idiot could build a smokehouse."

"Do you live near here?"

"Live wherever I happen to be," Aggie snapped. She glow-
ered up at the town again, then stared at Ceileigh as if trying to
decide whether or not to trust her. "A lot of us live on The
Flats," she said quietly. "Farther on down a bit, where the sight
of us won't offend those nice people."

"Och, God, here too?" Ceileigh sighed, feeling disappointed
and suddenly tired. "I figured there'd be no streets of gold, but
God, I did hope..."

"Where are you staying?" Aggie dared.

"I thought to spend the night right here."

"Christ, woman, you can't do that! They'll slit your throat
for the chance to steal your bit of blanket! But not before
they've made you pray for death with their foulness."

"They? Who?"

"Well, if we knew who we'd know how to stop it, wouldn't
we?" Aggie scorned. "The hard cases. The night-crawlers.
Who knows who they are? Some say they're the railroad police.
Some say they work with the city police. Some say..." She
shrugged again, made a rude noise, and didn't bother finishing
her sentence. She eyed Ceileigh warily, then, with an effort,
decided to extend the limits of her trust. "You can come back
with me," she growled. "Then, later on, when that fiddle has
made you rich and famous, you can tell the world you owe it all
to the one who saved your life."

Ceileigh was glad to leave the willows and follow the slender,
graceful girl with the personality of a snake. Even if Ceileigh
had no idea of where they were going, Aggie seemed quite at
home, and the thought of possible hard cases and night-
crawlers, the chance of getting her throat cut, did not appeal to
Ceileigh at all.

Aggie had called it The Flats, and when she saw it, Ceileigh
could well understand why. Mud. What seemed acres of mud
stretched along the bank of the river, and built on stilts up above

the mud, small shacks and shanties, some of them apparently held together as much by magic as by any talent for planning or construction. "When the tide comes in," Aggie explained, "the river spreads over the flatland. Then the tide goes out and the river goes back down. And in the springtime, as likely as not, half of what you see will be washed away, and who knows if people go with the junk or not."

"But it's springtime now!" Ceileigh blurted.

"The snowpack hasn't started to melt yet." Aggie gestured to the rim of white-capped mountains east of the smoke-smudge that was the city. "When it gets a bit warmer the snow will melt, the rivers in the hills will fill up and drain into the Old Woman here, and when she's full...it can get to be an adventure," she finished with a wry grin.

Aggie's shack was nothing more than a few poles, several logs, and some rough planks with a small fire-pit of stones. "It's not much," Aggie admitted cheerfully, "but the hard cases don't often come down here. There's too many of us river rats."

"But they do come?"

"Every now and again someone in town gets to maundering about the blight spreading along the banks of our fair river," Aggie intoned dramatically, "and the fat-ass police climb on their horses and come down to show us all the error of our misbegotten ways."

Ceileigh put down her violin and sat beside it on the rough flooring of evergreen branches and long, dry grass. The more she saw of the place, the less there was to look at. The roof hardly justified its name, just more branches and grass laid over a rough cross-frame of poles. Here and there a bit of sacking or a small strip of canvas, but the rain and wind would get through with no problem. "Not much, is it," Aggie agreed. "But there's plenty live in worse."

"I wasn't making judgement," Ceileigh fibbed.

"Don't bother me if you do," Aggie answered casually, "poor as it is, it's better than what you've got, right? Anyway, if you build anything very solid, you have to have someone stay behind to guard it."

"Your neighbours would steal it?"

"My neighbours," Aggie laughed, "would steal my teeth if I slept with my mouth open."

They talked quietly together, watching the sad-looking inhabitants of the shanties as they moved about their dreary business. Ceileigh wished she could feel something for them, wished she could care about them, but her entire life had been too full of this kind of hopelessness. Old world or new, it seemed as if the only way a person could have any kind of life at all was to have money, and lots of it.

"Grim, isn't it?" Aggie agreed, as if she could read Ceileigh's thoughts. "The only good part about it is it's a brief life. My mother didn't make it to thirty. Don't suppose I will, either."

"How old are you?"

"I don't know."

"How do you live? How do you make your money?"

"Any way I can." Aggie looked away, and Ceileigh asked no more. Instead, she reached for her violin case.

"Would it bother you if I played?" she asked.

"Please." Aggie lay back on the branches which pretended to be a floor.

Ceileigh played all the things she could not put into words. She played the slow, steady flow of the Fraser, she played the rhythm of the train wheels, the clatter of horse-drawn wagons, the push and shove of desperate humanity. She played the greasy sheen on the mud, the tattered clothes, the scarecrow figures, the bizarre tipped-and-tilted cabins, hoochies, and shacks.

"It's not as bad as all that in the summertime," Aggie said softly, "because once the floods are gone, the grass grows and there are berries on the bushes, birds singing in the trees, and the sun takes the ache out of your bones. We can catch fish and sell or trade them for other kinds of food. Sometimes," she smiled wistfully, "we even have some bread."

Finally they slept, and in the morning they left the shantytown and went back to the willow thicket where they had met. Ceileigh scrubbed herself as clean as she could but there wasn't much she could do about her wrinkled clothes. "Oh well," she decided, "if it's as good as it can be, it's the way it will have to be."

Aggie walked with her, back up the hill from the river, past the railway yards, the warehouses, the huge wagons drawn by massive horses who seemed almost unaware of the stacks of lumber or barrels of beer on the wagon beds. Ceileigh was uncomfortably aware of her wrinkled appearance, but nobody else seemed to notice. Even grubby Aggie passed unremarked in this busy crowd.

12

The town was no bigger than her own village had been, a few rough buildings on either side of a dirt road that seemed to start nowhere and end nowhere else. Trees and brush closed around one end of the street, where the river made a slow turn. She would gladly have avoided the place, but Elizabeth was ill and Su Gin knew there were things she absolutely had to get if the child was to have any chance.

She stopped in the bush, unsaddled the horse, turned the animals loose to graze on the grass and clover, then spread her blankets on the ground. Elizabeth limped over to them immediately. The child was pale, her eyes dark-smudged, and both feet were swollen and sore, the cuts badly infected.

"Sssshhh," Su Gin soothed, "just sleep, little girl, sleep and when you waken things will be so much better."

Su Gin had no intention of riding boldly into town on a thoroughbred mare or a distinctive buckskin quarter-horse, and flashing a lot of money for people to remember. She walked from the bushland, following the trail that widened to become the wagon tracks that formed the road. Then she went up one side and down the other side of the only street in town, looking in windows, planning her route and her purchases. One or two people looked curiously at her but nobody seemed to find her presence too outrageous. Nobody seemed even to suspect that

Su Gin was a woman. For all they knew, she was a young Indian looking to spend the money he had earned selling furs.

In one store she bought a large, sturdy pack, a pair of strong leather lace-front boots, a pot for boiling, a heavy black pan for frying and baking, and a huge, wickedly sharp skinning knife. At another store she bought a sack of rice, a small sack of black tea, beans, salt, dried fruit, and some wilted vegetables. At the same store, she got fish hooks and a big spool of heavy green twine she knew she could twist and knot into strong netting. On her way out of town she stopped at the livery stable and when she left she was leading a large-bodied, very ugly gelding, her purchases stowed on the pack frame strapped to the animal's strong back. She walked out into the bush, then made her way back to where the child lay sleeping, face slick with fever sweat. Su Gin unpacked the frame, turned the powerful ugly gelding loose with the other animals and built a fire to heat water in the new pot. While the water was heating, she sorted her purchases and nodded with satisfaction; she was prepared, now, as she had never been prepared in her life. Being passive and moving without purpose only mean that when the skies open and the shit pours from on high, it lands on your unsuspecting head. And she had been drenched once too often in her life. Besides, she had Elizabeth to consider now, and that changed everything.

She measured rice and water and while it simmered slowly, Su Gin mixed salt and a bit of vinegar with warm water. The enameled hand basin would be awkward to pack and carry, but it would be worth the bother. She wakened Elizabeth and sat her sideways on her own knee, then brought the basin to where Elizabeth could dunk her feet. Tears sprang to the small girl's eyes. She tried to pull her feet out of the basin and whimpered weakly. Su Gin grasped the small scarred ankles gently, shook her head, and spoke firmly in two languages. Elizabeth nodded, sniffling, put her feet in the water and wiped her nose with her filthy forearm.

The scabs softened and loosened, and blood-tinged pus began to leak from the small feet. Again Elizabeth whimpered, again Su Gin spoke to her softly in two languages, and again, the child nodded, sniffling. Su Gin slid the girl onto the ground and moved to the fire, busying herself with the preparation of a good meal. Elizabeth had never tasted anything like the food Su Gin handed to her, but a few tentative bites convinced her, and she ate eagerly, grinning often, nodding, the pain in her feet briefly forgotten.

The water was cold before supper was finished and the pots and plates cleaned. Su Gin lifted the child again, cuddled her, told her she was brave and beautiful, then steeled herself and began to clean the cuts and slashes on the small feet. She expected howling and yowling, she expected slaps and screeches, and the crack in her heart widened when, instead, the child squeezed her eyes shut and her hands into fists, paled, and just shook with pain, fear, and shock. The little feet jerked, the muscles in the skinny legs knotted, but the little girl did not throw herself into a tantrum. Su Gin, weeping, spread a sharp-smelling ointment on the poor infected feet, wrapped them with clean bandages, then cradled the child, hugging her, crooning comfortingly.

"Oh, baby," she mourned, "oh, poor baby."

"Don' cry," Elizabeth sniffed. "Don' cry, mommy."

Su Gin didn't trust anybody in this country except Elizabeth, so she packed quickly, distributing the loads as evenly as she could. Then she opened a last parcel, a small, flat, paper-wrapped and string-tied bundle.

"For you," she invited in the dialect of her own village. Elizabeth stared at the stiff new black trousers and grinned, stood on her bandaged feet, and reached slowly. Su Gin scooped her up and helped the little girl into the pants. They were too big, but they were the smallest she had been able to find in the entire town.

They left, moving away from the small town, heading north and pushing the rested horses across the rolling hills. Su Gin knew she had not shown too much money in any one place, but she knew, too, that people talk, and how many Orientals buy a hatchet in a town full of barbarians, how many Orientals were there in these hills, and how long would it take for the greedy savages to decide to find her camp and relieve her of the things she had bought, the pack horse she needed to carry it? She rode through the rest of the afternoon and most of the night, and the buckskin moved easily beneath her. Elizabeth chattered and giggled until she fell asleep, and wakened only briefly when Su Gin stopped to stretch her legs, drain her bladder and switch the saddle to the back of the dark thoroughbred. When dawn streaked the sky she stopped to rest the horses, cook a large breakfast, and share it with Elizabeth. Then, with tears from both of them, she again cleaned Elizabeth's infected feet.

She supposed she should rest, supposed she should sleep, but she wanted distance between herself and those she did not trust. She wrapped the child in a blanket, sang her to sleep again, then pushed forward stubbornly. The wild time, she knew, was finished. She moved through and into a time of quest, a time of searching for direction and purpose, and Elizabeth moved with her, the catalyst and the reason, the inspiration and the reward, the consolation Su Gin had never expected to find.

They moved steadily now, ten hours a day, every day, and Su Gin could not have said why the moving was so important, or where it was she was heading. She simply knew that staying in one place was impossible for her. She had to saddle up, mount up, and move forward. Elizabeth's feet healed slowly, but they healed, and the dark smudges vanished from her eyes. She sat easily in the saddle, whether riding double with Su Gin or perched by herself on Friend's smooth-moving back. When they stopped to make camp, Elizabeth gathered firewood without being told and stacked it near the fire-pit, and while Su Gin cared for the animals, Elizabeth spread out the slicker and the blankets, fussing to smooth out the wrinkles and make their bed comfortable and tidy. When it rained, the child rode with Su Gin under the slicker, peering out of a small slit fashioned at precisely the right place. She tickled Su Gin, she squirmed under the slicker, she buttoned and unbuttoned Su Gin's shirt, and she talked. She talked and chattered, demanding answers, making her own observations, teasing and sometimes annoying her new mother, and without either of them consciously being aware of it, they learned each other's language and began inventing their own. When Su Gin did T'ai Chi, Elizabeth copied her and the exercises strengthened her young body. When Su Gin sat in the evening knotting the growing length of netting, Elizabeth played games she had made up, running happily on her healing feet. She climbed trees, she chased ground squirrels, she raced in vain pursuit of low-flying birds, and she sang songs of her own creation.

They strung the net from one bank of the stream to the other, then went upstream and walked down, deliberately splashing and rattling the water-smoothed stones with their feet. Trout rushed away from them and were trapped by their gills in the net. Su Gin cooked trout for supper and made sticky rice balls around the leftover pieces of rich pink flesh. They gathered wild onion and chives, they found patches of wild garlic and peppergrass, they gathered miner's lettuce and wild sorrel, and made tea from the leaves and twigs of the huckleberry bushes. And every night before settling for sleep, they prayed together for the repose of the souls of the dead, the dead of Su Gin's home village, the dead of her family, and now, Elizabeth's dead mother.

They came out of the trees to the sand, and Su Gin gasped. Elizabeth squealed with delight and squirmed to be let down to run on the shore. The beach glistened wetly and shore birds of all sizes pecked in the shallow water warming in the sunlight. A group of eight herons stood knee-deep in water, eyeing them with no sign of curiosity or surprise. An osprey called fiercely, challenging the universe, angry at having her fishing disturbed, and her protest was echoed by the shrill scolding of a kingfisher, a brilliant blue zip above the surface of the sea, the black crest and white markings of his face startling contrast to the colour of his body.

Awed and overwhelmed, Su Gin dismounted. Elizabeth was already hauling off her trousers and shirt, bouncing impatiently. A red-shafted flicker cried welcome, the call bursting from it with each sweep of its wings as it up-and-downed across the sky toward a tall, naked spire of dead snag.

"One minute, one minute," Su Gin muttered. But Friend was waiting no minutes at all, she could smell fresh water and moved toward it. She stopped less than a hundred feet away and lowered her head to drink from a small rivulet which flowed across the shore to the glistening mud flats, dissipating into and becoming part of the shallow wavelets lapping the damp sand with kissing sounds. Su Gin stood alone, staring out across the heaving surface of the ocean, knowing that in that direction, half a world away, was her homeland. And she knew, without sadness or pain, that she would never see the place of her birth again.

They stayed six days but finally they tired of being in one place with nothing to do but gather food, cook it, and eat it. The horses were rested. Once saddled, they were eager to move off, stepping easily along the strand, moving north, following the coastline. Su Gin knew there was another cove just down the beach, then another, and another, and somewhere, she knew, there would be a place where they would want to stay. Neither she nor Elizabeth knew or cared that they had crossed a border, that they were now in a different country with a different system of government and different laws.

13

Ceileigh didn't really know what it was she had expected, but she was surprised to find half a dozen other young women at David Brownley's office. She stared at them and they stared back insolently.

"Ceileigh," David said easily, rising from his chair. "I'm glad you decided to come."

"I'm here," she said, still eyeing the other women. One or two of them, she decided, were more used to sleeping during the day and working at night.

"I've invited you all here," David said with a wide smile, "because I have a proposition to put to you." He ignored the knowing looks several of the women gave him, and pulled out a chair for Ceileigh to sit on. Then, after a long and speculative look at Aggie, he pulled a chair forward for her, too. "There's money to be made in the gold fields," he said blandly, "and not by standing in freezing water to your...waist...either." He smiled again and Ceileigh wondered if his face ever got sore. "If you agree," he said, looking from one to the other of them, "I propose to take you all with me. To the gold fields. To help separate the miners from the gold they find."

"A travelling whorehouse?" one of the women asked suspiciously.

"Nothing of the sort!"

"And what," Lily Nelson asked calmly, "do you have festering in that little scummy pool you call a mind?"

"Entertainers," David answered softly. "You and Ceileigh will play. Cora can sing . . ."

"I can dance," Aggie said clearly. David looked at her and his expression said more loudly and clearly than any words how unlikely he thought her claim was.

"She can," Ceileigh laughed. "If ever anyone could, it's our Aggie."

"You'll be paid well," David continued as if Aggie had never spoken. "After, of course, you reimburse me the cost of your passage and costumes."

"And who," asked Lily, "will decide how much these costumes are worth and how much we have to pay you for them?"

"Why Lily," David mocked, "you wound me."

"Oh, I will, for sure," she laughed, "if ever I find you cheating me. I'll give you, as they say, the unkindest cut of all."

David turned to Ceileigh with his usual broad smile. "Can you read music?"

"You know I can."

"Good." And he pulled some crumpled sheets from his pocket, made an attempt to smooth them, and put them on a chair for Ceileigh to read.

She played. The women listened and watched as David demonstrated the steps he wanted them to learn.

"You're not very good," Aggie challenged, her eyes glittering with something Ceileigh recognized as desperation. And before David could tell her to get lost in a crowd, Aggie was dancing, her tattered rags flapping, her dirty bare feet moving lightly. She spun and whirled, she dipped and turned, then Lily was moving beside her, watching Aggie's feet, copying her moves, then Cora was laughing and joining them, and David's disapproval and disbelief were replaced by calculating satisfaction.

"Give her the chance," Ceileigh said softly. "If what you're really after is dancers, then that's what she is, a dancer."

Aggie took them to the Chowder House and introduced them to the Celestial who had helped save her life when she was a small child. She spoke rapidly to the aging man. He nodded, grinned, spoke softly to her, and patted her shoulder approvingly. When they had all eaten as much as they could, they left and Ceileigh noticed it was not David who paid for the food but Lily.

David paid for rooms in the waterfront hotel, where Aggie was introduced to a bathtub, to hot water and soap, to a shampoo that left her hair soft and even gently curling. When she came from the bathroom wrapped in Cora's warm housecoat, Aggie looked as young as she really was, and Ceileigh stared in shock.

"Och, for God's sake!" she blurted. "Get the dirt off her and she's nothing but a baby!"

"But you said it yourself," David laughed, "she can dance. And that's all she has to do is dance. Dance and let them dream if that's what they've got a mind to do. They'll see hope and innocence, they'll see something they might once have had a chance to get, some kind of salvation, some kind of dream, and they'll pay for it."

"Christ Jesus in Heaven."

"No, Ceileigh," Lily corrected gently, "Christ Jesus and Heaven have nothing to do with any of it."

They took the steamship a week later—six dancers, a fiddler, a guitar-piano-mandolin-and-harp-player, and the master - of - ceremonies - booking - agent - choreographer - business - manager and self - proclaimed - general - factotum. The trip down the Fraser and up the coast was both exciting and uneventful. The scenery on either side of the steamer changed from hour to hour as they made their way past islands and islets, past towering cliffs and flat pebbled beaches. They saw seal and otter, black and white killer whales, and sea birds of every size, shape, and description. They saw inlets and fjords leading into the heavily wooded hills and they saw mile after mile after mile of heaving sea. But in spite of the churning water and the debris they encountered, in spite of the overcrowded cabins and decks, in spite of all predictions, nothing much happened. Even when David started a poker game and won consistently, there was no trouble. The other players just pleaded fatigue and left the table. Eventually, David was reduced to playing solitaire and trying to pretend he enjoyed it.

"Unimaginative bunch of louts!" he decided.

"No," Lily laughed, "but too smart to be skinned by you. They know they'll never get rich sitting in at a poker game. Their dreams are all focused on the gravel banks and sand bars. They're not going to be sidetracked by some sweet-talking slicker in a fancy flowered brocade vest."

They had left New Westminster in the third week in March when the first crocus were showing on the hillsides. To the west, the blue-green bulk of Vancouver Island hulked out of a sea of slate grey streaked with blue. By late afternoon the next day they were ploughing into Queen Charlotte Sound and the wind was blowing fiercely, the waves hammering over the side and onto the decks. The steamer stopped in a landlocked bay, surrounded on three sides by cliffs almost 200 feet high. With the engines turned off there was no heat in the cabins and they sat huddled in coats, shivering in a second-class cabin with ten rows of bunks three tiers high, the rows separated only by tables with solid benches.

When the crowding threatened to send them into spasms of nervous anger, they went out on deck and stared at the high mountains, the rocks, the thick covering of spruce, fir, cedar, balsam, and hemlock.

"It's a drear dark place," Ceileigh mourned. "As lovely as heaven except God forgot to give it any light or cheer."

They were storm-bound three days, then the wind dropped and the steamer was moving, the cabins again warmed by the heat of the giant engines. Day after day, night after night, past narrow channels with high mountains on either side, past rocks and sea life, through fog and rain, buffeted by wind and tide.

Wrangell, Alaska was a kaleidoscope of images, and few of them familiar ones. Totem poles lined the harbour, the huge graven faces scowling across the water, figures from a mythology unfamiliar to all save Aggie, who stared at the images and whispered to herself in a language only she understood, a language even she had begun to forget. Both sides of what was supposed to be the main street were lined with houses which were nothing but glorified tents, canvas stretched over wooden frames, many of them seeming to float on the mud only because of the rough wooden floors on which they were erected.

They stayed a day, then headed through the Wrangell narrows, and two days later docked in Dyea. It was three miles from the dock to the warehouse, and they hired several Indians with pull-wagons and sleds to skid and slither their freight and baggage through the mud. The way from Dyea to Skagway was five more miles of mud. They walked one and a half miles across the tidal flats at low tide, then were taken in a rowboat across the intervening channel, and after all that, Skagway proved to be two wharves, a warehouse, and some streets, along which lay saloons, saloons, more saloons, and restaurants.

"And why is it," Lily asked quietly, "you said nothing of any of this disheartening mess?"

"Oh, it's not as bad as all that," David soothed, but the spring was gone from his step, and the muscles in his jaw were knotted.

The hotel was a twenty-by-forty frame building, with walls one board thick to stop the wind and rain. It was icy cold inside and there was a puddle on the floor between the rows of bunks. Wooden frames with canvas stretched across, and so narrow there was hardly room to roll over in them. When the packers finally brought their gear from the warehouse, they left the hotel gladly, and rushed forward to reclaim their things.

"Dear God," Ceileigh prayed, "tell me I don't have to slog through this goo for the entire journey."

"It's not what I imagined," Aggie mourned. "I imagined..." She stopped, looked around, then laughed bitterly. "I could have had mud at home if mud was what I wanted!"

They stayed the night in the hotel, but it was impossible to sleep. Men came in and went out of the room at all hours, stumbling in the dark, tripping over boots left beside the beds. Other men shouted at the stumblers to for Chrissakes have some consideration and let people sleep. Noise continued from outside on the street as packers moved out with gear. Dogs barked and muleskinners cursed bitterly.

They were up and dressed before the dark had begun to fade, and as soon as it was light enough to see, they were ready to leave, bellies full of breakfast, bodies covered with warm woollen clothes. They headed out ahead of the team that was to haul their gear, and trudged forward grimly, over ice, over mud, over gravel, over more mud and yet more ice. Rain made the trail slippery, snow made it sticky, and mud weighed down their boots until it felt as if they were walking with bricks tied to their feet.

The first night they camped in a tent in a valley where forty or fifty other tents were pitched. Soaking wet and chilled through, they still managed to get enough fuel for a fire and to dry their socks before rolling up in their blankets and cursing themselves to sleep. A short time later, they were wakened rudely by what sounded like the end of the world. Cora was closest to the flap of the damp tent. She looked out into the night, terrified. A fine spray of powder-snow drifted into the tent, and Cora moaned softly. "Oh God," she prayed. "Oh God help them."

They took the time to pull on socks and boots, sweaters and jackets, then left their tent and stood staring in disbelief. The sound was mind-numbing, even as it slowly faded. Snow and rocks rolled down the slope, rolled inexorably, following the terrible mess already made by the front wave of the avalanche, following it down to the far end of the camp. The tents and sleighs were spread out on both sides of the path, the horses, mules, and dogs tethered near the sledges and runner-carts. And now the slide buried the far end of the camp.

"It could have been us," Lily breathed, awed.

"Dear Hag," Ceileigh prayed, "come quickly for their souls, and when it's time to judge them, remember, please, their death was an abomination. Have mercy on the poor bastards."

They wanted to stay away from the slide, to go back into the tent and cringe each time a piece of snow broke loose and thundered down the slope. Instead they raced toward the disaster area. They clawed with bare hands, they dug with anything they could find, they pulled and heaved, and the sweat froze on their faces, mixed with the tears that came hot from their eyes and turned to ice immediately. They pulled out a bearded man, face waxen, eyes open and staring. Lily looked at him, looked again, then slammed her fist on his chest, slammed again, and then again. "Breathe, damn you!" she screamed. "You're not dead, man, so breathe!" She grabbed his shirt, sat him upright, then pushed, slamming his back and shoulders on the hard-frozen ground. He gasped on impact, sucking air into his body, able to move once more. As soon as he was breathing, Lily rushed past him, caught a booted leg disappearing into the mess, and heaved. Cora moved to help her and they struggled desperately, but the teenaged boy they hauled from the slide was still, and nothing anybody could do would help him.

They almost thought they might have a chance, they might find more survivors, but the weather turned against them. The storm which had been threatening for days fell on them, wind howling, snow blowing, sleet falling, and each of them knew the tempest was growing. Aggie turned, raced back to the tent, rummaged in their supplies, and finally found the rope she remembered seeing. She tied it to the pile of gear stacked outside the tent, then fought her way back through the growing blanket of driving snow.

"Come on!" she insisted, grabbing at their arms. "Come on! You'll only get yourself killed if you stay."

"Christ, they're dying under there!"

"We're all dying!" Aggie screamed. "And we'll all be dead if we aren't under shelter in a minute."

Lily tried to protest, but the wind took her words and threw them into the whirling mess. They heard the deep rumbling that meant more snow and rocks were sliding down the mountain, and they felt the earth tremble beneath their feet, and they grabbed the rope and followed Aggie back toward the tent.

Without the rope they wouldn't have found it. In that brief space of time the world had vanished in a swirling horror of white needles. They couldn't have seen each other, let alone the tent. The ground rumbled, the canvas shook, and they stared in horror as the unmistakable sound of another avalanche, bigger than the first, came to their disbelieving ears. They sat, stiff with fear, waiting to be buried.

But the sound diminished. There was only the noise of the storm. Slowly, hesitantly, they began to breathe again.

"Shit," Aggie said. "I wish I was back on the mud flats!"

14

The town of Goose Neck depended on the cannery for its existence, and the cannery depended on the fishboats. And on the labour of the Chinese, Japanese, and Indians who stood knee-deep in fish guts, fish heads, fish scales, and fish slime twelve to fourteen hours a day, for wages so low only desperation would persuade a person to do the work. There was more money to be made logging or ranching or even labouring on the fishboats, but the law, conceived and enforced by those who benefit from it, denied this kind of work to those who were needed in the canneries.

Su Gin camped on a hill above the filthy town for two days, watching everything with suspicious eyes. So many Celestials. So many traditional enemies of her people. Chinese and Japanese living and working alongside each other as if centuries of war were forgotten. And who were the others, neither Chinese nor Japanese, who lived apart but looked almost like cousins? None of it could be trusted. Any of them could be like the ones who had co-operated with her father's cousin and sold her to the painted woman and her partners.

When she was ready to ride out of the hilltop camp, Elizabeth refused to stay there.

"I want to go with you!"

"You will be safer here."

"I will be safer with you," Elizabeth said firmly. "You know I don't like not being able to see you. What if I lose you?"

"Lose me?" Su Gin laughed. "And how will you lose me? Do you think I would leave you here and ride off without you?"

"I want to be with you."

In the end they rode together toward the river that flowed past the outskirts of town to the sea. They left the horses tethered in the bush and walked into town, Su Gin carrying just enough money to buy everything they would need. She walked head down, silent, determined to pass unnoticed. And might have, except for Elizabeth. People were just not used to seeing children, especially not children following a Celestial, especially not non-Celestial children accompanying a foreign youth. The cannery workers stared, the citizens stared, and, in turn, Elizabeth stared.

"Why do they do that?" She pointed at the huge stinking sheds where fish slime, fish blood, and fish guts oozed toward the water in slick streams across a beach devoid of life.

"I do not know," Su Gin answered sadly.

"I don't want to stay here." Elizabeth spoke firmly, in Su Gin's own village dialect.

They got the groceries they needed, and new clothes because their own were worn and faded, and they got a sack of peppermint candy. The carry-pack was stuffed to the top and heavier than Su Gin had thought it would be, and she almost wished they had ridden into town. She hoisted the pack to her shoulder, balanced it, and took Elizabeth's peppermint-sticky hand in hers.

"That man is staring at you," Elizabeth said quietly.

"You have good eyes," Su Gin said. "It is a pity you do not speak one word of their language. But then, how could you, being, as you are, the daughter of a foreigner?"

"Not one word?" Elizabeth asked.

"Not one."

"He is following us," Elizabeth whispered.

"Have I ever lied to you?" Su Gin smiled, her heart pounding in her throat.

"Never," Elizabeth agreed. "And I should have stayed in camp."

"Trust the gods and those members of our family who have gone before us."

"I should have stayed in camp," the child repeated.

"Perhaps we should both have stayed in camp," Su Gin agreed.

"Hey!" The voice cut rudely into their conversation. "Hey, Chink! You!"

Su Gin stopped and stood with her head bowed, submissive, obedient. The Lo Fan reached out, grabbed her chin roughly, lifted her head and stared at her. Then he stared down at Elizabeth.

"Where'd you get that kid?" he demanded roughly.

"*My* child," Su Gin lied. "My child."

"Bullshit, she is!" He released Su Gin's face. His hand flashed and he had Elizabeth by one wrist, lifting her from the ground. She screamed, kicking her small feet frantically. Su Gin dropped the sack of groceries but she was grabbed from behind before she could reach her child.

"Ma!" Elizabeth screamed.

"Trust!" Su Gin managed to shout. "Wait for me!" and then she was fighting savagely, twisting and squirming, her anger exploding. She jerked her body downward, bending her knees, focusing her energy in her legs, and the man holding her arms was pulled forward, off balance. Su Gin thrust upwards as hard as she could and the top of her head connected with the man's face. He gasped and the grip on her arms was broken. She whirled, and her outer leg took her weight as she bent sideways and kicked, her foot catching the man across the throat and sending him backwards to fall in the dust, his face pouring blood.

Three others were closing in on her. She whirled, kicked one of them in the knee, knocking his leg out from under him, dropping him to the roadway, his leg bent sideways, the loud crack of breaking bone sharp in the afternoon air. She ran toward him and he ducked, moaning as he lay flat on the road, and she jumped over his head, running as fast as she could, dodging in case anybody was aiming for her back, dodging again, down an alley, behind a small shed, unsure now of which direction to take.

"Behind the doorway!" a voice hissed. And the words were not the words of the foreign bastards, but of a dialect of her own people.

Su Gin dodged behind the doorway. A Celestial grabbed her hat and raced toward the cannery, ramming the hat on his head. She pressed herself into the shadows and heard booted feet racing heavily past the shed, heard a voice shouting loudly, and then the pursuers were racing after the rapidly fleeing Celestial. Only then did Su Gin dare to breathe again, but her arms and legs trembled with tension, the adrenalin still pouring through her body. At a slight sound she whirled, ready to kill if she had to.

"Sssshhh," the voice whispered. "You are safe. Come into the shed."

Su Gin did not want to go into the shed. She did not want to step into darkness, she did not want to be blind at a time of danger. But she could not stay forever behind a half-open door. She moved into the blackness, body tense and ready. A young woman stepped into the dim light.

"You have no choice but to trust," she said softly, smiling. Su Gin knew the young woman was right. There were no choices. She nodded, forcing herself to be calm. The young woman turned to walk toward the back of the shed and Su Gin followed. The woman knelt, heaved, and a section of flooring lifted.

"You expect me to crawl into a hole?" Su Gin growled. "Does a rat knowingly go into a trap?"

"Then stay where you can be caught," the young woman shrugged. "Stand here until they come back and start searching all the buildings." She dropped into the hole and began to lower the door, and Su Gin dared do what she had told Elizabeth to do. She trusted.

The young woman put the trap door back in place. Su Gin stood in total darkness, wondering if she had just made the biggest mistake of her life. A moment later there was the harsh scratch of a match and a flickering flare of light, and the young woman touched match to candle wick. Su Gin could see then, and the first thing she saw was the faces turned toward her.

"You see," the young woman said bitterly, "yours is not the only life which depends on the gods of fortune. If they find you, they find us. I do not know what they will do to you, or why, but I know what they will do to us!"

"I was wrong," Su Gin said, bowing respectfully, "to doubt your motives."

"Why are they chasing you?"

"Because of my child," Su Gin answered honestly. "I wanted her to wait, but she wanted to come with me and I was not strict with her."

"Why would the Lo Fan care about a child?"

"She looks like the Lo Fan," Su Gin admitted. Then, because a person cannot trust only partway, but must always trust whole-heartedly, "She is Lo Fan."

"Perhaps you should tell us the entire story," a voice suggested.

Su Gin nodded, brushed the tears from her eyes, and swallowed the sobs trying to burst from her throat. She told of her escape from the House of All Races, the bandit raid, and the long journey with Elizabeth. When she finished, the women stared at her for long moments.

"The people in your region have always been more than slightly insane," the young woman smiled. "It is well known."

"And you?" Su Gin asked politely. "How is it someone so certain of her own sanity wound up in the same hole as a lunatic from my village?"

"We were brought here," the young woman said, face and voice expressionless. "We were brought by theft and stealth, the same as yourself. The Lo Fan do not allow the wives, daughters, or sisters of Celestials to enter this country. They do not want the men to stay here, they bring them here only to work them to death, and if they do not die, they want them to go back again once they can no longer work."

"Then you are slaves?"

"There are other words for it, some nicer, some not nice at all," the young woman smiled humourlessly. "But anyone with no choices is a slave."

"And the man who took my hat?"

"Did not care to save you. He is the one who . . . owns us."

"And thought to acquire another slave," Su Gin said coldly.

"He probably ran to the cannery, threw your hat in the ocean, then took his place on the gutting line. He will be one more stinking Celestial, no different from any of the others. The Lo Fan will yell, will go out in boats looking for your drowned body, will bluster around the outside of the shed, but not go inside because of the stink. And tomorrow, or the next day, or whenever he thinks it is safe, the broker will make his way back here and . . ."

"And tell me what he demands for having saved my life."

"Who saves a life," a voice intoned, "owns that life."

"No," Su Gin said quietly. "Not this life."

"Insane," Ling Ying smiled.

"Not so insane as to live in a rat's burrow with nobody at all guarding us."

"Women of our nation are not allowed here," a woman whispered, terrified, "and if they see us, they arrest us, and . . . and what would happen then is sure to be worse than this."

"I am going to find my daughter," Su Gin said harshly, "if I die trying. I am already living on borrowed time. And I trust my gods and spirits."

"And if we asked to come with you?" another woman whispered.

Su Gin smiled, then laughed softly. "You have saved my life. Who saves the life owns the life ' she mocked. "It would only be fair if you gave me the chance to regain legal possession of my own life!"

They left the tunnel, left the shed, moved carefully and quietly down the alley, and dodged their way to the bush flanking the shoreline.

"I do not ask for good luck," Su Gin prayed, "I only ask that no bad luck visit itself on us."

They followed her through the brush and up the hill to the camp she had shared with Elizabeth only brief hours before. Ling Ying stared at the horses, at the supplies, then at Su Gin, unable to believe any woman could possess such wealth.

"I will give you most of what food there is," Su Gin said, "and most of the gear. I will keep the horse which has been my Friend, and the buckskin, and if you ride two together . . ."

"Are you not coming with us?" Ling Ying asked.

"I go for my daughter," Su Gin said stubbornly.

"You do not even know where she is."

"I will find out where she is."

"Your mother obviously told you too many stories of the White-Haired Girl," her new friend laughed. "She may have accomplished miracles alone, but you, insane woman, will need help!"

They waited until the town was quiet, the only light showing from the windows of the small jail. Then they rode boldly to the outskirts of town, and walked quietly to the stable behind the jail. Su Gin and Ling Ying listened carefully at the door of the jail for long minutes, nerves tight, stomachs knotted with fear. They heard soft noises from the stable, heard shifting and moving inside the jail, heard a faint clattering, then footsteps, then the squeak of a chair as someone sat down. Ling Ying held up one finger and Su Gin nodded. She reached for the doorknob and turned it noiselessly. Through the crack she saw a man sitting at a table with a mug of coffee in one hand, a small whiskey bottle in the other. She waited while he poured whiskey into his coffee, then corked his bottle and set it aside. He lifted the mug and inhaled the fragrance, his attention focused totally on his drink.

Su Gin threw open the door and leapt into the room. The man tried to turn, tried to draw his gun, tried to rise to meet her charge, but he had no time to do anything but spill his drink. She wanted to rip his head from his shoulders but contented herself with kicking him in the throat, stifling his yell and knocking him from his chair. She drove another kick into the soft place just under his ribcage, driving the air from his lungs, and then she had him on his belly, his arms pinned, hands almost between his shoulderblades.

"Where is my daughter?" she asked. He gasped and wheezed painfully and shook his head. She heaved on his right arm, pushing his hand up until he gasped with pain. "Where is my daughter," she repeated, pushing steadily. She had to dislocate his shoulder before he nodded, white-faced with pain and fear. She released the pressure on his arms, hauled him to a sitting position, took his own knife from its sheath, held it against his throat, and waited.

"Where?" she gritted.

They left him securely tied and locked in the single cell with a whiskey-reeking snoring drunk who hadn't stirred from his sodden slumber in spite of the commotion.

Su Gin reached up to a rack of rifles and ammunition and stacked the guns in her arms like firewood. Ling Ying nodded, piled the ammunition boxes in the tail of her shirt, and followed Su Gin from the jail, kicking the door shut tight.

Outside the women waited. Now each of them had a horse and several spares. Su Gin swung up on Friend and handed rifles to the women, none of whom knew how to use them, all of whom took them anyway. A dog barked somewhere at the other end of town, but the steady yap-yap-yap did not rouse anyone, not even the owners of the dog.

Su Gin and Ling Ying moved from where the other women waited with the horses and vaulted a white picket fence, landing on the short-clipped grass around the two-storey house. Su Gin tried the front door and found it locked. She went around the house to the back door and found it locked too. She knew the windows, too, would be locked and if she broke one of them, the noise would alert the people in the house, one of whom was certain to meet them, gun in hand.

She walked around the house looking for a way in, and finally her frantically searching eyes focused on the large clay pot near the front door. It was filled with soil and abundant geraniums. The wooden planking of the porch beneath and beside the pot was scratched where the pot had been moved repeatedly. Su Gin crept up the stairs, knelt, lifted the pot carefully, and grinned. A key glinted in the moonlight.

When Ling Ying was in the entrance hall with her, she closed the door quietly and moved deeper into the house. They checked every room on the first floor and found nothing. Together they moved to the second floor. The first room was empty. Through the door of the second room they could hear a man snoring, which told them everything they needed to know. The third door was padlocked shut, and Su Gin shook with fury.

Ling Ying hissed, then opened the second door, tiptoed inside, and moved beside the bed. She picked up a heavy brass candlestick, swung it, and hit the snoring man square on top of his head. The woman in bed with the man wakened, grunted in surprise and fear, and sat up, eyes wide. Ling Ying grabbed a handful of blonde hair. The woman didn't try to scream, she just swallowed several times, her face the colour of sour milk.

"The key," Su Gin demanded. The woman tried to speak and couldn't. "The key," Su Gin repeated, "or I kill him."

"I don't know!" the woman blurted. "I don't know!"

"Fool," Su Gin cursed.

It took less than minute to securely tie and gag the unconscious man and the surprisingly co-operative woman, but it took almost half an hour to get the hinge bolts out and push the door far enough ajar to allow Elizabeth to slither through to safety.

"I don't like this place," she sobbed, clutching Su Gin's legs, burying her face, snuggling into the warmth and security of love.

"We are not staying," Su Gin promised.

"I never thought," Ling Ying marvelled, "to see a Lo Fan who understood the civilized language."

"Elizabeth only looks Lo Fan," Su Gin said, her voice thick with tears of joy and relief. "Her heart is as our own."

She stopped in the second bedroom to check the knots holding the unconscious man and the near-frantic woman.

"He's dying," the woman sobbed. "She hit him too hard and he's dying!"

Su Gin looked at the man who had grabbed her daughter and knew the woman was telling the truth. There was a trickle of dark blood coming from his nose, trailing across his face, staining the pillow. Ling Ying had hit him too hard. She knew she could untie the woman and the woman would get help, she knew that help might save the man's life, but it would surely cost her own life and the freedom of her daughter and the other women. The decision was easily made.

"Tell someone," she said softly, "who cares."

She scooped Elizabeth into her arms and moved quickly down the stairs and out the front door, around the side of the house and across the lawn. She stepped over the fence, swung herself into her saddle, and, clasping her daughter firmly against her body, she moved away from the cursed town, away from the faint sound of a woman screaming for help, a scream less audible than the obsessive barking of the dog.

Su Gin estimated they would have no more than a four-hour head start, and then some early riser would find the guard locked in his own cell. As soon as the guard was freed, he would hotfoot it to tell the sheriff. The pursuit would be swift, skilled, and vicious. On her own she might have eluded them. But the women with her could not ride well, and were not used to being bounced, jounced, and jostled. She knew that within a heartbreakingly short time they would all be saddle sore and unable to continue. She couldn't leave them behind and surrender them to what was sure to be their fate.

Five miles out of town the ground sloped to the banks of a wide, muddy river. Stretched across the river, from one enormous tree to an equally gigantic one on the other side, there was an overhead cable, and fastened to the cable with strong lines front and back, there was a flat-bottomed ferry barge. Without bothering to check for a ferry master, Su Gin directed the others to dismount and lead their horses onto the barge. She studied the ropes and cables, then grabbed one and began to pull as hard as she could. As soon as the barge was clear of the landing and into the current, it began to move on its own, faster and faster, as the current pulled at it. Without the cables, the barge would have headed down-river and been smashed to pieces on the rocks in the rapids, but the cables held. The forward thrust of the current was changed into a sideways motion, pushing the ferry across the churning water.

Ten minutes later they were tying the barge to the landing on the far side of the river, leading the horses onto firm ground, and preparing to ride off again. Su Gin stared for a long time at the cable. Then she frowned.

"A strong man," she said, "could make his way across the river by way of the cable. Then free the barge...and it would go back across the river exactly the way it came over with us...and then...they would be after us."

Ling Ying quietly reached for the axe in the gear they had brought from Su Gin's camp. Wordlessly, she swung the axe. It thudded into the landing, splintering wood and fraying the cable. She swung again, then again, and the cable stretched, the fraying spread. "Stand back," she warned, and swung again. The cable snapped, the barge shuddered, and the current

grabbed the far end of the flat-bottomed craft. It slid slowly
into the river, then it half-turned and floated down, faster and
faster, caught by the river, borne swiftly out of sight.

They rode away from the river, heading into the forest.
When the first rays of dawn tinged the sky, they stopped long
enough to make tea and eat a rushed meal, then they were on
their way again, in spite of saddle sores, in spite of stiffness, in
spite of fatigue, pushing stubbornly and desperately toward any
hint or hope of freedom.

"I knew you would come," Elizabeth said clearly.

"I knew you would wait for me," Su Gin answered happily.
"For the rest of our lives, we are joined."

Day after day, from first light to last, they pushed on their
way with a clear idea of what they were leaving but no idea of
where they were going. Not one of the women complained or
said she could no longer keep up to the cruel pace. On the sixth
day, their horses tired, the women exhausted, they followed the
curving bank of the river through the fringe of trees to the
clearing where the ferry landing stood, almost hidden in piles
of stacked wood. They dismounted, loosened their cinches,
and hunkered, staring at the small wharf, the unpainted shed,
the heaps of cord wood. A woman with hair as black as theirs
and skin as dark watched them curiously, then moved forward
slowly.

That night the steamer arrived and tied up at the wharf. The
Indians began moving the cordwood to the ship, to be used in
the huge furnaces that kept the boilers steaming and the engines
turning. When the wood was loaded and daylight streaked the
sky, most of the Indians left, some of them riding horses. Half
a dozen Indians and one mixed-blood child boarded the river
steamer for the 1600-mile trip to Dawson. It should have taken
two to three weeks. It took six.

15

The rumbling thunder of repeated snowslides kept them awake all night and hampered any attempt to rescue those souls pinned under the rubble and ice. In the morning, the full extent of the horror was visible. The storm died, the sun shone, and the attempt at rescue began. They toiled in the rough mass, bringing out bodies, hauling out boxes and bales of supplies brought at such heartbreaking expense to this place of death. They worked until their clothes were soaked from the inside out with sweat, and from the outside in with snow melted by their body heat.

When they could do no more, they left the mountain of snow, ice, rock, and rubble, and went to one of the several fires where there was hot soup, hot tea, hot coffee, and a dry place to sit down. Clothes and boots steaming, they sipped the life-giving warmth as many of them wept quietly. They found their own freight and gear but there was no sign anywhere of David Brownley. Someone thought he had been seen playing poker in a tent with half a dozen other men, but where the tent had been there was nothing but snow, ice, rocks, and bits of shattered wreckage.

By late afternoon they all knew there were no more living people in that mound of horror. The identifiable bodies were wrapped in canvas and carried back to be sent to their families, the rest were sent to be buried elsewhere. Those whose freight was not buried or destroyed were advised to move on; the work of freeing the rest of the bodies and goods from the slide area would continue with experienced workers.

They moved out along the wide and muddy trail, following the mules which dragged their gear. Foot by foot they toiled up the trail. A motley throng of men, horses, dogs, mules, and even some oxen pulled sleds, sledges, and sleighs of every sort and description. Beside the trail, abandoned or stored piles of frozen bacon, sugar, clothing, tools, and hardware lay untouched.

They spent that night waiting for their turn on the cable, waiting for their gear to be weighed, waiting for what passed for a Customs and Immigration Department to check what papers they had, but at least they got to rest out of the cold and wind, and at least they had the chance to change into dry clothes and dry their soaked garments in the heat from a pot-bellied stove.

They saw their sledge and sleigh hooked onto the cable, and then they started up the gruelling climb again, toiling up the gouges cut like steps into the treacherous snow and mud. Halfway up, the animals could no longer pull the weight. The Chilkat packers unloaded the gear, piled it in the snow, and continued up the steep slope, leading the animals and carrying what seemed like impossible loads on their own backs.

"Well," Ceileigh sighed, "nothing ventured, nothing gained, old girl. Pack your heartbreak, and let's go."

They helped each other lash loads to their backs and then they walked, slipped, crept, and even crawled up, up, up, their breath harsh in their chests, their muscles burning, their hearts pounding with effort. They met the Chilkat packers coming back down and were brusquely directed to where the mules and the first loads were waiting. Half an hour later, they were sitting on the sledge, panting and gasping, unable to force themselves to start down for another load.

"Oh God," Ceileigh sighed. "I want nothing more than to just go to sleep."

"Do it," Cora said firmly. "You look like death warmed over."

"Not warmed much," Ceileigh agreed. "It's this damned walking for two does you in."

"You idiot!" Lily flared. "What are you doing in this outpost of bloody desperation if you're walking for two?"

"Trying to make enough money to eat for two of course," Ceileigh yawned.

She lay back and closed her eyes, and slept in spite of the cold, in spite of the noise, in spite of the hard sledge beneath her. Slept until a soft voice wakened her, and she opened her eyes to see the grinning face of one of the packers bent toward her, a mug of steaming stew in his gloved hand.

"Eat this," he said. "When you've finished, I'll give you another...they tell me you must eat for two."

"Say one word," she snapped, "and the world invents the rest of the story!"

He laughed easily and sat beside her, sipping his own mug of stew. "Son of a bitch," he agreed.

"Is it this bad every trip?"

"Some trips are worse. None are any better."

"How do you do it?" She could feel the warmth spreading from her belly out, warming her body, relaxing something clenched inside her. "It's work to kill a person."

"You get used to it." He looked sideways at her, hesitated, then asked anyway, "Why are you here? Where's your husband?"

"I don't have a husband," she answered softly. "And I suppose I'm here for the same reason you are. Bad as it is, the alternative seems worse."

"Finish your stew and I'll get you more. Then you sleep." He stretched and yawned. "We've got a tent up...and you sleep good and sound. Sleep extra hard, for me. It might be all the sleep I get tonight."

Ceileigh had three mugs of stew, then crawled into the tent, kicked off her wet boots, pulled off her wet socks, pulled on dry ones, and climbed into her pallet. She slept in spite of everything, slept until it was time to crawl out, pull on her still-damp boots, roll up her pallet, and go out to find breakfast. She ate, helped pack the gear, and then they were off again, hauling, pulling, lifting, carrying, packing a heap of gear to the top of the pass.

The way down was easier, almost ridiculously easy. The
snow and ice were worn in a groove cut by sliding boots, knee-
deep and wide enough only for one leg to pass the other. The
trail going down was forty or fifty feet from the trail going up,
the notch-steps as cruelly demanding here as they had been on
the other side. And then the pitch of the groove steepened and
they had all they could do to keep their balance, slipping, sliding, finally falling on their butts and slithering crazily until they
regained some kind of balance.

When they were at the bottom of that slope, they had to go up
so they could come down again, pressing deeper into the Klondike with each step. Several men drove a strong stake into the
top of the hill and attached a pulley block to it. Through the
pulley block they ran a length of rope, which was then taken to
the foot of the hill and fastened to the front of a loaded sled. An
empty sled was tied to the end of the rope at the top of the hill,
then several sturdy poles were put through the sled frame and
six men took hold of the poles, placed their chests against them,
and started downhill, pushing, running, bringing down the
empty sled and hauling the full one back up the steep slope,
moving five hundred pounds of freight up a hill with their own
weight, strength, and ingenuity. At the top of the hill they unloaded the freight and sent it to the bottom of the hill. Back and
forth, up and down, they moved freight.

When all the gear was finally in one place at the foot of the
treacherous pass, they ate. Then they ate some more. They
dried their clothes around a fire and then slept a full twelve
hours. The next day there was more, and then more. It became
a nightmare. The mules did what they could and the people took
up the slack. They loaded three hundred pounds on the sled and
hauled it fifteen miles a day toward the frozen lake waiting for
them. Day after day, until Aggie found a way to rig a sail on the
sled and the constant wind became a friend instead of an enemy. The sail filled, the sled moved, and all they had to do was
run alongside and steer.

Late one afternoon, after what seemed an eternity of toil,
they noticed smoke staining the sky ahead of them. An hour
later they heard the sound of axes, and minutes later they came
upon a group of men chopping down trees. Soon they were mov-

ing through a wasteland of litter and stumps, past miles of what had been bushland and was now nothing but discarded branches, churned mud, and filthy ice. By nightfall, they were part of a tent city cluttering the shore of Lake Bennett. They sat by the fire, shivering with exhaustion, poking hot food into their mouths, staring with disbelief at the mess.

"In the morning," one of the packers said, "most of us go back and start cutting our own trees. We have to make a barge for the gear. It's warming up, the ice on the lake is too rotten to trust. We might get across it, we might not. Probably not. So we go by barge."

"More work," Aggie sighed.

"Not you," the packer told Ceileigh. "You stay here, keep fires going, make meals, dry our clothes."

She opened her mouth to protest, but before she could say so much as one word, the others were agreeing with him. Ceileigh nodded, determined that if she could do nothing else, she would feed them and keep them dry.

She was up before the others in the morning. She got the fire going, put on the water for coffee, then started to make bannock. She was so intent on what she was doing that she didn't hear the approaching footsteps.

"Is that bannock you're making?" Mary Morgan asked pleasantly.

"It is," Ceileigh agreed, smiling. "And when it's done, would you like some?"

"It's nice to have a woman to talk to." Mary hunkered by the fire, warming her hands and smiling. "God, this is ugly country!"

"It probably wasn't until all these people got here. But it will be fifty years after we're gone before it looks like anything other than a wasteland."

When the coffee was ready, she and Mary Morgan sipped gratefully and talked softly together, but the others were stirring, coming from the tent, and conversation became impossible. Mary had bannock, hot beans, and coffee with them, then returned to her own tent and her own fire.

Ceileigh spent the morning drying clothes and boots while a fresh pot of beans and salt pork bubbled for supper. When the tree cutters returned dragging branchless trunks, Mary Morgan's packers were working with the ones Ceileigh had begun to think of as her own.

"A proposition." Mary moved to the fire and stood warming her hands, rubbing them together, trying to flex her work-swollen fingers. "You've got some freight, I've got too much freight and not enough packers; together, we can combine our energies and nobody's the loser."

"We've already talked it over," Lily laughed. "This is just by way of being a courtesy."

"No need to be courteous to me," Ceileigh said, "I just fiddle and cook food."

"No," Cora corrected, "you fiddle, cook food, and take care of our boots."

"Oh, right, the boots," Ceileigh agreed. "They're in with the beans, giving flavour in place of the onions we don't have."

There was enough supper ready for everyone to sit together, dipping hot bannock into the juice, eating hurriedly, as much to get some heat inside them as to fill their stomachs. And between bites of food and sips of hot strong coffee, the agreements were made, the handshakes exchanged, the partnership established.

For more than a week they toiled, cutting trees, dragging them to a deep pit in which one man stood holding one end of a saw, while another man stood on a log placed halfway over the hole. They whip-sawed planks from the trees, cutting the entire length of the logs, one plank at a time, and all of it hard, back-breaking bull labour. They cursed the pit, they cursed the damp, they cursed the blisters that formed on their calloused hands. They shoved the handle away, hauled it back, first the hands, then forearms, then elbows, upper arms, and shoulders numbing, tightening, then starting to burn with the dreadful damned toil of it all. Plank by plank, log by log, tree by tree until they had enough to build a boat on sled runners, a boat twenty-four feet long and six feet wide, and onto it they loaded three thousand pounds of gear. They ripped apart one of the tents and from the canvas fashioned a huge sail, to take their barge across the thick ice.

They skidded across Lake Bennett to Lake Tagish, then along Six Mile River and the twenty miles of Lake Marsh, along the river where they paid a pilot twenty dollars to take them down White Horse Rapids. Then they skidded across Lake Lebarge.

At Stewart they passed The Caches. Four small trees had been cut off some ten feet from the ground, and tin cans placed over the truncated trees to foil the mice and rats. On these supports a platform was built, and on the platform, piles of gear were stored. From here, many of the toilers headed out to lay claims and look for gold in the creeks and streams.

"God damn!" Chilkat Joe cursed, winking at Ceileigh. "If I ever figure out what it was I did wrong, I'll do anything I can to make up for it. Whatever it was, it must have been a godawful sin if this is the punishment I get."

"Your sin," Cora said clearly, "was in being so brainless and stupid as to have been born to poor parents. Poverty is God's punishment for not having had the forethought to have been born into a rich family." They stared at her, and then the grins began to spread, Chilkat Joe chuckled, and within seconds they were all laughing.

16

The shore of Dawson City was a trampled mess of mud. The banks of the Indian River were thick with boats, most of them empty, and not a tree was to be seen. They hauled their boats in anywhere they could find a place, acutely aware of the envious looks given to the teetering heap of peeled poles and strong branches they had tied to their freight. They all blessed whatever gods and goddesses had ensured they would make the trip in with experienced packers who knew enough to stop in a heavily wooded area and spend two days cutting and peeling the supports they would need for a decent, half-dry camp.

Dawson had been thrown together in a marsh of mud, the streets beaten in, around, through, and among the stumps left when the trees were cut. There were log-butts and rounds set in mud and stacked to form walls which, roofed with whatever came to hand, were called houses. There were log houses, pole houses, and board houses. Canvas walls, canvas roofs, anything that would stop or even slow down the wind and give some semblance of privacy, had been used to make shacks, shanties, cabins, hoochies, stores, hotels, and saloons. The hillsides were covered with tents, the streets were a press of anxious and tense men. Dogs, mules, horses, and oxen wandered the banks looking for scraps, unguarded food, forage, grass, green shoots, and if the animals had once belonged to someone, nobody claimed them now.

Everywhere Ceileigh looked, she saw stores and saloons. Two men stood swinging at each other in the middle of a muddy street, both of them too drunk to aim, too drunk to hit, too drunk to feel pain if they did happen to get hit, and too angry to stop flailing. A group of children stood watching, giggling, pointing at the mud-smeared inebriates.

"Children," Cora gasped, "in this place?"

"Sure," Chilkat Joe shrugged. "Come in on the steamer before everything iced up last fall."

Gambling halls, dance halls, blind pigs, brothels, and saloons vied for the gold dust the few fortunates had managed to wrest from the streams and rivers. Unemployed, desperate men with no money to file a claim, no money for supplies, no chance of persuading anyone to front them to a grubstake, and no way to either improve their situation here or get back out to civilization, stood waiting to do whatever needed done to make a few dollars to buy food.

They set up their camp, tents half floating in the mud, the peeled poles rafting them out of the goo. They shared a meal and sat dazed, unable to believe that after three and a half months of struggle and discomfort, this mud bog was what was waiting for them.

"I can have me a job," Ceileigh said quietly, "starting tonight, fifteen dollars a night, playing in a saloon." She shook her head in disbelief. "I never thought to make fifteen dollars a night guaranteed."

"What," Mary dared, "do you plan to do when your baby is born?"

"Who has a choice? I've got until October to make some money. After that...well, do as best I can, I suppose."

"What would you do, Joe?" Aggie asked. Chilkat Joe looked around at the horror that was Dawson, then spit carefully over the edge of the planking, into the mud. "If I was you?" He grinned at her. "I'd find me a millionaire, get married, then take his money out of this mudhole, put it in a bank in the south, and wait for him to either join me or die and leave me the whole kit and caboodle. I would *not* stay in Dawson."

"Why?" Lily asked.

"Because the cream's been sucked already." He tilted his head

in the direction of a ragged young man begging on a street corner. "He had dreams, too, I bet. And now...all the best op-
portunities are taken." He turned to Ceileigh and smiled apologetically. "Fifteen dollars a night sounds good but it's going to
cost you five dollars for supper. And it won't be worth eating.
And that's now, when the thaw's making travel easier. Wait
until winter when it's frozen solid. Fifteen dollars won't hardly
keep you fed, let alone give you a warm place to sleep."

"What would you do?" Aggie repeated.

"Serious?" He looked at her, then at the mountain of gear they
had toiled so hard to bring so far. "I'd move tomorrow. I'd
send my packers into the saloons to find out where the rumour
of strike is, then I'd get myself to that creek and I'd forget any
idea of a store! I'd build me a clean hotel, sell drinks and meals,
and I'd try for something that no place in Dawson has got.
Clean plates, clean cups, and good food."

"I don't have any money to hire..." Mary began.

"I do," Lily said quietly. "Mind you, I don't have a whole
helluva lot of freight. But," and she smiled slowly, "I bet it
wouldn't be hard to send some packers back up the river we just
came down...meet that steamer he was talking about...buy the
freight before it even gets here..."

"What I'd do," Cora said, bending forward eagerly, "I'd
round up all these abandoned and forgotten sleds, rafts, and
whatever else I could find, and I'd get those mules, horses, and
everything else left to starve, and I'd go meet those poor souls
trying to get here across the lakes...and charge 'em, either
cash or freight, I don't care, to bring 'em to Dawson. There
isn't enough wood left back there to float a flea, and the quicker
this place thaws, the wetter and muddier it's going to be."

"What we seem to have here," Ceileigh said thoughtfully, "is
some people with money, some people with ideas, and one or
two people with a bit of both."

"I got no money," Aggie laughed. "I don't even have many
ideas. Except," she looked at a gaunt ox wandering down the
muddy strip that passed for a street, "that poor animal might be
better off boiled up with some beans than it is dying slow like
that. I am," she confessed, "godawful tired of salt pork."

"The steamboat will be up from the south by the end of the

month," Chilkat Joe said, "and it'll be jammed from front to back with people who are going to need just about everything you can think of. The whole world wants to get rich panning gold, and all the claims around here are already taken. So the newcomers will spread out from Dawson. It would be a fine idea to be waiting for them."

"Why don't you pan gold?" Ceileigh asked. "You know this place like the back of your hand, and you'd probably get rich a lot quicker that way than you'll ever get packing other people's gear across the wasteland."

"Because no white man is going to let no Indian strike it rich and live," he said flatly, his eyes narrowing, his anger showing. "As soon as I stop being a mule for those people, I'm dead."

Ceileigh walked from one mud-smeared end of Dawson to the other, watching everything. Something inside her wanted to dispute Chilkat Joe's estimate, but she couldn't argue with the evidence of her own eyes. It wasn't just the mud. It wasn't even the desperate, penniless men. The place reminded her of what she had left behind when she headed away from the squalor of an eastern city. She looked at the prices scrawled on the few things still available for sale. She thought of what Joe had said about the price of food, and something squirmed inside her throat, a kind of contempt for her own folly, her own eagerness to believe that something other than bitterly hard work would get her what she wanted and needed. A warm dry place to call her own, and enough food to take the ache from her belly. "Ah, Ceileigh," she muttered aloud, "and to think after all you've seen, heard, and known you'd still fall for the bait."

She trudged back to camp, hunkered next to Chilkat Joe, and tried to grin. "Five dollars a meal, huh?" she managed.

"It's the hotel owners make the money," he agreed. "And sure, there's a few of the entertainers made a bundle; but they made it when Dawson was young, and new. Now..." He shrugged. "Well, you saw it. Mud, mud, mud, and half of that mud is shit."

"And it's only just started to thaw." She shook her head, suddenly bone-tired. "Thank you, Joe."

He poured a mug of tea for her. "You should get some rest," he advised.

"Rest. Right." Ceileigh sipped the tea, blinking back the tears threatening to drip from her eyes. "Where's everyone else?"

"Out seeing the sights," Joe laughed softly. "Ought to be back any minute. There isn't much to see."

They left Dawson before dawn, moving down Indian River to where it branched into a shallow stream nobody had yet bothered to name. Aggie followed them, shooing and shouting, prodding and poking her small herd of stupid and unwanted animals ahead of her.

"Damn," Cora cursed, "that kid is going to slow us down!"

"She'll follow us," Ceileigh said confidently. "She knows her way around even when she doesn't know where she is!"

"She isn't the only one doesn't know where she is," Cora snapped. "I haven't the slightest idea where I am and even less of an idea why I'm here."

"Don't know much of anything, do you?" Lily teased.

"I know a person has to be either a damn fool or desperate to stumble through country like this!" Cora laughed suddenly. "We might'a done better to go off looking for the pot of gold at the end of the rainbow."

"You mean to tell me that isn't what we're doing?" Lily stopped, put her hands on her hips and pretended to glare. "Then what in hell *are* we doing?"

"Don't ask me," Ceileigh panted heavily, "I'm just following the guy in front."

"*He* doesn't know what he's doing!" Cora objected.

"Sure I do," Joe shouted back, "I'm walking a bunch of tenderfeet through the bush in search of fortune and a life of soft living."

"That guy," Cora announced firmly, "is as crazy as a shithouse rat."

"What's more," Lily agreed, "he's not the only one." She sighed, shook her head, and trudged on down the path. "shithouse rats come in packs," she decided.

Aggie didn't mind being left behind with the unruly herd of skinny horses, mules, and oxen. She didn't mind moving slowly, surrounded by hopeful, starving dogs. She understood animals. She understood them so well she sometimes wondered if

she wasn't really an animal herself. They didn't ask to live exciting lives or meaningful lives or cultured lives, they just wanted a
chance to live.

Half a day from Dawson the pace slowed, not because the
animals were exhausted, and not because they wanted to go back
to the mud and crap they knew so well. The pace slowed because there were willow shoots to gnaw, there was moss under
the thawing snow, even clumps of dried grass exposed by the
thin, weak sunlight. More dead than alive, the stock spread out
and began to eat. Aggie didn't mind sitting on a tarp and waiting. She had food stuffed in her pockets, she had tobacco, rolling papers, and matches, she had a small sack of tea, and she
was never really alone. There was always a dog sprawled next to
her, mouth open, tongue lolling, as starved for human compan-
ionship as for food. She didn't have to hunt food for the dogs,
they could smell birds long before Aggie had any chance of
seeing or hearing them. They could find, track, and run down
rabbits, and, away from the noise and stink of the tent city, the
game began to show itself. Aggie sat for several hours, then
rose, rolled up her tarp, and shouldered her small pack. She set
off along the trail Chilkat Joe had marked for her, tapping the
bony rumps of the stock, whistling for the half-wild dogs.
With food in their bellies, the oxen moved obediently, the horses followed willingly. Only the donkeys and mules resisted, but
the dogs responded to the training they had every reason to forget, and came charging through the brush, noisy and eager,
and even the most stubborn of mules moved.

"Better stick with me," Aggie called, laughing, "otherwise
the dogs will think you're supper. Which," she added, "you
might well be before long." She moved on, content with her own
company, trailing after the others, following their tracks,
watching for their campsites, talking to the abandoned animals
she was saving from slow death.

They followed the shallow stream to where it branched into
another, then left it, and a week later, soaking wet, bone-
weary, and covered with mosquito bites, black fly bites, and
scratches, they hauled the first of the boats and rafts out of the
water and stared at the sluice boxes already set up to wash the
gold from the gravel. The bearded, filthy men barely took the

time to look up at the newcomers. They were fixated on their
toil, obsessed with finding the flecks of colour, the promise and
prayer that had brought them all these gut-wrenching miles.

South of an unnamed creek they set their tents, then started
working harder than they had ever worked in their lives. They
dropped trees, peeled them, notched the ends, and dropped
more trees. Ceileigh could neither chop nor saw, so spent what
seemed like endless days straddling raw logs, gripping the han-
dles of a draw knife, sliding long strips of bark from the trees.
Even covered with gloves her hands blistered, the blisters broke
and drained, and her raw palms bled. At night she sat with her
hands soaking in a mixture of vinegar and salt, tears streaming
from her eyes, the pain at least numbing the ache in her back.
She slept with her hands bandaged and woke in the morning with
her fingers swollen and stiff, her hands almost useless. Sometimes she worried herself almost sick about the strain on her
hands and wrists from the constant dragging of the draw
knife. She avoided her beloved violin because she was afraid she
wouldn't be able to play it, and if she couldn't play it, her heart
would crack down the middle. She unwrapped the bandages,
washed them, hung them on a branch to dry, and then she
pulled on her gloves, reached for the draw knife and moved,
already tired, toward the waiting logs. Then the walls began to
go up and the door frames began to take shape. Aggie arrived
with her stubborn herd of strays, which already looked less like
skeletons covered with scabbed hide. She turned them loose in
the brush to continue foraging on whatever they could find, and
joined the others in the sixteen hours of work each day.

"Pen those goddamn dogs!" Cora demanded, furious. "The
skinny buggers'll eat every scrap of food in camp if they get
half a chance."

"They're hungry!" Aggie defended.

"That's exactly what I'm saying," Cora agreed. "They're hungry. And they're big. And they're wild. And a big, wild, hungry dog is just as apt to eat the person guarding the food as they
are to eat the food. Pen them."

"They won't like it."

"They'll like it a hell of a lot less if I put a bullet in their
heads."

"These dogs will be worth money!" Aggie yelled. "Damnit, you think they grow on trees? As soon as it starts to freeze people will be begging for the chance to buy them."

"Yeah? And how much money will you make if I've shot them? Or if they've eaten all the goddamn food and you yourself have starved to death? Pen them!"

"She's right, Aggie," Joe said firmly. "These aren't house pets, you know. A good sled dog is maybe a half step away from being a wolf. Either pen 'em or chain 'em."

"They won't be able to hunt for food if I do that."

"No," he shrugged, "so you'll have to hunt it for them. Otherwise, no matter what you do, they'll raid the kitchen. I've seen 'em jump on a guy and take the food right off his plate! Take his hand, too, if he doesn't get it out of the way fast enough."

"They didn't do that to me," Aggie grumbled.

"Not yet. Come on, if we get started now we'll have them set up by this time tomorrow."

Two young men with no money for food came begging work. They stood, hopeful, their clothes worn and ragged, their boots half-rotted in the mud and damp of the spring thaw. Ceileigh looked at their hands, chapped and split by hours of fruitless toil in the frigid water of the creek, then looked at their eyes. Anger welled in her. She could see them as they must have been once, when they were children, with hopes and dreams, and she could not bring herself to think about what had dashed those hopes, ruined the dreams, and left them as pathetically eager to please as any homeless puppies. "We'll give you a good day's work, ma'am," one of them blurted, and she knew there would be a place reserved in hell for her if she turned them away. They were given a meal, then put to work hauling waste gravel from the sluice boxes to lay between the logs on which the flooring would one day be laid. The next morning there were four more unemployed and desperate men looking for a meal, and they, too, were fed and assigned work.

"Ah, God," Ceileigh mourned, "to think the poor buggers expected something better out of life if they came to this forsaken hole."

"Forsaken hole?" Joe eyed her curiously. "Some of us think it beautiful. I wish you could have seen it before they started digging it up and washing it bare. There were fish in the creek, Ceileigh, and all you needed to do to get a meal was drop in a baited hook or put up a little gill net. There were browsers and grazers, there were birds and birdsong. We called it the land of plenty, and it was our home."

"It's a bitter, cruel place!" she blurted. "Frozen solid for most of the year and swarming with biting flies the rest of the time!"

"Not bitter," he corrected, his tone still gentle, "and not cruel. Just... unforgiving of the stupid and careless. She only lets you make small mistakes, and not many of those."

Chilkat Joe went out into the brush with Aggie, then there was the sound of a shot, and they returned, dragging supper behind them at the end of a rope.

When they set up a cook tent to feed the workers, two miners came to ask if they could buy the meals they were too tired and too busy to cook for themselves. Ceileigh looked at their hopeful faces, thought of the stringy ox Aggie was skinning, and nodded agreement. The cook tent was a restaurant in full swing before the ground floor of the soon-to-be hotel was in place. Ceileigh could do none of the heavy lifting, none of the hauling, and very little of the hammering or sawing. But her belly, and the life growing in it, did not keep her from cooking. The stove was little more than a fire-pit surrounded by rocks with a piece of plate metal over the top, but she could make delicious stews and platters of fry-bread, she could cook rice by the gallon and even make pies with dried fruit and the first berries ripening on the bushes. And the miners, who had survived a winter of near starvation, ate hugely, grinning their appreciation. She had eager hands to help with the firewood, to clean the fire-pit and carry away the ashes, to haul water and wash dishes. She charged a pinch of gold dust to do the laundry of the toiling lucky, then got a man with more hunger than luck to do the scrubbing, the rinsing, and the hanging to dry, and paid him with a heaping plate of nourishing hot food. Ceileigh's hands healed, her fears evaporated, she picked up her violin and tuned it carefully, then, feeling hesitant and awkward, she drew her bow across the open strings. The sounds were wavering to her ear, but none of the others noticed. They drew closer, forgetting their fatigue, their hunger, forgetting for a minute or two even their greed. She snugged her chin more securely on the polished wood, whispered the old greeting to the soundpost and bridge, then began to play, slowly and softly, easing herself back into her music.

Minutes later she looked up and saw Chilkat Joe staring at her, his eyes bright with surprise. He nodded and Ceileigh smiled, suddenly reassured and made easy in places she hadn't known needed recognition or encouragement. Her bow quickened, the notes flew, and if her fingers were slower than they had been, if her touch was less sure, if her skill was diminished by the weeks of work and toil, only Ceileigh herself knew. And Ceileigh knew all she needed was a few hours of practice to get the callouses back on her fingertips, to get her elbow used to the proper angle, to get her wrists loosened and the muscles in the backs of her hands toned and firm.

By the time the hotel roof was on, there were four Chilkat women cooking and serving food, and two teenaged Chilkats busy buying up or salvaging the empty boats and sleds. Joe's packers took the boats back the bitter, sodden trail they had so recently travelled themselves, and charged desperate newcomers to bring them through the swamps, creeks, and sudden run-off lakes to Dawson, and the disillusion that awaited them.

"Ah," Ceileigh yawned, stretching her tired legs and arching her back to ease the discomfort. "And to think I could have been making fifteen dollars the night." Aggie laughed softly and winked. "And all I'd have had to do," Ceileigh continued, "is sing some songs, play some music, and enjoy life to its fullest."

"Yeah," Aggie agreed. "And life is full, for sure. They just didn't tell me what it was it was full of." She yawned, slapped idly at a mosquito, and scratched the bite on her arm. "You really unhappy, Cay, or just... nattering?"

"Nattering," Ceileigh smiled. "Sometimes there's this wee voice in my head nags on at me, as if scolding me. Nag, nag, nag, complain about this, complain about that, chastise me for thinking something or saying something or even being what I am...like my own Mrs. Grundy, constantly criticizing. If I keep silent, it wears on me. If I say out loud what it is Mrs. Grundy is saying to me, if I really do hear it with my own ears,

I can shrug it off and just go about doing what needs to be done."

"Yeah," Aggie nodded. "Anyway, someone once said what can't be cured must be endured. Although," she shrugged, "I don't think it was really intended to be that way."

"What are you going to do when you're filthy rich, Aggie?" Lily asked quietly. Aggie laughed and scratched her bug bites.

"A place," she said wishfully, "near the chuck, so I can go fishing any time I want. If I can't find a place by the chuck, I want a river or a lake. I have to have water, lots of it." She blushed, suddenly shy. "I guess being a river rat you come to need it."

"Go on," Cora yawned, "tell me more about this place."

"A good roof so I don't get leaked on when I'm sleeping. A garden, for fresh vegetables and stuff. And flowers." The blush deepened. "I don't think I'll ever have too many flowers."

"What kind of flowers? Roses?"

"Sure. Why not? Roses and lupins and foxgloves and all kinds. I don't know the names of many of them," she admitted. "There weren't many flowers growing on the mud flats and not many people who knew the names, or if they did know, they didn't tell me!"

"Flowers," Ceileigh agreed. "And a nice floor. All my life I've stubbed my toes on warped boards, or driven slivers into the soles of my feet. Nice floors with maybe some rugs to keep the chill from shocking me awake when I finally get around to getting out of bed. I think maybe noon would be a good time to get out of bed."

"Early riser," Lily accused. "I probably won't get out of bed for, oh, the first year or two, at least."

"And food," Mary said suddenly. "My God, but I am going to eat! Roasts and browned potatoes and desserts covered with whipped cream and I will not do one single thing about the cooking of it, either! Nor do the dishes, nor anything except just pack it away, forkfuls and spoonfuls and cupfuls and platefuls and me just chewing and swallowing." She yawned, stretched, and stood up, still yawning. "Ah, well, and if we're dreaming we might as well go to bed and do it properly, with our eyes shut and the blankets pulled under our chins."

The yellow split peas Mary had brought were soaked in a washtub, and to them was added raisins, yeast, and precious sugar, then the fermenting mass was covered with a piece of cloth. Three weeks later they strained off a clear, yellow-tinged fluid that would become the mainstay of the hotel, a powerful brew some might call wine, guaranteed to make anyone's eyes water. They added more water to the mash and put a second batch on to ferment.

"And if they're too proud to drink this," Mary laughed, "we'll add a drop of two of bad rum to change the taste and colour and . . . charge 'em twice as much!"

Miners trudged in, walked in, boated in, and were followed by others who had paid their fifteen-dollar entry fee and hundred-dollar permit to prospect and mine gold. The hotel rooms rented for twelve dollars a night, and if that was too expensive, there were cots in tents for fifty cents a night. Steak supper was five dollars a plate, beans and bacon twenty-five cents, coffee and dessert extra.

Ceileigh played the violin each night. Lily played guitar and mandolin. Aggie, Cora, and even Mary danced, sang, and chatted up the weary men who came to the hotel for something hot and good to eat and drink, then stayed and spent their gold for a chance to be warm and dry in a welcoming place where they could hear the sound of women's voices and laughter. When the hotel closed at night, Chilkat Joe barred the doors and the women went to bed and slept until it was time to get up and start the next day's duties. They each did as much as they could do, working incredible hours, and then it was time for a good scrub in a tub of hot water, time for clean clothes, time for supper and a half hour to digest it, then back to the music and dancing and more hours of work.

"Would you teach me the guitar?" Ceileigh asked hesitantly.

"Any time," Lily agreed. She shifted her weight on the bench, patted it, and Ceileigh sat beside her. "Here." Lily handed the guitar to Ceileigh, then corrected her grip on the instrument. "Hold it a bit higher," she said softly.

"Like that?"

"Like that. Now see if you can find some of the notes yourself." Lily watched as Ceileigh experimented with the strings and frets. "Amazing," Lily laughed. "Just like that!"

"Och," Ceileigh scoffed. "All I've done is find a few wee notes. It's the chords I want to learn, and how it is you can shift position so quickly when your hand is at such an awkward angle."

"An awkward angle?" Lily poked Ceileigh in the ribs. "Have you looked at yourself with that little thing of yours tucked under your chin? Now if you want awkward . . ."

"It's not awkward, it's just like cuddling, is what it is."

"Cuddling! You want to cuddle? Look, bend your head a bit . . . there . . . now hold it softly against you . . . see? That's it, find the melody lines first, then we'll build on them . . ."

Lily sat beside Ceileigh, watching carefully as years of practice and skill on a four-stringed instrument without frets were adapted and transferred to a six-stringed instrument with frets.

"The fingers of my right hand are clumsy," Ceileigh fussed. "There's no callous on them and already they're sore from the strings."

"You didn't learn to play the violin in an hour," Lily teased, "and you won't learn the guitar in an hour, either."

"You sound like my gran," Ceileigh laughed. "If it was easy," she chanted, "the whole world would be experts at it."

"Cay, it was my great-gran made me learn. And I had the best teachers a body could find. I enjoyed it, but it wasn't . . ." Lily frowned slightly, searching for words. "It wasn't for me what the fiddle is for you. It wasn't . . life, it wasn't . . . it wasn't my identity, my . . . it was just fun. I had to learn it a step at a time. You don't play like that." She smiled suddenly and patted Ceileigh on the knee. "It's a pity you couldn't have had the lessons I had. My God, woman! We'll get you a piano one of these days. Ah, my great-gran would have loved you."

"My gran would have been daft for you, too," Ceileigh said.

Gold dust and gold nuggets came to them in trickles and pinches, in dribs and drabs. They collected the bits in rawhide pouches, which they stored under the floorboards in the barred storeroom where Chilkat Joe slept lightly, his loaded guns near his powerful hands. The gold was worth less than one-hundredth here what it would be worth outside. In Dawson, cash was worth more than its face value; somehow it was real money and gold wasn't. Lily's store of cash dwindled but still there were workers to pay, supplies to buy, and the frustration of knowing that if they just had more ready cash they could triple or even quadruple their profits.

"Damn, damn, damn," Mary gritted. "Even if we send dust and nuggets out on every steamer that arrives in Dawson, we're close to being sewered. By the time it gets to the city, gets to the bank, gets assayed, weighed and fol-de-rol, then gets turned into cash and sent back up here...the time we lose is terrible! And once the rivers ice up and the boats can't get in we'll be months without cash."

"Och," Ceileigh agreed, "the whole clanjamfrie of them is daft! Put their faith in a piece of printed paper but treat the very thing they're killing themselves to get as if, once it was in hand, it was nothing but common soil."

"Clanjamfrie?" Cora gaped. "What is a clanjamfrie?"

"Oh for heaven's sake," Mary laughed, "now we have to teach her to talk along with everything else! A clanjamfrie is a shiterooni." She tried to keep her expression serious and might have succeeded except for Ceileigh's sudden hoot of loud laughter. Cora, knowing she was being teased and not resenting it in the least, looked over at Ceileigh and wondered what kept the laughter alive in her exhausted body. There wasn't an ounce of fat left on Ceileigh's bones. Her cheekbones stood stark and strong in a face tanned by sun and wind. Her hands and arms were whip-cord strong, but there were shadows beneath her eyes and when she closed them, small blue veins showed on her eyelids. In spite of her fatigue, if there was a joke to be made Ceileigh made it, and if there was a chance to laugh Ceileigh laughed. We'd be at each other's throats without her, Cora realized. She moved quickly to the stove, pushed the kettle onto the heat and set about making Ceileigh a cup of tea. "You should eat something, too," she chided. "After all, you might not think you're hungry, but what about that swelling under your pinny?"

"What's a pinny?" Aggie asked. They all turned, stared at her, then looked at each other. "Well," she flared, "what is it?"

"It's short for pinafore," Cora said carefully.

"Yeah? What's a pinafore?"

"A sort of an apron," Mary offered gently. "No sleeves, no collar, and usually you just slip it on and pass the fasteners around your waist, then tie them."

"It's to keep your dress clean," Ceileigh laughed, "if you happen to have a dress to keep clean." She plucked at the worn pair of oversized trousers she was wearing, curtseyed deeply, and winked. "Thank heaven I don't need one."

"Nor me, either," Aggie agreed, her anger forgotten.

The steamers arrived regularly at Dawson, and the newcomers moved out like spokes from a hub, buying worked-out claims, buying worthless claims, working in frenzied desperation, gambling their lives on the dream. And some of them arrived at the unnamed creek, found the hotel, and came in looking for hot food and a dry bed.

"My God," Ceileigh whispered, her hands folded on her swelling belly, her eyes wide with amazement.

"Celestials," Aggie breathed, smiling suddenly. She moved forward, speaking words only the newcomers understood.

"Another Lo Fan who speaks the civilized tongue," Ling Ying marvelled.

"Greetings," Su Gin laughed. "I am glad to see that if we are about to drop off the edge of the world, we will not be dropping off alone!"

They sat together at the long table in the restaurant and drank hot honeyed tea together. In spite of inadequate vocabularies and heavy accents, in spite of differences of every sort, their conversation was pleasant, the outcome satisfactory to all.

"Competition," Mary said quietly, "only drives prices down, and that cuts profits, which is good for nobody."

"Competition," Aggie translated as best she could when Su Gin's vocabulary fell short or faltered, "would require us to start now, building what you already have."

"A partnership?" Cora suggested.

"Partnership," Su Gin agreed. She hesitated, then put a travel-worn saddlebag on the table and pushed it gently toward Lily. Lily opened the saddlebag, looked inside, raised her eyebrows in surprise and relief, and smiled at Mary.

"They have," she breathed happily, "American dollars."

"How...?" Mary clamped her lips shut, swallowed, and never did ask the question.

Chilkat Joe and a crew of packers went to Dawson with the American money and the accumulated gold dust. They shipped the dust out to a bank in New Westminster, and with the money bought mountains of supplies. The desperate men begging for food in Dawson were given a week's supplies and instructions on how to find the hotel. When they arrived they were fed and given a cot in the huge tent that was beginning to be called the bunkhouse. The next morning they were given jobs for a dollar an hour, a cot in the tent, blankets if they needed them, and two hot meals a day. Other employers complained the women were setting a bad example by overpaying their employees.

The leaves were starting to turn colour and rustle drily in the wind, the mountain peaks were drifted with new snow, and the miners were talking of ways to keep the ice from sealing the creeks. Some invented wild and jackassed ways to set cans, metal drums, or even stoves on platforms, hoping the heat would keep their section of stream thawed; others ordered extra axe heads from Mary's store, so they could chop away the ice to get to the rich gravel beds.

"Teach me your dances," Ling Ying said. Aggie nodded and reached for Ling Ying's hand. "Watch my feet," she said happily, "then do what I do."

"If I could do what you do," Ling Ying replied, "I wouldn't have to ask you to teach me. I cannot *see* your feet, you move them so fast."

17

Joe and his crew of freighters headed for Lake Bennett, taking with them the boats and sleds they had salvaged or built through the short summer. Even crates from the steamer freight were useful to experienced packers: they knew how valuable trash was once winter seized the country and closed off all but the gruelling overland routes. With bags of gold dust they bought up freight abandoned at the top of the pass by the broken-hearted who could go no farther. Any gold left over was deposited in Dawson, in the recently established assay office and chartered bank.

The steamboats were still coming in, off-loading freight and passengers, taking out the dust and nuggets being wrenched from the gravel banks and stream beds, but everyone knew each steamer could be the last. Cora bought flour for two dollars a pound, knowing they could sell bread at five dollars a loaf, and the sugar that cost thirty cents a pound now would bring two dollars a pound when winter hit. She traded two yards of cotton cloth for a fresh-killed moose which the Chilkat cooks turned into steaks, roasts, and cubes of meat for the endless cauldrons of beans they cooked and sold in the restaurant.

"Keep the silk, though," Mary cautioned. "They'll be bringing in fox and marten before long, and they aren't going to settle for anything else."

Aggie and Cora organized a group of workers and went into Dawson and the surrounding camps, taking cash and gold and buying up any scrap of freight Chilkat Joe might have over-looked. Whatever it cost now, they would get four times as much for it once the snow and ice closed the country.

Ceileigh was mixing bannock in the kitchen when a pallid-faced miner stumbled in, his face sheened with sweat, his lips discoloured almost blue.

"Great God in heaven, man," she exclaimed, "sit over here near the stove where it's warm, and get some of this inside you." She reached for the ever-present pot of strong hot tea and handed a mug of it to him.

"I'll just sick it up again, Cay," he protested weakly. "Everything I eat just sicks up again."

"Man, you need a doctor." She felt his pulse hammering quickly and thinly in his wrist. "There's none of us can help."

"There's no doctor." He drew in a breath, almost sobbed, his body shaking with fever and pain. "I think I might die, Cay."

"Damned if you will!" she said. "Drink that tea, and if you sick it up, you'll have to clean it up yourself, I warn you, now."

Ceileigh went for Mary and the two of them went to Lily. Within the hour the man was loaded onto a travois hitched to a strong, gentle horse, and taken to Dawson by three of the Chil-kat freighters. In his pocket he had money for passage out on the last steamer before freeze-up, and money for a doctor when he got to Vancouver.

"Give me an address," Lily insisted, "some relative I can send your share to."

The day after he left, the women put a crew of carpenters to work building a rocker box to sift the gravel through a slat-bottomed container by means of a handle on the side, a handle which rocked the box back and forth like a cradle, shaking and washing the precious gold from the riverbank.

"My God," Mary sighed, "our own claim, our own rocker-box, our own gold."

"Our own pain in the face," Lily agreed.

"I suppose whoever we hire to run the rocker box will steal half of what comes out of the sand and gravel."

"Half a fortune is better than no fortune at all," Ceileigh teased, "and you never know, it might be a bust and he won't have anything to steal!" They all grinned, as prepared for nothing as they were for something. The first night the rocker-box brought in twice what they had put out to get the sick miner to safety. Ceileigh looked at the dust in the small rawhide pouch, then looked at the once-ragged young man they had first hired to haul gravel for the floor of the hotel. He grinned widely, as proud as if he had made the gold himself.

"Here." Mary reached into the pouch, brought out a bean-sized nugget, and handed it to the astonished youngster. "You'd better keep this for yourself. For luck."

"You pay me good wages," he protested.

"You telling me you don't want this?"

"No!" he blurted, his fingers closing over the nugget. "I want it. Damn sure I want it. Thank you, Miss Mary." He shook the nugget gently. "One day..." he promised. "One day..."

Every day the Chilkat brought them deer, brought them elk, moose, bear, rabbit, and ptarmigan, and went off with their lengths of cloth, smiling widely. Cora supervised the salting and smoking of the meat, and Mary put a crew of carpenters to work building a storehouse. "When the creeks freeze," she grinned, "we'll rent out crews of axemen to knock the ice from the creeks, then bring the ice to the storehouse and pile it around the edges. And not lose so much as a scrap of food to weevils or mice."

"You're going to charge the panners to remove the ice, then..." Ceileigh shook her head, grinning. "And I thought my gran was Scotch!"

"There's more than the Scots can be Scotch," Cora agreed. "I didn't come here for the scenery, nor even for your own fine company, Cay. I'm not here for a good time and I'm sure as hell not here for a long time. I'm here to get enough salted away that I never again in my whole entire life have to worry about whether or not there will be a tomorrow."

"But can you not have a wee bit fun in the doing of it, Cora dear?" Ceileigh spoke softly, gently. "We're all here for the same thing. It's just yourself is so...so fierce about it."

Cora turned, opened her mouth to reply sharply, then blinked rapidly, took a deep breath and nodded. "That bad?" she asked, uncertain and suddenly frightened.

"No. Not bad. Not bad at all," Ceileigh soothed. "Just fierce."

"Sometimes I feel fierce, Ceileigh. Sometimes I feel as if . . ." Cora shook her head and Ceileigh hugged her briefly, tightly.

"Aye, we all do," she agreed. "And with good reason."

The fine flakes of snow stuck to the ground now, and every day the layer of white was thicker. By the middle of the first week of October, the streams were covered with a half-inch of clear ice. And Ceileigh McNab's daughter was born in a second-storey bedroom just after breakfast, with the important people in Ceileigh's world gathered to welcome her.

"Relax with it, Cay, you're fighting yourself."

"Relax? Lord God!"

"Easy, darlin'," Mary soothed, "Cora knows about this, everything will be fine."

"Never mind Cora," Cora objected, "pay attention to the midwife."

Ceileigh heard their voices, but the words meant nothing to her. She was focused on her own struggle, watching the muscles twist the tight drum of her belly, feeling the pressure building, pushing, forcing. The Chilkat midwife calmly tied a length of rope around a support beam and handed the end of the rope to Ceileigh. "Pull on the rope," she smiled. "Do not push on the child, pull on the rope."

"It's the same thing!" Ceileigh gasped.

"It does the same thing," the woman agreed placidly, "but it is better for the child. Do not push her out of you, help her into the world. Make her welcome."

And then nothing anybody said meant anything to Ceileigh, there was only this thing she had to do and the hands of the Hag, fastened to Ceileigh's neck and to the back of her knees, folding Ceileigh, jack-knifing her, with no need of the rope or anything else. It was all out of her control, and the Hag was doing it, folding her, folding her, three times, four, with time for a gasping rest between, then again the pressure and the folding.

"A girl," Su Gin breathed, tears sliding down her cheeks. "See, Liz-Bef, a girl, just like you." Elizabeth watched, her face bright with wonder, as the marvel was wrapped in a soft cloth and laid on her mother's belly.

"What's her name?" Aggie asked eagerly.

"I don't have a name chosen," Ceileigh said flatly. "I wasn't sure was it a boy or a girl and..." She swallowed rapidly, swallowed again. "I wasn't sure it would live," she admitted.

"Oh, Ceileigh, she's lovely! Strong and..."

Ceileigh stared down at the little girl, trying to find some hint of which of the two drunken fools had been responsible. The soft golden fuzz on the child's head told her everything she needed to know. "Ah, well." She lifted the child and held her close, feeling the soft new skin against her cheek. "It's a fair enough bargain," she crooned, surprised at the power of her emotions. "I marked him for life and he's marked us both, my hinny, and none of it to be held to your account." She wept. The others thought they were tears of joy, and Ceileigh told nobody then, or ever, that she was crying for all the times she had cursed and detested the child she now knew she would fight to the death to protect.

"You could call her Mavis," Aggie suggested shyly. "You know, like the bird in that song you played."

"Mavis?" Lily repeated. "What in hell kind of a name is Mavis?"

"It's a lovely name," Aggie insisted.

"It's a stupid name," Lily argued.

"I'd call her Liza after my grandmother," Ceileigh said, "but Liza is so much like Elizabeth and we've already got a wonderful Elizabeth. My mother was Flora, and much as I loved her, I never thought the name was all that nice, not strong enough, somehow. I think it might take a few days before she has a name. See what suits her best."

"I still like Mavis," Aggie insisted stubbornly.

"Then have your own and call it Mavis," Lily said reasonably. "You like it. I think it's a dumb name."

"Then when you have your own, don't call it Mavis," Aggie argued. "Call it Fido for all I care."

"You must not argue," Su Gin said firmly. "You will teach this child to argue, and we do not need that. We have enough to put up with just listening to you two."

"I'm not having any babies," Aggie said. "If I live to be a hundred years old I'm not having babies."

"Well, we agree on something," Lily laughed.

The dogs Aggie had saved from certain starvation in Dawson were kept in a large pole-and-brush fenced enclosure a fifteen-minute walk from the hotel. The bitches whelped, the pups tumbled, yapped, and tussled with each other, the male dogs fought, howled, barked, and growled at everyone who came near them, even Aggie. "If you had to have some pets," Cora said disgustedly, "couldn't you have picked something else?" But Aggie persevered, feeding the dogs the scraps from the restaurant, and the bones and offal of the animals the Chilkats brought for trade. The horses, mules, and oxen she had fed generously on brush and grass she had collected herself. All summer they had worked hauling lumber and helping pull trees, logs, and posts from the bush. Without them, almost every job would have been five times as hard and taken ten times as long. With them, even the gathering of firewood for winter was made easier. Chilkat children laughed and cut grass, gathered moss, collected leaves, and stored the feed in a canvas shed protected by an overhang of evergreens. The dogs nobody had wanted became worth their weight in gold as soon as the snow was knee-deep. They could run on the glittering crust and drag sleds piled with hundreds of pounds of freight, breaking trail for the horses and mules. The slow-moving oxen fared less well, their cloven hooves prone to splitting and bleeding.

"You sold that miserable snarling thing for how much?" Lily stared at the widely grinning young woman. "I wouldn't have paid a nickel for a hundred just like him."

"He'll be the second-best lead dog in the Klondike," Aggie bragged.

"And who will be the best?"

"This one." Aggie lifted a half-grown shaggy pup, held him close, and laughed as the pink tongue licked at her face.

"How do you know he'll be the best?"

"I just know." She looked up shyly, then looked down again. "He'd be an even better guard dog," she ventured.

"Uh huh," Lily teased, stroking the pup's head, rubbing his ears. "And I guess the only way he'd learn who and what to guard would be if we took him back to the hotel and...got to know him?"

"Well," Aggie wheedled, "what with the gold and all. Money and food and stuff. You know. I mean, really, there are a lot of low-class people moving in."

So Faro came to the hotel on the other end of a piece of rope. Cora fed him scraps, Aggie fed him raw meat, Ceileigh gave him the surplus oatmeal she cooked for her own breakfast every morning, and Elizabeth spoiled him totally.

The nights got colder, and Mary brought out her store of hot water bottles. Su Gin painted a number on each and looked after the rental. Miners who wanted the precious warmth were required to put down a five-dollar deposit, then pay twenty-five cents a night, hot water included. When the hot water bottle was returned, the deposit was returned, minus whatever was owing for rental. One miner tried to cheat them and keep the hot water bottle without paying rent, filling it with water he heated himself over a small fire. He was rudely wakened in the middle of the night, the hot water bottle was taken from him by force, and he himself was dumped into a snowbank by four of the Chilkat freighters. Two nights later he was back, apologizing profusely. He paid a ten-dollar deposit and twenty-five cents in advance, trotted back to his cold sleeping bag with number sixteen, and returned it the next night with a smile on his face. He slid the quarter across the counter, smiled at Su Gin, and politely asked, "Another night, please?" Su Gin nodded as if there had never been any trouble at all, emptied the cold water, added hot water, and handed it over with a small smile.

Faro filled out. His coat thickened and he obeyed the women without hesitation. He spent hours near little Margaret's basket, staring worshipfully at the sleeping baby, his wolf-slanty yellow eyes glittering. But all Elizabeth had to do was clap her hands and Faro was on his feet, moving with her, mouth open, tongue lolling, enormous teeth exposed. Even Su Gin no longer worried about Elizabeth's safety. They might be surrounded by fierce or dangerous men but nobody was going to make a move against Elizabeth, not with a hundred pounds of power and fury padding beside her protectively.

The night they discovered Faro really was a watch dog, it was coincidence, but only the women knew, and they told nobody. Faro was lying near the baby basket in the warmth of the kitchen, more asleep than awake, his tongue lolling, his tail wagging slowly. In the saloon two men began to argue, and the argument turned into a fight. A table crashed to the floor, the baby wakened and began to howl with fright, and Faro went into action, determined to defend her from whatever was making her cry. He hit the swinging half-door with the bulk of his chest, his fangs bared, his growl reverberating, and charged into the rolling tangle of battling drunks. The combatants separated and backed away, knocking over more furniture. The noise of the falling furniture frightened the baby more, she howled louder, and Faro went into a frenzy.

"Get the baby!" Aggie gasped, "Shut her up or he'll kill them all." Ceileigh raced for Margaret and picked her up, patting her back, talking quietly to her, hushing her howls. As the baby's cries diminished to a thin wail, Faro calmed slowly, and Aggie was able to get hold of him before every customer in the place had been unceremoniously chased out into the whirling snow and frozen wind.

"That dog's vicious," one of the men complained, climbing back down from the bar where he had taken refuge.

"Sure is," Lily agreed happily. "And he can't abide strife!"

Behaviour in the bar calmed noticeably from that evening, and even the most bush-crazed celebrants opted for pacifism once it became known if there was any fighting at all in Lil's Place, the damn dog got into the fight, too. The women knew the brawl would have gone on until dawn if Margaret had not been wakened, but they told nobody. The peace was too precious. "Let them think the dog's a po-liss man," Ceileigh yawned. "Nothing else seems to keep them from wanting to bang on each other's heads with our chairs."

Packers came in almost daily, bringing freight overland along the same heart-rending route the women had taken. Sacks and sacks and sacks of yellow peas arrived by dog sled or were carried in on pack saddles by toiling mules. Chilkat Joe had a relay system in place that cut weeks off the time needed to haul supplies. Each time it was necessary to cross a lake or go down a frozen river, the supplies were off-loaded, the mules and horses sent back to the last pick-up spot, and the freight sent down by wind-sail barge. There were fresh horses and mules waiting to portage the load to the next place where only a sled or barge could travel. And the supply of peas, beans, rice, and lentils was assured. Su Gin taught them how to make rice wine, which they mixed with whiskey and molasses and sold by the quart for thirty dollars gold.

They sold a mixture of their strange pea wine and rum for fifty dollars gold a bottle, they sold cigars for fifty cents each, they sold tobacco for ten dollars a pound and butter for four dollars a pound. But they never turned away a hungry person, and they paid their workers top wages and fed them the same food they ate themselves.

The claim Ceileigh had bought from the sick miner continued to produce a steady trickle of gold, and when the opportunity presented itself to buy out another claim, the women moved quickly. They pulled out the rough sluice box and replaced it with another rocker box, bigger than the one on what they now called the Sick Miner's Claim. The second rocker box began to show more than traces of gold, it began to bring in real colour. Su Gin and Ling Ying worked the handle in one-hour shifts, and were relieved by two of the other Celestial women for the off-hour. When they had put in a full day, they returned to the hotel to get ready for the evening shift of dancing and a crew of men took over the rocker handle. The men were paid a dollar an hour, more than any other employer paid, and given generous bonuses for extra production. By the beginning of December the Sick Miner's Claim was bringing in a thousand dollars a day clear profit. Ten per cent of it was sent faithfully and regularly to the recovering miner in Vancouver. The second rocker box brought in almost as much profit. All of the gold, after wages and bonuses, was stored in rawhide pouches in the room where Joe slept, with Faro stretched across the doorway.

"It's probably safer there than in the bank in Dawson," Joe said.

"Take a fool to go up against you and the dog," Ceileigh agreed. Joe grinned and winked.

"You're one hell of a woman, Ceileigh," he said softly. "One hell of a woman."

"You're one hell of a man." Ceileigh looked at the oilcloth-covered tabletop, her face flaming. Joe's weathered hand reached for hers and she squeezed his fingers softly. They sat in the warm kitchen, sipping tea, holding hands, and smiling.

18

Phillip Hewlett learned quickly and well. He grew up being taught things everyone expected would prepare him for life as one of the pillars of the empire. His wastrel father and his two charming but useless uncles wined, gambled, and frolicked away the family fortune and then died in tacky and boring ways. No brave charge of the cavalry brigade, no graceful parabola over the neck of a charging horse, not even the doubtful glory of being gored by a wild boar. They died of alcohol and stupidity, one found drowned in a ditch, the other lying on his back with his lungs full of his own vomit, and one in circumstances which involved a bed, a doxie, and a heart exploding with exertion.

Phillip knew he could not possibly live on the small salary he made in his socially correct little job. He hadn't been intended to live on the money he actually earned himself, he had been intended to fill a position and live on the family's wealth. The job required he dress well, speak well, and be charming, but it did not pay well. Only someone with Phillip's upbringing and education could have done the job, but only someone with family security could have survived on the pittance the job provided. Phillip was, not to put too fine a point on it, broke.

He did what too many men of his class did. He left his native country and headed to the New World to seek his fortune. He learned quickly that the accent he had cultivated so carefully was a guarantee of a punch in the face. He learned quickly that the manners he had learned were a guarantee of a kick up the butt. He learned very quickly that everything about him was an insult and a pain in the face to the low-class toilers in the new land. Phillip was no fool. He changed his accent, he changed the way he smiled, he changed the way he combed and parted his hair, he even changed the way he ate his food. The nasal drawl vanished and was replaced by a soft, purring brogue. The punches in the face stopped, the kicks up the butt stopped, and Phillip actually became welcome in a few places.

When his accent was comfortable and his attitude properly hidden, Phillip stopped trying to vanish into the woodwork and sat down at a table where a number of men were playing cards. Several hours later, Phillip left the table and the bar with more money in his pocket than he'd had when he walked in. It wasn't much, but it was more than he had seen in weeks. The next night, in the same bar, he sat at the same table and won a bit more. He moved from bar to bar, winning a bit here and a bit there, never so much that anyone got suspicious, never so much that anyone got angry, and certainly never so much that anyone was tempted to slam him along the side of the head and rifle his pockets. When Winnipeg began to bore him, he moved west, and when he had gone as far west as it made any sense to go, he headed north.

With his pockets well lined, he arrived on the first steamer to land in Dawson in the springtime. He spent two weeks in Dawson sitting in on card games, winning comfortable amounts, and listening to everything everybody had to say about everything. Then he packed his clothes, slung the pack on his back, and headed for what he knew was the big chance of his life.

Mary Morgan worked at her desk for three hours every morning, checking the account books, going over the receipts, keeping track of the supplies, ordering more supplies, and watching every penny, every two-bit piece, every dollar that came in or went out of the business. When the books and papers were done, she met with anyone who needed to talk to her about business, and discussed everything from Aggie's plans to enlarge the kennel to Su Gin's plans for a fresh vegetable garden. And when that was finished, Mary Morgan got something to eat and went for a good long walk to clear her head and prepare her for the crowd which would arrive soon after dark.

She was totally relaxed and absolutely without defences, strolling along the unnamed creek looking at the first bright green shoots on the bushes, feeling happy and lucky to be alive, when she heard a sound, turned, and looked into the large blue eyes of Phillip Hewlett. He smiled with what Mary Morgan thought was gentleness, and spoke with what she interpreted as friendly shyness.

"Excuse me, ma'am," he said in the accent he had learned offended nobody and pleased almost everybody.

"Yes," Mary managed.

"I understand that if an honest man wants a job, you're the one he should see."

"What kind of a job?"

"I can read and write, ma'am," he said truthfully enough, "and I can do accounts, balance books, and draw up contracts. If you don't need someone who can do that, I can tend bar, balance the cash, and tidy up after closing. If you don't need someone who can do that, I can play piano and sing passable-fair. And if you don't need someone who can do *that,*" he smiled again, "I can use the proper end of a shovel, chop down a tree, or whatever else needs done."

"Really," she said, for lack of anything more sensible to say.

"Oh, yes, ma'am," he nodded, then the smile was turned on her one more time.

Phillip started out polishing glasses and pouring drinks. He moved from that to head bartender, keeping track of the stock and supplies, the money and gold coming in, the bottles and kegs emptying. He watched Mary Morgan, studied her more carefully than he had ever studied his lessons, and made damn good and sure he said the right things at the right time. Faster than anyone who knew her would have thought possible, Mary was mired in Phillip up past her neck. Mired so completely and obsessively she was frightened.

"Mary, Mary, Mary," Lily chided softly. "It's not as if you were contemplating blowing up the houses of Parliament."

"But..." Mary shook her head, her face flaming red.

"Oh, Mary." Lily flopped onto the bed, wriggled and squirmed, got herself comfortable on the pillows, then reached out, took Mary by the shoulder, and pulled her down next to her. "So there's nobody here could marry you. So? It isn't really a sin, you know. Or if it is, well, there are worse sins in the world."

"I've never...I mean, I don't know...I just..."

"Darlin'." Lily lit one of the long, thin, stinky black cigars everybody wished she would stop smoking. "For a start, let me say, I would feel much better about the whole thing if you had fallen madly in love with someone else. Anyone else. I don't like Philly-Willy. But I don't like blond men, so there you are."

"Don't like him!" Mary was shocked. "But he's wonderful!"

"Yes, and do you ever ask yourself why he works so hard being so wonderful?"

"Oh, Lily, if you just took the time to know him..."

"No, thank you." Lily laughed, pulled on her little cigar again, and breathed deeply, drawing the smoke into her lungs. She blew the smoke out in a fine stream, then waved her hand, dispersing the smoke. "I grew up in a house full of women who had all, at some point in their lives, met someone who was wonderful, someone they took the time to know. And I saw Silly-Philly a dozen times a night. If not him, someone just like him. And I think you're making a huge mistake...but I think you're going to make it no matter what anybody says, so if you're going to make the mistake, make the bastard! Don't feel bad, don't feel guilty, don't feel sinful, don't feel...wrong. If it's a sin, it's a sin, whether you feel bad or not. If it's wrong, it's wrong, whether you do it apologetically in the dark or joyfully in broad daylight. So..." She hugged Mary close and kissed her cheek softly. "*Do* it, darlin'. In flaming reds and brilliant greens, in bright blues and purples, with gold and silver and lots of laughter. Not in greys, for God's sake! Besides," she winked and Mary blushed, "it'll do more for you than a week's holiday. Get the old juices flowing, put some bloom in your cheeks. Everybody goes a bit crazy in the springtime." Lily examined the ash on her awful little black cigar. "I'm going a bit crazy myself," she admitted quietly, "and I think Ag is about to go absolutely out of her weak little mind. Su Gin is not what anybody would call normal right now, and Cora, well...Cora never was what anybody would call ordinary or normal."

"Aggie?" Mary was puzzled. "Aggie doesn't pay attention to anything or anyone except her animals."

"And her language lessons," Lily agreed.

Mary shrugged, examined her hands, then looked up, hopeful and frightened. "You don't think it would be...a sin?"

"Sin." Lily rolled her eyes. "Sin, in my experience, is something other people get very upset about when someone else is doing something the shocked and outraged would dearly love to do but don't have the imagination to think of or the courage to do."

"He's so...beautiful," Mary smiled softly, "and so..."

"Yeah," Lily nodded. "Yeah, they usually are."

"Oh, you're just pretending to be hard-nosed," Mary laughed. "Everybody likes Phillip! Even Faro is starting to like him!"

"Yeah," Lily nodded, unsmiling, "but unlike Faro I can't be bribed with a piece of meat or a big plate of biscuits."

Mary Morgan went crazy in the springtime. She stayed crazy all summer. Her friends might have tried to drag her back to sanity, but too many of them had gone crazy, too. Aggie and Su Gin started out teaching each other more of the languages they shared only sketchily, and wound up sharing at least a room and doubtless more. Cora and Lily might or might not have been involved with each other, nobody knew for sure. What they did know for sure and worried about was that Ceileigh and Chilkat Joe were sharing a room, and if anybody else found out, Joe might well wind up with his throat slit or his skull split.

"Ceileigh," Aggie tried, "Ceileigh, it won't matter how many people think Joe's a nice guy. He's Indian and you're not!"

"To hell with the lot of them," Ceileigh said stubbornly. "He's twice the man of any ten of them!"

"Cay..."

"Aggie, stop it." Ceileigh took a deep breath and shook her head. "You'd think there was something special about white skin! And the stupidity of it all is we all started out in the same place."

"They aren't going to listen to Bible stories about the Garden of goddamn Eden!" Aggie argued.

"Never mind the Bible and never mind the Garden of Eden either." Ceileigh wiped tears of anger from her eyes. "We started in Africa," she insisted, "all of us started there. Or at least all of us who have or used to have the Gaelic. And moved out, for whatever reason, over years and centuries, moving and moving, getting farther from Africa all the time, farther from the colour we all originally were, fading into what we are now. So those who curse them with dark skin are cursing their own foremothers and forefathers. And are too damned stupid to know it, believe it, or figure it out for themselves!"

"That's all very interesting, I'm sure," Cora said quietly, "but I doubt if you'll have time to explain it all if they find out you're helping Joe guard the gold in that little room at night."

"Worry about yourself," Ceileigh advised.

"Oh, I do," Cora agreed. "I worry about myself a whole helluva lot! Because if they even suspect what I'm up to they'll kill us both. You've only got to worry about Joe. They won't kill you."

"God," Aggie raged, "and they pretend to be our friends."

"They aren't pretending." Ceileigh wanted to believe what she said, but she couldn't lie to the others, let alone to herself. "I don't care," she said firmly. "He's the best thing ever happened to me."

"Pray God you aren't the last thing happens to him!"

"Nobody will find out," Ceileigh said desperately. "Faro won't let anybody go near the door, let alone open it."

"I hope you're right."

Su Gin held Aggie close, stroking her back, speaking softly to her, words less important than the sound of her voice, the comfort of her touch. "Is it true?" Aggie sobbed. "Is it true they'd kill him if they knew? Kill Cora and Lily? Us?"

"It's a way to get rid of a question they don't have the time or courage to answer," Su Gin replied. "If they can't ensure they are the most powerful and wonderful, they can at least ensure someone else isn't. And if they can prove to themselves someone else is less, then obviously they, themselves are more."

"More what?"

"I don't know."

"All I know," Aggie smiled, wiping her eyes, "all I know is everything was rotten and then I heard Ceileigh's music. I thought I'd died and gone to heaven. And that music isn't a patch on what we have!"

"What does that mean, not a patch?" Su Gin teased.

"It means," Aggie said, "if anyone tries to get mean with me about us, I'm not going to try to explain, or justify, or ask for forgiveness or understanding. I'm just going to do what Faro does. Go for the throat."

"How can anyone so fierce be so gentle?" Su Gin laughed. Aggie snuggled beside her, pulled the quilt higher, fussed it up over Su Gin's shoulder, and burrowed closer. They fell asleep together, warm and unafraid.

Elizabeth was learning to read and write two languages and to speak Chilkat, little Margaret had learned to crawl, and there was more work than there was time to do it. The two Chilkat teenagers who were hired to look after the children managed to keep them out from underfoot most of the time, but there were still more things to do than time to do them.

"My God," Cora yawned, "when I think of the days and days and weeks of boring nothingness I used to think was going to drive me insane...well, I wouldn't mind having a few of those days. It's a blur. I feel like I leap out of bed at top speed and just go like hell until I fall into bed again."

"And then," Lily teased, "you really go like hell."

"Oh," Cora shrugged easily, "that's all your fault."

"Me?" Lily stubbed out her stinky little cigar, smiling widely. "How do you figure that?"

"You can't make a fire with sodden wood," Cora announced. "You could light every match in the world and you wouldn't get a flicker. But if your wood is prime, all it takes is a spark." She slid closer, her strong hand stroking Lily's waist. "I don't go like hell. I just provide a little bit of a spark and you do the rest."

Mary rose in the morning wishing she could stay in bed with Phillip, who was sleeping soundly, looking to Mary like an angel visiting from heaven. She dressed, went to the cookhouse for coffee and breakfast, then went to her office and tried to concentrate on her work. She would rather have daydreamed about Phillip, but the sooner the bookkeeping was done, the quicker she could get back to him. She went to her room and wakened him. They painted the world in scarlets and purples, then rose, washed, dressed, and went to the cookhouse. They walked together, smiling and whispering, finding a dozen different places in the privacy of the bushland and painting the world in bright golds and verdant greens.

"Sunshine and civilization," he breathed against her throat. "Decent food and clothes, good wine, theatre, music. Real music, my darling," he promised, "not some fiddles and banjos."

"They grow oranges and lemons," he insisted, "and you can pick them off the trees and eat them fresh."

"There's stores there as big as this entire hotel," he elaborated, "and all they sell is women's pretties. And we'll live in a huge brick house on top of a hill, looking down on the city and the bright blue ocean beyond it. We'll have fresh flowers in the bedroom every day and at night you'll wear nothing but silk and everyone will say Look, there, now, look, it's the beautiful Mrs. Hewlett, the most gorgeous bride in the city."

"Paris, my treasure," he whispered, "and then we'll get in our private train car and go to Italy."

Now there were three claims, and crews working day and night with rocker boxes, there were hotel rooms and cots in tents, there were fingers in pies all over the settlement, and the gold dust and nuggets came in from three or four dozen different sources. Chilkat Joe was in charge of several crews of packers and freighters and he no longer went out himself, but stayed in town, organizing and directing, ostensibly working for the women, but actually running his own enterprise.

And Mary Morgan had never been happier in her life. She had everything she had ever wanted, and more than she had dared dream, she had work, she had money, and she had Phillip. She loved him as she had loved everything in her life, totally and openly.

Mary got up, dressed quietly, and went down to the cookshack for her coffee. Halfway through the first mug, she was amazed to see Phillip coming in, smiling at her.

"I thought you'd sleep until. . ." she blurted.

He leaned over and kissed her, stopping her words. He sat beside her, ordered breakfast, and smiled his slow, gentle smile. "I couldn't sleep," he shrugged. "So, I thought I'd go for a good long walk, get some fresh air, enjoy the last of the good weather. It'll be freeze-up soon," he said sadly, "the last steamer is due any day. After that...we'll be stuck in place for months." He sipped his coffee, he patted her hand, he smiled at the Chilkat woman who put his breakfast in front of him, and then he packed away enough food for two hard-working men. "Could you pack me a lunch?" he asked the smiling cook. "I might decide to stay out for a few hours."

Mary looked up from her books in time to see him ride off in the direction of the creek. He did not turn to wave, but why would he, there was no way he could know she was watching. He was wearing a sweater and had a warm jacket tied to his saddle, and the cook must have packed him enough lunch for six hungry men, because the saddlebags were stuffed.

Mary didn't see Phillip at suppertime, and he didn't show up for his shift behind the bar.

"Maybe he's hurt," she worried.

"And maybe he isn't," Lily said evenly. "Maybe he's just got sense enough not to try to ride the horse back home again in the dark."

"But..."

"Mary, think! He probably rode and rode and rode, then sat and ate and ate and ate, then lay down to have a rest. And it gets dark sooner every night, now, it's almost time for freeze-up. He started back and it got dark quicker than he expected. Maybe he slept longer than he intended. He's got food, right?"

"Oh, yes," Mary laughed, "his saddlebags looked positively stuffed."

"Well, then, there you are," Lily shrugged, patted Mary's shoulder. "Don't be a nag, darlin'," she drawled, and moved away slowly, puffing on her cigar and waving to Chilkat Joe.

Joe moved to the bar, had a few words with Lily, and then they both nodded and walked behind the bar, toward the store-room. Mary sighed and prayed to all the gods and goddesses that Joe and Lily weren't going to get involved in something that would break Ceileigh's heart and possibly send Cora into a screaming rage. Cora was just too good with a rifle for anyone, even Chilkat Joe, to dare get her angry. And Ceileigh did not deserve to have any kind of horror come down on her head, especially not the kind that could come from having her lover go into the storeroom with her friend.

But Chilkat Joe and Lily came back out of the storeroom within a few minutes, and there was no sign that they had been up to anything they shouldn't have been doing. Mary stopped worrying about them and went to chat up some of the customers.

"See you a minute, Mary?" Chilkat Joe asked softly.

"Something wrong?"

"Not wrong." He nodded to the customers and turned, leading the way across the floor of the saloon, toward the stairs.

Mary followed, wondering what needed looking after at this hour of the night. Joe opened the door to the room he shared with Ceileigh and Mary walked inside, puzzled. Lily sat on the bed, puffing furiously on one of her stinky little cigars.

"Better sit down, darlin', I'm going to dump something on your head," Lily said quietly. Mary sat on the bed, folded her hands in her lap, and waited to hear almost anything except what she did hear.

"I don't believe it," she said flatly.

"You don't have to believe it," Lily said, her voice level. "Doesn't matter if you believe it or not. It is. Like fire, pestilence, or flood. Whether you want to believe it or not, it is."

"There's got to be some other explanation."

She went into the storeroom and watched Chilkat Joe lift the floorboards, exposing the storage hole hidden between the support logs. She counted. Then counted again. She left the storeroom and went up to her office, pulled out the account books and went over them, then over them again, then again. Her hands and feet were cold, her stomach empty, and there was a dull roaring in her ears, as if a cold wind from hell was blowing on her. No matter what she did, no matter what she checked, no matter how often she counted and recounted, there it was. Someone...not Phillip!...had gone into the storeroom, lifted the floorboards, removed eight rawhide sacks of dust and nuggets, put the floorboards back, locked the storeroom door again, and left. But not Phillip! God, not Phillip!

"I figure," Chilkat Joe said softly, "there's damn close to three million worth of dust and nuggets just took a hike."

"No!" Mary flared. "No, damnit!"

"Sure, Mary, whatever you say," he answered agreeably, but she knew from the look on his face, the look in his eyes, that he was saying it only to keep her from screaming. Both of them knew that if she started screaming she might never stop.

Joe took his jacket from the peg on the wall and shrugged into it. He kissed Mary on the cheek, then kissed Lily. "Guess I'll just head into Dawson," he said softly, "see if I can get there before the last steamer leaves for Seattle."

"Want me to get Ceileigh before . . .?" Lily began.

"No." Chilkat Joe fastened the buttons on his jacket. "You tell her I'll be back as soon as I can. You tell her.." He shrugged. "You know what to tell her."

His packers brought him home a week later. He had been found face-down on the frozen mud in an alley near the steamer landing. The bullet had gone in his back and out his chest, ripping his heart apart.

"He didn't feel it," Lily tried to console Ceileigh, who just sat, her spine stiff, her hands folded in her lap, staring holes in the log wall, saying nothing. "Jesus Christ, Ceileigh!" Lily sobbed, "Let it out! Cry!"

"And what good will that do?" Ceileigh asked numbly. "I could cry until my throat bled, and it would change nothing. That goddamn smiling piece of shit shot him from behind and now he's off on the last steamer. He'd been gone a week before they got back with Joe's body. He's made it. He's gone. We can't even go after him until . . ." She drew in a long, shuddering breath and shook her head angrily. "And if we had him right here, with my hands around his lying neck, what good would it do?" She moaned then, and the sound of it made the hair on Lily's arms stand on end.

"Oh, dear Hag," Ceileigh prayed, "collect him and ease his pain." She took the mug of tea they handed her, and she drank it, she even took the bowls of soup they pressed on her, and she ate the soup, but she just sat, staring at the log wall until they all feared for her sanity.

Mary sat beside her, folding and unfolding the handkerchief

she had found forgotten in a corner of Joe's shelf. She rubbed her fingers over the fine stitching, seeing nothing, feeling nothing, just rubbing, as if trying to erase something, trying to erase everything.

"I'm sorry," she said finally. "It's my fault."

"Don't be an asshole," Ceileigh said faintly.

"I gave him a job," Mary insisted. "I trusted him. I . . ."

"Och, God, woman, it wasn't you took the key, it wasn't you stole the sacks, it wasn't you ran off like a terrified flea, and it wasn't you shot my Joe in the back. I know it wasn't you." She reached for Mary's hand, took it and squeezed as hard as she could. "You were right here with me the whole time."

"I'm the one said he was wonderful . . ."

"Aye, well, we're all fools at times in our lives. And none of us any bigger the fool than any of the rest. It's his sin, not yours."

"If I had him here I'd rip his throat out myself," Mary vowed.

"And would that give me back my Joe? Or give you back what you thought you'd found? Oh shit!" she exploded, "if all the bastard had taken was money I wouldn't mind! But he stole so much more than some pretty rocks the fools value more than honour itself!"

Ceileigh was back at work a week later, playing her fiddle and speaking pleasantly to the customers. She saved her tears until the morning she wakened to find her moon time on her. Then she wept. "And would it have been such an awful lot to ask," she sobbed, clinging to Su Gin desperately, shaking with the finality of it all. "It was two men for no time at all, against my will in the muck and mess," she raged, "and as quick as that I was pregnant. And this time, when I wanted . . ."

"The gods do what the gods do," Su Gin said quietly. "And who can ever understand them?"

"Damn them, then!" Ceileigh screamed. "Damn them all!"

The packers and freighters heard every bit of gossip that surfaced from Skagway to Dawson, and by Easter they knew as much as could be known about the affair. They knew that Phillip had caught the river steamer out, they knew he had paid for his passage with nuggets, and they knew he bought passage as far as Seattle.

"He's out of the country, then," Aggie gritted.

"He won't stay in Seattle," Mary countered. "Seattle is as raw as New Westminster, Vancouver, or Victoria. He'll go to San Francisco. And then he'll go back to where he came from and live the life he thinks he deserves to live. And who knows," she sighed, "maybe it is what he deserves!"

The work continued in spite of the ice forming on the streams. The choppers went out every morning and smashed through to the gravel, and the jackassed inventions worked to a greater or lesser degree. Pot-bellied cast iron stoves were set in the shallows, the water not quite to the fireboxes, then stuffed with dry pitchwood and slabs of bark. The stoves heated, the ice retreated slightly, but as soon as work stopped and the fire was allowed to go out, the ice formed again, and had to be chopped or melted in the morning.

The days shortened, the nights lengthened, the men tried to work by lamplight or firelight, and the gold was wrenched from the gravel. Then, bit by bit, the promise returned, the promise of light, the promise of warmth. The days lengthened, the nights shortened, and one day the branches of the evergreens began to drip as the ice and snow melted in the light of the sun. The first steamer of the season made it to Dawson and there was a fresh flood of newcomers. Among them were four well-dressed men who supported themselves with decks of cards and skilled, slender fingers.

"If I catch you cheating," Lily warned, "I'll not only bar you from the place, I'll break your hands."

"You won't catch us," one of them grinned. His eyes slid from her face to the bar where Su Gin was serving customers. "We don't cheat," he amended.

"I hope not," Lily smiled falsely. "But you have to understand my side of it. It can ruin a place to have tinhorns running dishonest games."

"Your bartender," a second man asked suddenly. "She isn't Chilkat, is she?"

"Chilkat?" Lily turned slowly, looked at Su Gin, then looked at the gambler. "No," she said easily, "she's from farther north. Different looking, isn't she."

"How much farther north?" the second gambler asked casually. "Mongolia?"

"She's an Aleut," Lily lied. "But you're right, she looks like she's Mongolian. A lot of them do." She was afraid she was talking too much, unable to stop. "Maybe that old land bridge theory is true. Maybe they did walk across the ice or something."

"Or something," the gambler agreed, riffling the cards, smiling suddenly. "You won't have any trouble with us," he promised. "We won't be here long. Just long enough to make our fortune, find the pot of gold at the end of the rainbow. You know how it is."

"Sure," Lily agreed, leaving their table, glad to get away from them.

And one morning Aggie was gone. And Faro was gone with her. Su Gin just shrugged and shook her head when questioned.

"Come on, Gin, you know something!" Cora yelled, stamping her foot on the floor. Su Gin shrugged for the umpteenth time.

"There's no money missing," Lily said quietly, "so why are you so upset?"

"I'm upset," Cora hissed, "because Aggie is gone. Aggie's clothes are here, Aggie isn't. The last time one of us headed off like this, he didn't come back."

"Aggie is no thief!"

"I didn't say Aggie was a thief," Cora responded, "all I said was there was no money missing."

"That is the same as saying Aggie . . ."

"It is not the same as saying Aggie stole money," Cora snapped. "What I'm saying is, without money she couldn't go anywhere. Unless someone stole *her* and is holding her for ransom."

"Then where is Faro?" Lily laughed. "Anybody steals him will bring him back in one hell of a hurry."

"Not if he's been shot in the head," Cora argued.

"Oh Jesus." Lily stopped laughing, her face pale.

"She has not been stolen," Su Gin said.

"Then where did she go without money?"

"She had money. I gave it to her."

"Where did she go?"

"If she had wanted you to know she would have told you."

"Jesus Christ, Gin, if you keep on like this I'm going to lose my temper and rip your hair out by the roots."

"You try," Su Gin laughed, "and you will wish you hadn't."

"Oh wonderful," Ceileigh shouted, tears springing to her eyes, "it isn't enough that every son of a pimp from here to Europe is trying to ruin what we've got, you two have to fight like this. For God's sake, Su Gin, stop what you're doing, whatever it is. And you, Cora, use your brains instead of your mouth. Aggie's gone off looking for Phillip."

"I did not tell you that," Su Gin said complacently.

"Oh, bugger you, too," Ceileigh gritted. "I had a working brain before you came into my life and I haven't lost it in spite of being up to my armpits in lunatics."

"Well, damn her!" Cora slapped her hand on the tabletop. "She could have said something. I might have liked to go with her."

"She didn't want you," Su Gin grinned.

"Didn't want *you*, either, I notice," Cora retorted.

"Of course not," Su Gin shrugged. "I am not allowed to be in this country, how could I go across the border to another country where I am not allowed? And who had time to find ways to sneak across?"

"We could have all gone," Mary said softly. "We could have all..."

"Been as obvious as cooking cabbage, I suppose," Ceileigh said. "My God, Aggie's only a child. She has no idea what she's heading off into or what she'll find when she gets there."

"She's got Faro," Cora consoled her.

"And won't that be fun?" Lily lit a cigar. "I can see her now, trooping down a city street with *that* huge ball of muscle and fangs snarling along beside her."

"We could go into Dawson and catch the next steamer," Mary suggested quietly.

"What good would that do? We'd always be a week or two behind her. We don't know where she's going. By the time we found her it wouldn't do any good to find her. And when we got back we'd find ourselves out of business. Better we let her do it her way and just make sure that when she gets back there's something for her to come back *to*." Ceileigh wiped her eyes, sniffed, then tried to smile. "I'm sorry if I insulted anyone."

"Oh, piss on that," Lily laughed. "It's okay. You were upset."

"And you weren't?" Su Gin teased.

"I," Lily glared, "am not apologizing to anyone for anything I might have said here today."

"Sometimes," Cora smiled sweetly, "you are a pain in the ass."

"That," Lily said, hugging Cora gently, "must get you in exactly the same place other people get a headache."

19

Aggie enjoyed every minute of the trip on the river steamer. With the nuggets Su Gin had given her, she paid for a first-class cabin for herself and Faro, even though the purser insisted she had to pay full adult fare for the dog if he was to stay in the cabin with her. When the purser asked her name, Aggie smiled widely. "Hunter," she said pleasantly, "Aggie Hunter."

On the way to San Francisco they passed through New Westminster, and she stood at the rail of the steamer, staring across the river to the mud flats she had once thought would be her home all the days of her life. Then she turned her back on the dismal scene and went to her cabin, where she stayed until the steamer left a few hours later.

Aggie kept to herself. She took her meals in the cabin, grinning as Faro licked his own plate clean. "Some dog," she teased, "sleeping on a bed, eating human food off pretty plates. They won't even know you when you get back." Every evening, when the other passengers were either celebrating in the lounge or dancing, she strolled the decks with Faro. She spent hours soaking in the tub and sometimes she wrestled him into the warm water to scrub him clean. He sat glaring at her, his eyes slitted, his lips curled in a near snarl, but Aggie just poured more water on him and lathered his thick fur again, getting the wild Klondike smells off his fur, making him marginally more socially acceptable. "They've seen bush dogs in this tub before," she scolded, "but when we get to San Francisco we'll be in foreign territory and we don't want them deciding you aren't toney enough for their tastes."

In spite of her efforts, it was obvious that the desk clerk in the big San Francisco hotel did not take kindly to having an enormous shaggy beast with a noticeable strain of wolf in him as a guest in the hotel. Aggie just smiled wider and put two more nuggets on the desk. The clerk looked at them, then at Aggie, and then at the dog. "I do hope," he said coldly, "your dog is house trained."

"Oh, he is," Aggie agreed mildly, "his manners are probably better than your own."

Aggie Hunter left Faro in the hotel room while she went out to buy herself some appropriate clothes. She wasted no time wondering what women her age were supposed to wear, she wasted no time worrying about fashion. She walked into a store, zeroed in on an elegant older woman, and walked up to her with a big smile. "I have just come out of the Klondike," she said truthfully, "and I need some clothes. Nothing overboard, but nothing...boring." The woman looked at Aggie and nodded. "You're right," she smiled, "you certainly do need some clothes." Two hours later Aggie was back in the hotel with half a dozen boxes, her shopping spree finished. She had almost everything she needed.

That night she left Faro in the hotel room and, dressed in her old clothes, she headed for the streets. It took her thirty American dollars and three-quarters of an hour to find what she wanted. She supposed she ought to be afraid to walk into the place alone, but she walked in anyway. The Celestial men sitting in the dim room looked up at her with expressionless faces. When she spoke to them in their own language they gaped in amazement. It took her fifty more dollars and ten more minutes to get what she wanted. Then she went back to the hotel, had a bath, put on one of her new outfits, and went down to the lobby.

The desk clerk who had been so superior when she and Faro checked in was preparing to go off shift when Aggie crooked her finger at him and motioned him to one side.

"Madam?" he asked politely.

"I need an escort," Aggie smiled. "I don't think people would think it quite proper for me to go where I want to go without a...gentleman...accompanying me. Ten dollars an hour, and I pay the tab."

"Madam!" he blurted. Then he smiled, thinking of the ten dollars an hour. "I would be delighted," he assured her.

He was. Aggie took him to the restaurant he recommended, bought the wine he suggested, and asked his advice about the menu. Then she slipped him more than enough money under the table, and allowed him to appear to pay the bill and leave a generous tip.

"Is there a concert hall or an opera house?" she asked.

"The best," he assured her.

"Good." She grinned and took his arm.

He waved down a cab, and by the time they arrived at their destination she had again slipped him the money. The driver was paid and tipped and the clerk paid their admittance to a place he had dreamed of going but only been able to walk past until now. Aggie even gave him enough money to take a cab to his own lodgings when the concert was over and she was ready to go back to her hotel room.

"Is there someplace else we could go tomorrow night?"

"Yes, ma'am!" he smiled.

Aggie went up to her hotel room, changed her clothes, and took Faro out for a good long walk. Several hours later she went to bed, remembering every note of music she had heard and every step of the dancers, every turn, every move, every gesture.

That night, dressed as well as any woman in San Francisco, Aggie accompanied her escort on a whirlwind round of clubs. Again she gave him the money so he could appear to be the one picking up the tabs. And again she gave him his ten dollars an hour plus cab fare home. And again, once back at her hotel, she changed her clothes and took her huge, savage-looking dog for a good long walk.

Phillip was sound asleep right up until the very second Faro jumped from the carpeted floor to his chest. And then Phillip was wide awake, staring in horror at the snarling wolf-face mere inches from his own.

"Don't make a sound, Phil," Aggie suggested softly, "or he'll have your throat for supper."

"How in hell did you get in here?"

"Oh, you know how it is," Aggie shrugged, "a pinch of dust here, a pinch of dust there and you can get just about anything you want. Where's Mary's gold?"

"Go to hell," he gasped.

"No, no, no," she chided. "Nothing like that at all."

She tied his hands behind his back, then ran the same rope down to his ankles and tied them.

"And now," she laughed softly, "I'm gonna put a slip-knot in this rope and tie 'er around your neck. Move and you'll strangle yourself."

"You evil bitch," he hissed.

"No, no, no," she repeated mockingly, "nothing like that at all or I'll just give you to Faro."

She gagged him. She shoved one of his own crumpled socks into his mouth, then tore a strip from his best shirt and wrapped it around his face, knotting it securely at the back of his head. Then she sat down in the comfortable stuffed chair beside the bed. She put her feet on the bed, told Faro "Guard," and went to sleep.

In the morning she told the chambermaid that her "uncle" was still sleeping. The chambermaid nodded wordlessly, tidied the other two rooms in the suite, and left, her generous tip in her pocket. It was none of her business if the gentleman wanted to exhaust himself with someone hardly old enough to know what time it was.

Aggie had breakfast sent to the room, and sat next to the bed eating it while Phillip watched every move she made. She offered him toast, and he shook his head no, but when she offered him a cup of coffee, he accepted gratefully and drank it thirstily. So Aggie poured him another and held it while he sipped quietly, aware that nobody would hear any sound he made, and that he had no wish to invite Faro to attack him.

"You ever hear the story about the guy found this really odd-looking critter?" Aggie asked conversationally, shoving the gag back into Phillip's mouth and tying it tightly in place again. "Well, what it was, this guy found this thing, a bird, all bright colours and fluffy feathers and a bit like a parrot but a bit like a great turkey vulture. You know, kinda good-looking but kinda mean-looking, too. So he asks around to find out what it is and this guy who knows just about everything says Oh, he says, that's what you call a Crunchbird. Well, says the guy who found it, what in hell is a Crunchbird. Oh, says the guy who knows everything, let me show you. And he takes this big chair and he puts it in the middle of the floor and he points at it and he says Crunchbird, the chair, and just like that, poof, the chair is ripped all to hell. And the guy who knows everything, he takes this big fancy desk, and he points at her and he says Crunchbird, he says, Crunchbird, the desk, and poof, like that, the desk is in little bitty spoon-size pieces. So the guy who found this bird is pretty impressed and he says thank you and he's walking down the street and this big cop comes up to him and says to him What have you got riding on your shoulder. Well, says the guy, this is my bird. I can see it's a bird says the cop, but what in hell kind of a bird is it? Oh says the guy who found it, it's a Crunchbird. And the cop sneers, the way they always do, and he turns away and he says Oh Crunchbird, he says, Crunchbird my balls."

Aggie snickered happily. Phillip stared at her. Aggie winked, took a piece of toast from the breakfast tray, placed it on the floor then pointed at it. "Faro," she said softly, "the toast." Faro leapt from the bed with his mouth open and the toast was gone. "Now, Philsy-Wilsy," Aggie mocked, "if you don't smarten up, you might be the cop, and Faro might just be the Crunchbird...if you get my meaning."

By mid-morning Phillip's bladder was threatening to burst, but no matter how much he grunted, Aggie just laughed at him. Finally, to his shame and his horror, he could hold it in no longer. He soaked himself and the bed on which he lay. "Tsk tsk," she laughed, "look at you." Phillip groaned, but he didn't dare try to move. He had tried several times during the night and each time the only thing he had accomplished was to tighten the rope around his neck. His back ached, his arms ached, his legs ached, his neck ached, his head ached, and he was lying in a cooling puddle of his own piddle.

"Pretty soon," Aggie predicted, "your guts are gonna start

rumbling. You'll want to take a crap. You'll hold it in. Your guts will start to ache. But you'll hold it in. Maybe a day. Maybe two. Eventually, Phil-Old-Fart, you are going to shit. And you are going to lie in your own shit. You'll lie in it until I get ready to cut your clothes off you. You'll lie in it until the very minute I put on a pair of your lovely grey gloves, pick up that shit and ram it in your mouth. And then, Phil," and she stared him in the eye, "you will either eat that shit or Faro will eat your face."

He pissed himself twice more before he broke. She knew the very minute he snapped. She let him cry for half an hour, then she got a piece of paper, a small bottle of ink, and the pen from the bedside table. When the letter was written, she untied his hands long enough for him to sign it. Then she tied him up again and left him on his bed with Faro sitting right next to him, his slanty yellow eyes fixed hopefully on Phillip's handsome face. "Please," Aggie laughed, "do yourself a favour. Behave."

She took a cab back to her hotel, changed into her best outfit, and proceeded to the bank where, Phillip had admitted, he had deposited the gold he'd stolen from Mary. The bank manager almost asked some questions of the elegantly-dressed young woman, then decided he liked his job and left the questions unasked.

Half an hour later, Aggie left the bank and took a cab to another bank. "I'd like to open an account," she said pleasantly. The teller looked at the certified cheque, then at Aggie, then back down at the cheque. "Certainly, madam," she said quietly.

Back in her own hotel, Aggie put on her old clothes, packed her things, and went down to the lobby. The desk clerk smiled when he saw her, and Aggie grinned widely at him. "I'm leaving today," she said. "And I'd like to thank you very much for being my escort." She gave him two hundred dollars which he didn't want to take, then handed him a gold nugget. "A good luck charm," she grinned.

She went to the steamship office, booked passage to Dawson for herself and her dog, took her boxes to the stateroom, and took a cab to Phillip's hotel.

"Well, well, Phil-Old-Fart," she said cheerfully, looking down at the miserable, broken-spirited wretch lying in the stinking mess on the bed. "I guess I didn't get back in time. Not to worry, old shitter," she laughed, "I've paid your hotel bill. You have until tomorrow morning to get your educated ass out of here, and nobody but you, me, and Faro knows about this. Why, I bet you can even scrub the evidence off the sheets and have them dry and back on the bed before you leave. But you get in my way again, and the entire godforsaken world will know all about this." She cut the ropes, then dropped a hundred dollars on the filthy bed. "Judas only got thirty pieces of silver," she hissed, "so you're doing better than he did."

"Aggie..." he blurted, holding out his hand imploringly. "Aggie, please..."

"If it was up to me," she said coldly, "I'd leave a corpse in this shitty mess, but Gin says that would just make me what you are. And whatever I am, or will be, it won't be what you are. I'd rather be nothing. Ceileigh cried, you bastard, we all cried. Joe was worth two hundred like you." Aggie wiped at the tears flowing from her eyes. "I really would like to kill you for what you did to Joe, and I really would like to kill you for what you did to Mary, but I'm not going to. Just don't get in my way ever again."

"Aggie, for God's sake..."

"God's got nothing to do with it," Aggie answered easily. "You might have got away with it, Phil-Old-Shit, but you were so busy impressing the entire world with your importance you left a trail a mile wide. It was easier finding you than I thought it would be. If I was you," she suggested gently, "I'd use that fancy straight razor to slash my wrists. Or my throat. You could have had it all, you fool. She'd have given you her entire world."

"I didn't want to spend the winter in that hell hole!"

"She'd have come out with you. All you had to do was ask. But you were too damn busy scheming. You broke her heart because you could do it. Not because you had to. Because you could. Well, enjoy the memory. But you'd better go get a job. A hundred bucks won't last long in this town!"

20

The gamblers were sitting together at their table, sipping drinks and talking. Not a playing card in sight, but they looked as if they'd just won the jackpot. Lily didn't trust them as far as she could throw the entire hotel. Still, when the tallest of the four smiled and waved her over to the table, she moved forward, a smile on her face. Business, when all was said and done, was business.

"Something I could do for you?" she asked pleasantly.

"Oh, yes, ma'am," the tall one said politely. "You can sign over the hotel, lock, stock, and barrel."

"Be glad to. As long as the price is right."

"The price?" he laughed. "How about our co-operation?"

Something in the tone of his voice wiped the smile from Lily's face, took the laughter from her voice. "In what way?"

"You sign the place over," the spokesman said firmly, "and we won't tell the law you've got Illegals as partners."

Lily gaped.

"We checked it out," he warned her. "You're in shit to your eyebrows, lady."

"Perhaps," a second man suggested, "we should explain."

"Perhaps you should," she agreed.

"It's against the law for Celestial women to be in this country," the tall one said quietly. "What's more, it's against the law to bring 'em in, or to aid, abet, or shelter them if they sneak in."

"Arrest," said the third, "prosecution, conviction, jail... or," he smiled unpleasantly, "sign over the hotel and restaurant."

One yell from Lily and the men in the bar would gladly beat all four blackmailers to bloody pulps. Faro would happily scar or even cripple any or all of them. She could even have them killed. But there was law in Dawson now, and that meant it would soon be here, too. Besides, who knew how many more of these men there were. Lily knew the men were laughing at her, reading her thoughts as easily as if she had spoken aloud.

"Why don't we give you a few hours to discuss this with your friends," the second one suggested. "After all, people are like eggs, aren't they? Treat 'em rough and they crack. And when people crack they do silly things. And we wouldn't like that."

Lily walked to the bar, spoke quietly to Cora, and headed for Mary's office. She wanted a minute or two alone before she dropped the bomb on the others. A minute or two alone with a stiff drink and a strong cigar.

They all knew they were stretched over a barrel. And they all knew that the men knew, and worse, that the men knew the women knew that the men knew. And everyone knew there was nothing much could be done.

"We all know," the spokesman said gently, "that your friends are not Chilkat nor Aleut but Celestials."

"And," Ceileigh put it into words, "all we have to do is sign everything we own over to you, and you'll forget to inform the police?"

"Exactly." The cold grey eyes turned to her, the neatly-trimmed head nodded, and the manicured hand reached inside the jacket and brought out a thick document. The women knew without asking that it had been dictated by a legal expert, knew there wasn't a loophole anywhere in it.

"And if we tell you to take a flying leap at the moon?" Lily asked, her voice husky with suppressed fury.

"Your friends will be arrested, they will be deported, and, I expect, they will be in very deep trouble when they get back to their own country."

"Do not do it," Su Gin hissed. "There will be no trouble for us when we get back. We have done nothing wrong."

"You will have done by the time you get back!" the spokesman answered, his impatience showing through the thin veneer of sophistication. "Anything can be arranged for a few dollars."

"Besides," another man said with a grim smile, "we checked it all out. There is still slavery in your country. They buy and sell women like you for less than the price of a half-dead dog."

"And you'd arrange that, too, I suppose," Mary said bitterly.

"Oh, lady, you know it," the third gambler agreed.

"Do not sign," Su Gin insisted.

But Mary reached for a pen, dipped it calmly into the bottle of ink, and signed the document in all the indicated places. Ceileigh scrawled her name beneath Mary's. Then Cora signed, then Lily, and finally Aggie.

The spokesman returned the papers to his pocket. "One week," he said, rising and moving toward the door. "To tidy up your affairs."

"My affairs," Cora drawled, deliberately insulting him with the tone of her voice and the defiant tilt of her head, "are none of your business. Why," she laughed, "I don't even *have* affairs with people like you!"

The men glared, stepped from the room, and closed the door firmly. "One of these days," Ceileigh warned, "you'll make a remark like that and the god-praising bastard will have you burned for a witch."

"So?" Cora sighed deeply. "I'll be in good company when I fry."

Lily took one of her foul cigars from her shirt pocket, carefully clipped the end of it, lit it, and inhaled deeply. "I would really like," she said tiredly, "to rip off their faces and ram them up their asses, but what good would it do; there are probably six more like them at home."

"You should not have signed," Su Gin mourned. "Now you have lost everything."

"The paper," Cora trembled with rage, "isn't worth shit until it's registered. All we have to do is blow them to hell and leave them in the bush for the bears to eat."

"No self-respecting bear would eat that kind of offal," Ceileigh shook her head.

"Well, hell," Cora argued, "there's other ways to get rid of them. There's piles and piles of gravel, mountains of gravel left from the workings. Just lay the buggers on the ground and shove the gravel on top of them!"

"And what do we do with the next bunch?"

"We'll leave!" Su Gin blurted. "We'll go somewhere else!"

"Where?" Ceileigh challenged.

"Ah, piss on it." Aggie reached up, took the cigar from Lily, puffed on it, and coughed before puffing again. "I mean, what are we here for, anyway? Who needs this shit? We've all been working so hard for so long we've forgotten what it's like not to be tired and aching! You should have been there with me! You should see it for yourselves! If we walked out without getting two dried peas for the place we'd still have more than enough money to live like real honest-to-God human beings for the rest of our lives!"

"It's the principle of the thing," Lily argued. "I hate to be screwed."

"Piss on the principle of the thing." Aggie chewed on the end of the cigar and Lily sighed, reached for another, clipped it, and lit it, thinking furiously.

"You'd walk away just like that?" she probed.

"I'll *run* away just like that if the rest of you will come with me!" Aggie waved the cigar for emphasis. "Ah, God, Lily! I never heard such music in my life! It was like a dream. What did we come here for? We came to strike it rich. Well, how rich do we have to be before we're rich enough? For God's sake, there's so much money in the bank we don't know how much money we've got unless we haul out Mary's books and look for the total!"

"And let them get away with it?"

"Oh, I didn't exactly say *that*," Aggie winked. "You know me. I am not a nice lady. They'll get their comeuppance one way or the other, I promise. But damned if I'm going to let them know that I feel bad. I won't give them the satisfaction."

"Did your mother feed you on raw meat?" Cora asked, reaching for the bottle of whiskey on the desk top.

"No, she didn't feed me at all," Aggie snapped. "Most of the time I didn't have a mother. Couldn't afford one."

"Why are we arguing with each other when it's *them* we're mad at?" Mary rubbed her eyes, stretched and yawned. "It's signed, it's legal, and that is that."

"I am sorry," Su Gin wept. "If we weren't..."

"If you hadn't shown up with good hard cash when you did," Mary countered, "this place would be one-tenth the size it is, and we'd have six others bigger and more profitable in competition with us. Maybe Aggie's right."

"Of course I am," Aggie said confidently. "After all, how much more can be washed out of the gravel before it's all gone?"

They poured themselves small glasses of whiskey, sipped, and stared at the floor. Cora got up, frowned at Lily and Aggie, went to a window, and threw it open. "Goddamn you both," she said without anger, "but you sure can stink up a room in a hurry."

"Oh yeah?" Aggie laughed, "so why do you share a room with her?"

"The big question is, why does Su Gin share a room with *you*," Cora retorted. "I wouldn't. You're a brat."

"Hey, never mind you sharing a room with me," Aggie countered, "Didn't anybody teach you it's manners to wait until you're asked?"

"Oh, do shut up, please," Ceileigh begged. She drained her whiskey and stood by the window, looking out at the cluster of tents and the bustle of activity. "I hate to leave him here," she confessed, swallowing quickly. "It's going to be frozen cold and thick with snow in a month, and..."

"Well, then," Aggie said, "wait until it is, then have him shipped out to wherever it is we wind up."

"They have places for people like you," Mary said quietly. "And we could probably get a ten-dollar reward for turning you in."

"Use your head for something other than a place to put a hat." Aggie reached for the whiskey bottle and held it up. "This is the same colour as cold tea," she said, laughing softly. "And there are barrels of it down there. And we could dig up Joe, drill a little hole in his box, fill the box with whiskey, then seal the whole shiterooni with tree pitch and ship him out. Nothing to it, really."

Ceileigh turned slowly, and looked at Aggie as if she had never seen her before in her life. "I'm sure we'd get twenty dollars, not ten," she said, shaking her head. "What in hell would Joe want with a coffin full of whiskey? He wouldn't want to be buried anywhere other than here. He was born here, for the love of God! He belongs here! Whiskey in his coffin my ass!"

"Atta girl." Aggie rose, stubbed out the cigar, and moved to put her arms around Ceileigh, cradling her gently. "Come on," she urged, "let's just pack our stuff and hit the road. We've enjoyed about as much of this place as those assholes will allow."

"God forbid," Cora said thoughtfully, "anybody ever get the idea I agree with even one-tenth of anything the brat thinks up, but...we seem to have only two choices. Kill the buggers, or just...eat this."

"Three choices," Su Gin argued. "We will go and..."

"Shut up, darling," Aggie suggested.

"Yes. Shut up, darling," Lily agreed.

"We could very easily," Mary suggested softly, "pack our things, go into Dawson, see a couple of old friends, buy a drink or two, catch the steamer out to Vancouver, and be halfway there before this place burned to the ground."

"Och, aye," Ceileigh grinned, "and everybody knows everything in this country goes up in flames as soon as the damned cold hits."

"Things happen." Lily sipped her whiskey. "There you are, and either it's the worst thing ever happened to you, and the end of everything, or it's a good thing, and a beginning. And it's always up to you to decide if you're going to face the end of your life or the start of a new life."

Mary walked to the unnamed creek and along the bank to the first of the three rocker boxes. She handed the toiling crew a bottle of whiskey and a handful of cigars. "We leave tomorrow afternoon," she told them. "If you're interested, come see me when you're finished for the day. We'll sign some papers." She grinned. "Unless of course you don't want to own sixty per cent of this claim."

"You're kidding!" one of them gasped.

"No, my friend, I'm not." She held out her hand, "Good luck to you all."

"Jesus, Mary!" He shook her hand happily. "We're hauling seven hundred dollars a day out of this box."

"It used to be a thousand," she reminded him. "Someone want to take a run up the creek and tell the other crews?"

"This got anything to do with those guys in suits?"

"Yes," she said honestly.

"We can bury them for you."

"And be what they are?" She shook her head. "Think about it. Every week or so the profit from this box goes down a bit. By spring..." Mary swallowed, blinked back tears. "But thanks for the offer. Look, we're having a little going-away party. Everything free-gratis, as they say. With any luck the joint'll be dry before those bastards come back to claim it!"

The food was there for all to share, and the drink flowed freely. Not the pea wine and rum mixture, but the kegs of good whiskey and the cases of expensive bottled wine. Miners, labourers, workers, and the down-and-out came early and stayed late, feeding their faces and filling their bellies. "The new owners don't take possession for a week," Ceileigh told everyone repeatedly, "so make the most of it. In fact," she laughed, "do what the squirrels do, and take some with you for later."

"Eat up," Mary urged. "You'll never get better at this price!"

"There is," Aggie laughed, "more than one way to skin a cat." And she jumped on the bar, singing loudly, dancing happily.

The party was in full swing when the sun rose, and was still swinging when the freighters brought the pack horses to the front of the hotel.

"Time to go!" Aggie yelled. "Come on, we've got a steamer to catch!"

"Not me," a deep voice replied, "I've got an invitation to a party!" The young man who had faced death by starvation before he was put in charge of the Sick Miner's rocker box put his arm around Mary's shoulders and hugged her firmly. "You're leaving just in time," he said. "I hear tell there's gonna be one helluva goddamn fire in this place in about a week. Right to the ground is what I hear. Total loss, the way they tell it. Shame," he grinned, "a real pure-dee double-dog dirty damn shame!"

"Everybody in this country," Su Gin said clearly, "is quite mad."

"Oh, you can bet we're mad," the young man gritted. "But we ain't crazy. Gonna miss you."

"Look us up when you get down south," Aggie invited.

They hauled up the floorboards and brought out the accumulated profit, packed the sacks in sturdy boxes, and tied them shut with strong rope. Ceileigh carefully wrapped her fiddle in a soft otter pelt, put it in its case, and packed the case inside the battered wooden box with the scratches on one end of it where Margaret's father had left his teeth and his handsome face. She looked at her daughter, who sat on the bed, watching gravely. "Come along, my hinny," Ceileigh smiled, "we're off, now."

They rode away from the hotel, the sounds of the party following them, and not one of them looked back. Five days later they left on the steamer, first class from Dawson to Vancouver. Half the passengers on the steamer knew them as friends. By the time they debarked in Vancouver every passenger and every member of the crew called them friend.

The desk clerk looked at the women, then at the enormous dog, and sighed. "Will you be staying long?" he asked politely.

"Not long," Lily promised. "And don't worry about the dog, he's house trained."

"The rest of us are, too," Aggie whispered.

"Of course, madam," the desk clerk agreed, not sure whether he had heard right.

They left Faro in the suite and went to the store the chambermaid had recommended. Two hours later, bathed and dressed in their new clothes, they went to the hotel dining room for supper.

"What's that?" Margaret demanded, glaring suspiciously.

"Milk, my darling," Ceileigh smiled.

"I don't like it."

"You've never tasted it!" Cora protested.

"I don't care. I don't like it."

"Tell you what," Aggie bargained. "You drink the milk and I

promise you something for dessert that you will *love*."

"What?"

"Drink your milk and find out."

"Show me and I'll maybe drink the milk. Maybe."

"You know those nice dresses I got you?" Ceileigh smiled maternally. Margaret nodded her head happily. "Well, if you want to wear any of them," and Ceileigh's voice hardened, "you'll drink the goddamn milk."

"And then get the dessert?"

"And then eat your dinner and get the dessert."

"I might be full of dinner and not have room for dessert."

"Margaret. You know Aggie's story about the Crunchbird. Want me to go buy one and bring it here and say Crunchbird the child?"

"Oh, for Christ's sake." Cora picked up the glass and drained the milk. "There, now can this just stop?"

"Momma!" Margaret wailed. "Cora drank my milk!"

Aggie rolled over in the big soft bed and put her head on Su Gin's shoulder. "You sleepy?" she asked softly.

"No." Su Gin turned to rub her face against Aggie's. "I was thinking about when Elizabeth and I were making our way north. About the sky being so big and so blue, and how nice it was to just sit on Friend and feel the sunshine warm on my skin."

"I've never ridden a horse like that," Aggie sighed. "Not for days and days like that, not for miles and miles. Not just to be riding; just, you know, get on it and go somewhere and get off it again."

"It's wonderful. And the long grass swishes, the grass seeds blow off like dust in the wind, and it's only when you get off the horse you realize that you weren't a part of the body of the living animal."

"I'd like that," Aggie yawned.

Cora cuddled close to the curve of Lily's back, nuzzled her face against the warm skin, and smiled sleepily.

"We could get a piece of land," she suggested.

"A big piece," Lily agreed.

"Build a house."

"A big house."

"And grow lots and lots of flowers?"

"Lots and lots of flowers."

"We could travel."

"Twice around the world," Lily yawned.

"Sleep in the biggest bed anybody ever had."

"Sleep," Lily suggested, "would be very nice."

"Momma?"

"Yes, my darling."

"How come Liz'Bef and I sleep in a bed, and Su Gin and Aggie sleep in a bed and Cora and Lily sleep in a bed and Ling and . . ."

"Go to sleep, Margaret, please."

"But how come you sleep by yourself?"

"I like it that way."

"But why don't you want to sleep with someone?"

"I don't have the energy," Ceileigh sighed. "Now go to sleep."

"Momma?"

"Go to sleep, Margaret."

"You could sleep with Faro."

"I don't want to sleep with Faro!"

"But Faro's got nobody to sleep with."

"He doesn't need anybody to sleep with! Go to sleep, Margaret!"

"Could he sleep with us?"

"Yes."

"If Faro's going to sleep in this bed," Elizabeth said crossly, "then I'm going to sleep with Ceileigh!"

"Goodbye, then!" Margaret snapped.

"Oh, Christ," Ceileigh sighed. "Try not to kick, please, Liz."

"Do you think the hotel burned down yet?" Elizabeth asked conversationally, snuggling herself under the blankets.

"With my bloody luck," Ceileigh yawned, "this one will catch flame before I get any sleep."

"Momma?"

"Go to sleep, Margaret."

"But I want to ask you something."

"Faro!" Ceileigh called. "Faro, the child!"

Elizabeth giggled, Margaret laughed, and Faro wagged his huge tail on the coverlet. Ceileigh closed her eyes and fell asleep thinking of the unnamed creek and Chilkat Joe's grave, covered now by a foot of ice-crusted snow. Spring would come again. The snow and ice would melt, fresh green willow shoots would grow, and even the cold empty place inside her would vanish.